MW01235780

Finding Salus

Book 1

Chloe Chadwick

Meg M. Robinson

Dedication

This is for Granny, the best woman I've ever known. I miss you.

Acknowledgements

I absolutely must thank my husband, Andy, first, as he's put up with a lot. From me rambling about plots and ideas, to days where I would hole up and simply ignore him as I wrote. He's supported me even when I doubted myself, and I couldn't love him more.

I'd also like to thank my publisher and friend, Michelle, who has done more than anyone could ask to make me feel like I could really do this, and then to actually help me do this. You're one of the main reasons this book exists.

And my family, thank you. Mom, you have been supportive through the journey for me to get here. Kimberly, you were my first fan, and I promise I won't forget that, especially as you turned into my editor. Vickie, I couldn't ask for someone better to give me honest feedback, and I'm thrilled you volunteered.

And to everyone else who has read my stories, given advice or support, or just been there for me, thank you.

Chapter 1

"So, as you can see, your grandmother left everything to you. You are her sole beneficiary."

Chloe barely heard the lawyer. She didn't care about *things*, not even Granny's things. She wanted her grandmother back. To make matters worse, she felt guilty because she hadn't visited as much as she should have the last few years. She'd been too caught up with getting her private investigation business, Chadwick and Hall Investigations, off the ground and had only made the trip from Philadelphia to Boston a few times a year. Granny had deserved more. She'd deserved better from her only grandchild. But even with the guilt riding her, Chloe couldn't cry.

A hard knot of numbness and anger writhed and grew inside her. She was officially alone. There had never been any sort of male relative in the picture and her mother was killed in a car accident when Chloe was just a baby. Now, almost twenty-seven years later, she'd lost her grandmother the same way as her mother. It wasn't right. It wasn't *fair*. And instead of being able to process, being able to grieve, she had to deal with a lawyer talking about *things*. The same day she'd put her grandmother into the ground, no less. That had been a trial all on its own. Unfortunately, her grandmother had requested the will be read the same day as her funeral. Chloe had no idea why, but she wasn't going to go against her grandmother's last wishes. It was the last thing she could do for Granny.

Lydia Chadwick had been a good person, a friendly and compassionate woman with a tight-knit group of friends, but her funeral had been full of unfamiliar faces. Part of that Chloe chalked up to how little she'd visited, but too many of those faces had been focused on Chloe rather than the casket buried in flowers. More than a few of those strangers had been giving her odd looks and whispering to their companions. Between dealing with the loss of her last family member and the unusual behavior of the people she assumed were Granny's friends, Chloe was close to snapping. Even the flowers sent from her friends and people she worked with hadn't taken the edge off.

"Her estate includes the house she was living in, which is paid in full, all her possessions, and a tidy sum of money. Some of that will go to paying any existing debt she left, as well as taxes, but it looks like you'll receive about two hundred and seventy thousand dollars when all is said and done," the lawyer continued, even though Chloe's mind was elsewhere until he gave the amount.

"I'm sorry, how much did you say?" Chloe asked with a frown. She had to have heard him wrong. She didn't care about the money—she'd never really been materialistic or greedy—but the total given just didn't make any sense to her.

"Two hundred and seventy thousand."

She shook her head. "That can't be right. Granny hasn't— hadn't," she corrected, "worked for years and she never gave me any indication that she had that sort of money. She clipped coupons and tried to shop during sales whenever she could."

The lawyer spread his hands and shrugged. "I don't know what to tell you there, because that is the amount you'll receive. After the debt and taxes, of course," he reminded her. "She also left you this," he said, setting a cream-colored envelope on his desk and pushing it across to Chloe.

The envelope was made out of heavy paper and had Chloe's name written on the front in neat handwriting she recognized immediately. When she turned it over, she almost smiled.

Granny had loved doing things the old-fashioned way, which included closing letters, when possible, with wax and a seal. Staring up at her now was a dollop of hardened blue wax with a detailed symbol she knew very well—a tree of life with a raven perched in the branches.

His face softened, as did his demeanor. "She requested you open that when alone," the lawyer explained gently. "I'm sure you want to get out of here, so if you can just sign a few things for me, I'll give you the keys and you can go. It'll be a little bit before you get the check, but I can have that sent to you."

"Yes, that's fine," she agreed and hurriedly signed the papers he set in front of her, took the keys, and left the office. Once she was back in her car, she looked at the envelope, brushing her fingers across the familiar script. It was tempting to open it now, but she expected that reading the last words from her grandmother might cause the dam on her emotions to break. She didn't want to cry her eyes out while sitting in the lawyer's parking lot. Instead, she started the car and drove to her grandmother's house.

She walked up to the front porch and paused, absently toying with the keys the lawyer had given her. She had her own key, given to her when she was little, but used the key that had been her grandmother's to let herself into the house.

It still smelled like Granny. The subtle scent of her perfume invaded every corner of the house and was almost enough to make Chloe lose it. Her eyes grew damp but she blinked the tears away, determined to at least read Granny's letter before she broke down. She moved through the familiar home with the familiar things—the knick-knacks, the photos, the landscapes that Granny had painted. Making her way into the kitchen, she set her messenger bag and the letter on the round table before she opened the fridge, unsurprised to find it stocked with Cokes. Granny hadn't liked soda, but Chloe did, and even when Chloe didn't visit often, Granny made sure she always had some on hand.

She grabbed one and sat down at the table, taking a sip before she broke the seal on the envelope and took the letter out. Her

3

breath caught at the sight of her grandmother's pretty handwriting—the large, looping cursive, neatly penned—and she started to read.

> *My dearest Chloe,*
>
> *I'm so sorry that reading this letter means I'm gone and you're alone. It's not what I would have wanted for you, but few people are able to choose the time and place of their death. I've done my best to ensure you're taken care of, though I know that's of little comfort at the moment. But I want you to know that I have always loved you, will always love you. Death doesn't change that. I've been so proud as I watched you grow up, go to college, and find your path. When you opened the doors of your own business I almost burst with pride. You have always been so strong, so smart. And stubborn, but I think that's where some of your strength comes from. I like to think the rest of it came from your mother and myself.*
>
> *Unfortunately, you're going to need that strength, that stubbornness. I'm afraid there are many things I haven't told you, my dear. At first, I did it for you. You simply weren't ready. Then I did it for myself, because I couldn't stand to see you suffer. I should have told you, so you could be better prepared, and I'm sorry for that as I'm sorry for nothing else in my life. Unfortunately, I can't tell you everything in a letter. It wouldn't truly help you, and there is entirely too much to put on a few sheets of paper.*
>
> *I know I always told you to never go into the attic, but that is precisely what I need you to do now. You'll find a box with your name on it. Open that and nothing else, at least for now. What you find in there will help you discover what I was too selfish to tell you myself. I hope that when this is done, you will forgive me.*
>
> *Remember to be strong, to be smart. I know your world has just changed, but you are more than up for the challenge of dealing with your new reality.*
>
> *Always with love,*
> *Granny*

Chloe lowered the letter, rested her forehead against her arms, and let the tears come. She didn't sob, her shoulders didn't shake, but the tears flowed down her cheeks. She cried until she felt drained and purged. The grief remained, and she mourned the fact that she'd never see her grandmother's smiling face again, never feel her arms wrap around her in a hug that made everything better. She would regret not visiting as often as she could for the rest of her life.

Several minutes later she lifted her head and wiped impatiently at her cheeks. Her eyes were swollen and tender, but she folded the letter and slid it back into the envelope. Grief was still her primary emotion, but shock and curiosity were beginning to build within her. She wasn't dumb, she knew everyone had secrets, but she hadn't thought there were any big ones between her and Granny—aside from her grandmother's refusal to discuss Chloe's father—but now she was being told there were things that had deliberately been kept from her. And for it to involve the attic?

She stood, her steps slow as she made her way up the stairs and to the door that led to the attic. All her life this was the one room that had been off limits to her. She'd never gotten a true reason why, which had been unusual. Her grandmother had been firm, but fair, and gave a reason for everything else. To this day Chloe had no idea what was up there. Her curiosity had driven her to pester Granny when she was younger about what was in the attic, why it was forbidden. She'd even considered sneaking up on more than one occasion, but she never could bring herself to go against Granny's strictest rule. Disappointing her grandmother? No, just no. Granny had always had a way about her that made the mere thought of disappointing her the worst thing in the world. Kicking a puppy wouldn't have made her feel quite that bad, and Chloe had always had a soft heart when it came to animals.

Still, the taboo against the attic was so strong that she had to force herself to actually reach out with a lightly trembling hand and open the door. In front of her was a perfectly ordinary set of stairs. So ordinary it was more than a little anticlimactic. Cautiously she started up and was further surprised to see normal attic things—cardboard boxes, stacks of books, even a couple of trunks and chests. Nothing struck her as a reason to forbid her from stepping foot in this room.

Though her inquisitive mind wanted to snoop, to see what was in those boxes and trunks, she made herself focus on the task at hand. It wasn't hard to find her name, but it wasn't on one of the cardboard boxes, despite Granny's letter specifically mentioning a box. Instead, it was one of the wooden chests, not quite a foot square. She knelt in front of it and lifted her hands, pulling it closer. It was latched but not locked, as she saw some of the trunks were, and she opened it slowly, equal parts nervous and excited to see what it contained. To her confusion, all she saw was another sealed letter with her name on it. Her first thought was why such chest this size was needed for a single envelope. Her second reaction was mild annoyance.

"Why would she write a letter telling me to read another letter?" Chloe murmured as she took the second letter out and sat down to open it.

> *Chloe,*
> *I apologize for your confusion, but I had to be discreet. My lawyer is a good man, and while I trust him in all legal matters, he couldn't be trusted with this. No one could. I own a second house on an island called Salus and need you to go there. I have a friend who lives in town and she has agreed to explain things to you in the event of my death. Go to Salus, find the house, then find Emma Mitchell. Don't bother trying to locate the town online, you won't find anything. Instead, use the directions I've included.*
> *Again, I'm so sorry, and I love you so much,*
> *Granny*

Chloe stared at the writing, more lost than ever. Her grandmother had never been exceptionally secretive except for visiting the attic, so Chloe couldn't figure out what all this was about. Her mind raced with ideas, but each was more unlikely than the last. There was no way Granny had been involved in anything illegal, which ruled out a lot. Nor could Chloe see her in espionage, witness protection, or anything like that, which didn't leave a whole lot of options. None that were plausible, in any case.

She glanced at the second page and saw very detailed directions that led to an island off the coast of Connecticut. Not only did her grandmother include roads and turns, but landmarks. There was no way to know when the letter had been written so there was no telling how accurate the directions were. Despite her grandmother's words to not try to find Salus online, Chloe pulled her phone out to see if she could do just that. Unfortunately, none of the sites she was able to find where useful. She learned the word was Latin for safety, and there was a bed and breakfast in southern Connecticut called Salus Bed and Breakfast, but that was it. After more than an hour of searching she admitted defeat. Temporarily. Then she did a search for Emma Mitchell. Unfortunately, that wasn't an uncommon name, and she found dozens. Since several of them were in Connecticut, and with nothing else to go on, she changed direction. Instead, she pulled up a map site and tracked the path to this Salus place. It would probably only take about two hours to reach. Assuming the directions were good and she didn't get lost.

A quick look at her watch showed it was nearly six, so if she left now and didn't get lost, she'd reach Salus around eight. It wasn't likely things would go perfectly, though, so she decided to wait and head out in the morning, to give herself plenty of time. And to be honest, she wasn't sure she was up for any more major revelations at the moment. After all she'd been through that day, she was beyond exhausted, both physically and emotionally.

At least Chloe didn't have to worry about work. When she'd been informed about the accident, she'd called up her business partner—who also happened to be her ex—Adam Hall. Though they hadn't worked as a couple, they'd been able to remain friends. Then they'd discovered they worked much better professionally than they ever had romantically. So, when she knew she was going to be out of town for a few days, minimum, he'd agreed to take over her cases.

7

She closed the chest and carried it and the letter downstairs to the room that had been hers since birth. It had changed over the years, of course, as her tastes had evolved, but it had been the same for almost a decade now. More, it was home. The chest was set on the nightstand, the letter put on top, before she stripped down to her underwear and tee-shirt and crawled between the sheets. It was early, yes, only dinner time, but she just couldn't keep her eyes open any longer.

As she waited for sleep to claim her, she thought about Salus, wondering why it had no online presence, and why her grandmother had owned a house there. Was it some sort of cult? Or an island full of people who didn't believe in technology? Then again, to keep something off the internet, it was more likely the government was involved.

No matter how hard she thought, she couldn't come up with a scenario that fit the few facts she had and made sense for her grandmother. So, when sleep finally claimed her, her mind continued to work, and she dreamed of an island she'd never seen.

Chapter 2

W hen Chloe woke the next morning, she forgot her grandmother was gone. Waking up in her old room, surrounded by a hint of her grandmother's perfume, had her, just for an instant, smiling and expecting to see Granny downstairs. She threw back the covers and prepared to jump out of bed and go down to see her. That was when reality hit her. Her chest tightened painfully and her eyes stung as she was faced, once more, with the loss of the most important person in her life.

She sighed, forced herself to get out of bed, and headed into the bathroom. She leaned against the sink and stared into the mirror. There were dark circles under her teal-blue eyes and her shoulder-length blonde hair was a halo of tangles around her face. Since it tended toward crazy curls when left to its own devices, she normally tied it back, but she knew it would be useless to attempt doing so until she'd showered. She could only tame it when it was damp.

Part of her wanted to delay going to this Salus place, no matter how curious she was. It sounded like Granny had been keeping some major secrets and she was a little worried about uncovering them. Granny was gone, so if Chloe learned something that warped her view of the woman who'd raised her, there wouldn't be a chance for her grandmother to explain.

On the other hand, she was no coward, and she was more than a little nosy.

Unable to convince herself to stall, she brushed her teeth then stripped down and got in the shower. She took her time, but eventually she'd dried off and pulled on a pair of jeans, a tee-shirt, and a much-loved gray hoodie to combat the autumn chill. Once her hair was pulled into a ponytail, she looked at herself in the mirror again. Normally she was tan, given how much she loved being out in the sun, but the last few days had left her drained and pale. It didn't help matters that she'd only eaten one real meal in the past three days. Her jeans were a little loose on her now, and she couldn't afford to lose the weight. Keeping in shape wasn't exactly necessary in her line of work—it was basically a desk job—but she still considered it a priority. Because of that she resolved to at least hit a drive-through and grab a biscuit on her way to Salus.

She tossed her keys, phone, the directions to Salus, and her pistol into her messenger bag before she slung it over her shoulder and grabbed the suitcase that held her clothes. She started to head out to her car but stopped and looked at the chest bearing her name. It was empty except for Granny's letter, but she took both chest and letter with her. She couldn't tell herself why she wanted it, but she felt better when she put it in the passenger seat with her bag.

On her way out of town she stopped for coffee—she couldn't start her day without her iced caramel coffee—and got the biscuit she promised herself to get. She also put off her arrival in Salus a little longer by going inside to eat. Yes, biscuits could be messy to eat in a car, but she knew it was just an excuse she was trying to sell herself. Unfortunately, though she was a good liar, she couldn't lie to herself, so ate quickly and got back in the car.

The directions were more up to date than Chloe expected them to be. She only made one wrong turn before she reached the ferry mentioned in the directions. She could see the ferry waiting at the dock, and a small booth set nearby for people to buy tickets. It didn't look busy, which surprised her a little. It wasn't that early, and surely there should be either residents of the island coming to the mainland for things they couldn't purchase at home, or tourists wanting to visit. Still, she parked and headed for the booth.

It was six feet square, but the door took up a whole wall, swinging to open it fully when the weather was nice. The small structure was only big enough for a chair, mini-fridge, and a shelf with some odds and ends. In the chair sat a man in his mid-twenties. His skin was the color of her coffee, his hair short and even darker, but his eyes were a startlingly pretty green, the shade of new leaves in spring. He wasn't dressed in any sort of uniform but wore a pair of faded jeans and a sweatshirt. His chair was propped up on the back two legs, his feet resting on the edge of the shelf while he watched something on a laptop. It wasn't until Chloe said 'Hello' that he noticed he was no longer alone.

The front two legs of the chair hit the floor hard as he sat forward. "Who the hell are you?" he asked, sounding equal parts surprised and annoyed.

Not expecting that sort of reaction, Chloe blinked at him. "You need my name to sell me a ticket to the ferry?" she asked dryly.

The man frowned at her. "Why do you want to get on the ferry?" he asked, eyes narrowed in suspicion.

"Uh, to get to Salus?" Chloe pulled the directions from her pocket, skimmed over them, then looked over the area for any sort of signage. She didn't find any. "This is the ferry to Salus, right?"

Rather than appeasing him, it seemed to make him even more wary. "How do you know about Salus?"

"I don't, really," she admitted with a shrug. "I couldn't find a damn thing about it. You guys must *really* like your privacy out here. What, is it just a bunch of rich people living on the island or something?"

"Something like that." The man studied her for a moment then thrust his hand out. "I'm Ted."

Automatically Chloe took his hand. The instant she did she wanted to take it back. She didn't shake hands with rude guys as a rule, and this particular guy was giving her an entirely too distrustful look.

"Chloe," she said as she gently extracted her hand from his.

"Chloe what? You got friends on the island or something?" Ted asked.

"No, or at least I don't think I do." Chloe shrugged. "My grandmother just passed away, and she left me a note telling me to go to Salus, that she owned a house there," she explained, waving the directions in her hand.

Ted's eyes softened and he visibly relaxed. "Lydia Chadwick was your grandmother?"

Chloe took a step back, startled. "Yes, how do you…"

"I knew her. I know the funeral was yesterday, but I couldn't make it. I did send some flowers. Lilies."

"She loved lilies," she murmured, her chest tightening.

"I know." He tore off a ticket and handed it to her. "No charge for the ferry this time. It's the least I can do for Lydia's granddaughter. Just drive around to the yellow poles, give the ticket to the guy, and drive on. Ferry should be leaving in fifteen, so you've got time."

"Thanks." She started to turn, then paused. "Um, before I go…are there a lot of people on the island who knew my grandmother?"

"I won't say everyone knew her, but a lot of people, yeah," Ted confirmed with a nod.

That potentially explained all the unfamiliar faces at the funeral. "Thanks," she repeated, giving Ted a quick smile before she headed back to her car. She sat there for a moment, processing. With a groan she lowered her head to the steering wheel and closed her eyes. There had been way too much to process lately, and she knew it wasn't done yet. She still had to learn Granny's secrets. Hopefully she'd learn them all at once, like ripping off a Band-aid.

Steeling herself, Chloe sat up and drove to the spot Ted had indicated. The other man took her ticket in silence before she drove onto the ferry. It was chilly enough that she opted to stay in her car. There were no signs of the island in the distance, not yet, so there was no point in getting out. Ten minutes later she felt the ferry begin moving away from the pier. It was another ten before she got her first glimpse of the island. At first all she saw was green and gold. Trees, she realized. Lots of trees. It didn't look inhabited, really. It just looked like a densely forested island. When they got closer, she saw a couple buildings and another pier.

A few minutes later Chloe carefully drove off the ferry. Once she was on the island, a wave of dizziness hit her, followed by jitteriness and an insistent tingling over her entire body. She felt like she'd downed several pots of coffee, and every inch of her skin hummed. She slammed on the brakes and threw the car into park. For a full minute she did nothing but breathe and grip the steering wheel hard enough to turn her knuckles white. Gradually the feeling began to fade, receding until she felt almost normal. There was still a sense of something being off, but nothing she could pinpoint.

She tried not to panic. Was she sick? Or maybe the stress of everything had simply decided to hit her all at once? It would be a better option than her being sick, though she knew stress could cause all sorts of physical issues.

She was working herself up to a major freak out when there was a tap on her window. Chloe jerked in her seat and whipped her head around. A man's face peered at her from the other side of the glass. He was wearing a tan uniform and hat that shadowed his face. What she could see of his face was worth a second look, though. His hair was kept short, just barely curling against his collar, but even shadowed by his hat she could tell it was black. He had a neatly trimmed beard and tanned skin. She couldn't tell what color his eyes were other than light, though she was betting on blue. His nose was a touch crooked, like it had been broken at some point, but it didn't detract from his appearance. If anything, it made him look more masculine, more rugged. However, he was looking at her like she was crazy, which docked a point or two from his hotness rating.

Chloe cleared her throat and rolled down the window. "Yes? Can I help you?" she asked in a voice that was a little tight.

"You do realize you're blocking traffic onto and off of the ferry, right?" he asked mildly, and she felt some of the tension fizzle out. His voice matched his appearance perfectly, low and a little rough. Almost a growl, but she liked it. She added those lost points back.

"There isn't anyone waiting to get onto the ferry," she pointed out.

"Not the point. You're blocking access," he said as he straightened, and it clicked then that he was a cop. Normally she could spot a law enforcement officer a quarter mile away. Her only excuse now was that she'd been distracted by the anxiety stroke thing she'd suffered only minutes ago.

"Sorry. I just…wasn't feeling well," Chloe explained. "It seemed better to stop than crash into something."

He cocked his head and considered her silently for a minute. "Fair enough. Are you feeling okay now?"

"I am, yeah."

"Good. Well, while I have you stopped, and since, as you pointed out, no one's waiting, why don't you take a minute?" he suggested. "We don't get too many strangers around here."

She made an annoyed sound. "I'm getting that," she said dryly. "I got interrogated before I could even get a ticket to the ferry," she muttered.

The man's lips twitched. "Ted's protective of us like that. Did this interrogation include your name?"

"I'm surprised you're not asking to see my license and registration," Chloe quipped.

"Don't tempt me," he said, though it sounded like he was kidding. Mostly.

She rolled her eyes. "Chloe Chadwick. And since apparently my grandmother was well known here, yes, I am Lydia Chadwick's granddaughter."

"Ah. I'm sorry for your loss. Lydia was a wonderful woman. She's going to be missed, even if she hadn't lived here in a while."

Chloe frowned. This man looked like he was in his early thirties, mid-thirties, tops. As long as Chloe had been alive, her grandmother had lived in Boston. What in the hell was going on here?

"I'm Sheriff Adams, by the way. Wesley Adams."

She pulled herself out of her thoughts. "Pleasure to meet you, Sheriff. I don't mean to be rude, but it's already been a long day in an even longer week. I just want to get to my grandmother's house and try to relax a little."

"Sure thing," Wesley said. "You know how to get there?"

"I've got directions. They don't sound difficult," she said, tapping the paper that lie on the passenger seat.

"All right. You need any help, let me know," he said, stepping back.

"I will. Thank you," she told him before rolling up the window. Everyone seemed so curious about her, a newcomer. And when people were this wary of strangers, it tended to mean they were hiding something. She put the car in drive and started to follow the directions.

As she drove, a smile began to curve her lips. If they really wanted to hide something, they shouldn't have piqued the curiosity of a private investigator.

Chapter 3

As Chloe had hoped, the directions to her grandmother's house weren't difficult, and the drive there was actually pleasant. There were no more odd occurrences or interactions, and the island was surprisingly pretty. There had been a few buildings around the ferry, but none were exceptionally large and they blended well into the trees. After she got away from that area, the trees took over. The leaves were turning, so she drove past walls of emerald, garnet, and gold.

It was a good mile from the ferry before she reached the town itself. There were fewer trees here, but still some, spaced along the buildings. Like at the ferry, none of the buildings were extremely tall, and she only saw one that even reached three stories. Probably City Hall, she figured, though she was a road over and couldn't tell for certain. She also passed a diner, a veterinarian clinic, a few small shops, and one larger two-story building that was the hospital. At the edge of town, just before the road disappeared into the trees once more, she saw the sheriff's department.

All in all, the town couldn't have been but a mile from one end to the other. It was a little creepy for someone who had always lived in big cities, but kind of appealing as well. And it seemed normal enough. There was definitely electricity and technology, though they could still be crazy cultists.

A few minutes later she turned down a dirt driveway, surprised by how even the road was. She didn't hit any large bumps or potholes, though it still wasn't as smooth a ride as the paved streets. The trees opened up to reveal a home that could only be classified as a cottage. Instantly charmed, Chloe parked and studied the house. It was small, though two stories high, with stone walls and a chimney. The door was rounded at the top and solid wood, which gave it an old-fashioned look she was surprised to discover she liked. The windows had planter boxes in front of them, even the one on the second story. What surprised Chloe the most was how tended everything looked. Unless Granny had been sneaking away to clean and maintain the place, someone had to have been caring for it for her. The windows sparkled, the grass was neat, and the flowers in the window boxes were lush and colorful despite the autumn chill.

She noticed a crow perched on the edge of the roof and smiled. To her, that just added to the cottage in the woods ambiance the house had going for it. But as quickly as the smile appeared, it disappeared. Charming or not, this was still baffling.

"What the hell, Granny?" Chloe muttered as she grabbed her messenger bag, the travel bag from the back, and chest before she headed toward the door. It was only when she reached the door she realized she had no key for it. It was possible one was hidden somewhere, and certainly a neighbor—or this Emma woman—had one, but that didn't help Chloe at the moment. "Wait a second..." She fished in her bag for the keys the lawyer had given her. Yes, one had been the key to Granny's house in Boston, but there was another key on there. It looked older and definitely wouldn't have fit any of the doors at the other house. Curious, she gave it a try, only to roll her eyes when the key turned and she could open the door. "She couldn't have just told me that in the letter?" she grumbled as she nudged the door open and stepped inside.

She found a light and flipped it on. While the cottage didn't look identical to the house in Boston, it still looked like her grandmother's. The furniture was comfortable looking, the colors homey, soothing, and it was full of the pretty things her grandmother liked placing around to brighten up the place. Then there were the pictures of Chloe on the wall, along with more paintings that had to have been done by Granny. And most of all, the subtle scent of her perfume remained. It wasn't as noticeable as it had been in Boston, but the smell of it further relaxed Chloe.

Her things were set by the door after she shut it, and she started to explore. Aside from the living room there was a kitchen, bathroom and bedroom on the first floor. The bedroom was obviously the one her grandmother had slept in, because the perfume was stronger here, and Chloe saw a bottle of it sitting on the vanity. None of the rooms were large, but they didn't feel cramped. Nor did she see a speck of dust anywhere, further reinforcing the idea that someone was taking care of the place in Granny's absence.

There was a door in the kitchen which led down to a cellar, though other than some shelves, it was empty. Probably a root cellar, or had been at one time. Upstairs held a bathroom and two bedrooms. One of the bedrooms was currently lacking a bed and was full of boxes and trunks. Chloe made a note to go through them later and peeked in the other bedroom. This one, she knew, was meant for her. Though the walls were a soft white, the decor was done in purple and blue—her favorite colors, and the colors her room in Boston had been done in. The choices were all soft, so the room didn't seem too bold or too dark, and she immediately loved it.

She went downstairs to gather her things and brought them up to her room. There wasn't much to put away, so she just set her travel bag in the chair sitting in the corner, and her messenger bag and chest on the dresser. She plopped down on the bed and sighed. So far, she'd gotten no answers, just a whole lot more questions. Though this friend of Granny's, Emma, was supposed to tell her whatever had been hidden from her, Chloe doubted all her questions would be answered. For that she'd have to stick around a while. Since she worked for herself—

mostly—getting time off wasn't a problem, but if she wasn't working, she wouldn't be making any money, and the one thing this home lacked was food. Then she remembered what the lawyer had said. She had almost three hundred thousand dollars coming to her. The thought of using her grandmother's money didn't sit well with her, but it would allow her to stay and get some answers, and Granny had wanted her to come here. Maybe she'd even approve of the use.

Not one to procrastinate, she got up and slung her bag over her shoulder. She wasn't sure where to find this Emma Mitchell, but she knew where she could likely find out while getting some lunch at the same time. She did so enjoy killing two birds with one stone.

Back in town, Chloe easily found the diner she'd passed earlier, Salus Diner. She parked and glanced in the window. It looked normal. Given that it was half past noon there were plenty of people inside, and so far, no one was giving her odd looks or demanding her life history. Maybe it was just ferrymen and cops who were so nosy? Either way, after the vertigo she'd experienced after leaving the ferry, she needed to eat.

She went inside and saw several pairs of eyes flick up to her, away, then slowly return for another look. A small sigh was all she allowed herself as she took a seat at the counter, set her bag on the seat beside her, and picked up a menu. Nothing surprising jumped out at her, just the standard diner fare. She could do without all the staring, but if the food tasted as good as it smelled, she'd be happy.

The waitress, whose name tag read 'Lexi', wandered over and smiled, though there was curiosity in her gaze. "Hi!" she asked, her tone friendly, at least. "What can I get you to drink?"

"A Coke, please. And I'm ready to order, actually."

"Oh sure, go ahead," Lexi said, pulling out her order pad.

"Can I get a cheeseburger with cheddar and a side of fries?"

"Absolutely. You can't go wrong with that combo," Lexi said with a grin. "I'll be right back." She delivered the order to the cook before bringing Chloe her Coke. "Food will be out soon," she promised before going to check on another customer.

Chloe sipped at her drink, but she could *feel* the other customers staring at her. It was starting to make the back of her neck itch, not to mention pushing her temper closer to boiling. She did her best to ignore it, but five minutes later, when her food was set in front of her, she'd had enough.

"Here you go. Enjoy," Lexi said with a smile, though it looked a little tight now.

"Thanks," Chloe muttered, but she didn't touch the food. Instead, she turned around so she could see the rest of the diner. Some of the customers looked away quickly, but others made no move to hide the fact that they'd been watching her. "Yes, that's right," she called, making sure her voice carried. "New person in town. Scary! So let me save you guys some time and gossip. I'm Chloe Chadwick. I'm twenty-seven and graduated from Northeastern. I'm a Pisces, if you're into that sort of thing, and my favorite colors are blue and purple. And yes, I'm Lydia Chadwick's granddaughter. That should do you for a few minutes, so can you all stop staring at me so I can eat in peace?" She looked around and saw a few shamed faces turn away. "Good. Thanks."

She turned back around and picked up her burger. Before she could take a bite she saw Lexi grinning at her. "What?"

Lexi shook her head. "Nothing. That was just funny. And kind of impressive. Burger's on me," she said, never losing the grin.

Chloe couldn't help but smile. "Thanks." She took a bite then remembered her other reason for visiting the diner. "Do you know where I could find Emma Mitchell, by any chance?"

"I do, yeah. Normally you can find her at the boutique she owns, but it's Monday, which is her day off, so she'll probably be at home."

Chloe pondered as she ate, barely tasting the burger. "Think you could give me directions? My grandmother told me to go see her when I got into town."

"Yeah, I can do that. She lives right by the house your grandmother used to live in."

Finally a bit of good news. "That's easy then. I've already been there."

"Oh good. Then just turn down the second driveway past your grandmother's house and you're good," Lexi said with a smile.

"Cool. Thanks, Lexi."

"My pleasure. Yell if you need anything else."

"I will."

When she'd finished eating, she fished out a tip. Lexi had been useful and could, potentially, be an ally, so she deserved the ten.

Back on the road, she slowed after passing her grandmother's driveway. Only a quarter of a mile down the road she found the second driveway and turned down it. Much like at her grandmother's house there was a short drive surrounded by trees, but Emma's driveway was paved. The house, however, was in the same style—stone cottage—and just as tidy and homey looking, though it was at least twice the size of Granny's. A blue SUV sat at the end of the drive and smoke curled lightly from the chimney.

"At least someone's home. What are my chances it's the right person?" Chloe murmured before she grabbed her messenger bag and got out of the car. She didn't hesitate to knock on the door. She was so done with secrets. It was time for answers.

A moment later the door was opened by a woman in her late-forties, one who stood a few inches shorter than Chloe's five foot six. Her skin was only half a shade lighter than mahogany, while her eyes were a little darker. Her black hair was cut short so it framed her face. A face which brightened when she saw Chloe. "You must be Chloe. You look so much like your grandmother," she said warmly.

Chloe frowned. She didn't think she'd looked much like her grandmother. She had blonde hair and blue eyes while Granny had been a brunette with green eyes. "I am Chloe, but…"

21

The woman laughed softly. "Oh, I know, your colorings are very different. But here," she said, reaching out and lightly touching beside Chloe's eye, "this is all Lydia. It was Cynthia, too. I'm sure you've guessed I'm Emma. Would you like to come in?" she asked, motioning for Chloe to do just that.

"I would, yes. I have questions," Chloe said as she started inside.

"Oh, I'm sure you do. I intend to answer them all."

Chapter 4

Chloe was surprised to find Emma's house was similar in decor to her grandmother's. She even saw a painting with Granny's signature at the bottom. There were a lot more plants in Emma's place, both flowering and non, but that was the major difference. The house itself was larger, the rooms more spacious, but it felt just as comfortable.

"So, you were friends with my grandmother?" she asked as she followed Emma to the kitchen.

"Oh yes, good friends, for many years," Emma said with a smile.

"I'm not going to say this right, because I'm pretty much all out of tact after the week I've had, but how is that possible?" Chloe asked. "She hasn't lived here for at least twenty-seven years, so you would have been what, ten when she moved away? At the oldest?"

Emma clucked her tongue and shook her head as she filled a kettle with water and put it on the stove. "Oh dear. Lydia really didn't explain anything, did she?"

"Considering I have absolutely zero idea what you're talking about, I'm going to say no," Chloe answered dryly. "She even apologized for not telling me. Said she was being selfish or something. So, what is it that she's been keeping from me?"

Emma sighed and motioned to the table. "You're going to want to have a seat, Chloe. This is going to be hard for you."

"Harder than my grandmother dying and admitting from beyond the grave that she's been keeping some big secret from me for all my life?" Chloe grumbled as she sat down.

"Yes," Emma said without hesitation or humor as she took the chair next to Chloe. "You're not going to believe me, but that's okay. I can prove everything I say, though I'm sure you won't want me to."

Chloe sighed. "Just tell me. I'm sick and tired of all the secrets."

Emma pursed her lips but nodded. "Very well. You're not human. Neither was Lydia, your mom, or myself."

Chloe snorted. "You know, I always wanted to be a unicorn. Am I a unicorn? They look cool and can stab people with their heads," she said sarcastically.

That brought a laugh to the older woman's lips. "No, dear, you're not a unicorn. I'm sorry to say they don't exist as far as I know." She sobered. "There are quite a few races coexisting with humans. Most of those races are represented in Salus. It's a haven for supernatural people."

"You know...you're right."

Emma cocked her head, mild surprise showing on her kind face. "About what?"

"I don't believe you," Chloe answered bluntly.

Emma nodded, unsurprised. "I know. But you will. Let me explain a little more then I'll prove what I'm saying, all right?"

Chloe sighed and slumped back in her chair. "Sure." This wasn't what she expected when she first read Granny's letter. She wondered if her grandmother had known her friend was a few slices short of a pizza.

Emma chuckled softly as the kettle began to shriek. She got up and took the kettle off the stove and began making tea. "As I said, there are multiple races. I'm a witch. Your grandmother was an elemental."

"Okay, I'll play. I know what a witch is, but what's an

elemental? I never saw Granny do anything supernatural."

"There are subsets to elementals, dear. Each elemental has a single element," Emma explained. "Water, earth, air, and fire, of course, but also stone, lightning, metal, and aether."

"Aether?"

"Short answer? The essence of magic and life. The spark. Some might call it chi," Emma explained. "Lydia was an aether elemental."

"Uh huh. So why did I never see her do anything…aethery?"

Emma stopped what she was doing and turned to look at Chloe, her expression solemn. "Because she was determined to give you a normal life. She wanted you to be yourself before you got dropped into this world. Our world."

Chloe tapped her nails on the top of the table and considered Emma. "Right, moving on. You said quite a few races. That's just two."

"It is," Emma said as she carried two cups over to the table and set one in front of Chloe before she sat. "There are also shapeshifters—not just the wolves you might have read about, but shifters of a wide variety of animals—vampires, psychics, gods, ghosts, and demons."

If this was some sort of elaborate joke, it wasn't funny. Worse, Chloe was starting to doubt that it was a joke. There was something so credible about Emma. Although…"Gods? Like…god gods?"

"Mmhmm. Zeus, Hera, Poseidon…the whole lot," Emma confirmed. "And like I said, most of those races are represented here in Salus. This island, and towns and islands like it, are places where supernaturals live openly. Salus is protected by wards, magical barriers that keep humans away. Safely."

Chloe rubbed her fingers against her eyes. "Okay, you said you would prove everything you're saying, right? I'm giving you five minutes to do that before I walk out of here, grab my things, and head back to the real world, where people aren't nosy or feeding me bullshit."

"Lydia said you were stubborn. She was right," Emma murmured. "Very well. Luckily, witches do tend to have magic that's a bit more visible than some." She stood and walked to the sink, turning the water on. "One of my powers is the ability to manipulate water."

A motion was made toward the stream of water, and it stopped flowing straight down, instead looping up and out of the sink. It shot toward Chloe and circled around her head, teasing at her ponytail before it whirled around and back into the sink.

Releasing her control of the water, Emma smiled at Chloe. "Was that enough, or should I come up with something a bit more...flashy?"

Chloe gaped at Emma, her mouth moving, though no sound came out for another minute. "The...the water. It...you..." She made a spinning motion with her index finger.

"Yes, I manipulated the water, just as I told you I could," Emma said as she shut the water off. "Do you believe me now?

"I'm stubborn, but I'm not stupid," Chloe snapped as she stared at the faucet. The burst of temper faded quickly, and she shook her head slowly. "I don't get it. Okay, not telling me when I was a kid? Maybe. But I'm twenty-seven. Why didn't she tell me sometime in the last few years? Why leave me in the dark only to toss me in the deep end once she was gone and I was alone?" Painful as it was, it was still an easier thing for her to focus on than the supernatural being real. A fact she wasn't convinced of. She could be having a psychotic break due to stress, for all she knew.

Emma sat down and covered Chloe's hand with her own. "She couldn't bear to see your world turned upside down. You seemed happy, she said. You went to college, started working as an investigator, then opened your own firm. She was proud of you and didn't want to do anything to derail your life." She sighed softly. "I think if she thought she could have gotten away with it, she would have let you live your life as a human."

Chloe frowned and shook her head, confused. "What do you mean? Why couldn't she do that? I've never shown any sort of...powers. I've never seen or heard anything that even hinted to the fact that this was real. So why not let me live in ignorance?"

Emma smiled, but it didn't reach her eyes. "You never showed any powers because she had them bound for your protection. But powers or not, there's one aspect to being supernatural that you would have noticed eventually. She didn't want you ignorant when it happened."

"What's that?"

"We don't live the same lifespan as humans, Chloe. We live much, much longer."

Chloe went still. "How much longer?" she asked slowly.

"Brace yourself," Emma murmured, and the apology on her face had Chloe doing just that. "I'm eight hundred and fifty-seven. Your grandmother was almost twice my age," she said gently. "And there are those who live to be three times my age. And some, like gods and vampires, never age."

Chloe drew back, shaking her head rapidly. "No. Just no. The magic, okay, I'll buy that. People have been wondering for years if the human brain isn't showing its true potential. But people living to be two and a half *thousand* years old? No. It's just not possible. And immortal gods? Vampires? This isn't some cheesy horror flick," she snapped as she shoved to her feet.

"No, it isn't," Emma agreed, "but it's all very true. If you stay here for any length of time, you'll see things you can't explain with anything but the truth. And I'm sorry I had to be the one to tell you, I truly am."

Chloe just shook her head again. "No," she repeated. "I've gotta go. Thanks for the tea," she said, rushing toward the door, leaving her cup of tea untouched. Emma called her name, but she didn't stop. She left the house and got into her car. After starting it she just sat there. She couldn't outrun this. What she'd seen, what she'd been told, would just follow her. So, hightailing it back to Boston, or even Philadelphia, wouldn't do any good.

Especially since she believed Emma. She didn't want to, but she believed every word.

"Dammit, Granny," she whispered before she turned the car around and drove down the driveway. Despite her first instinct being to run, she headed back to her grandmother's house. There were all those boxes in the spare bedroom. Maybe some of them had more answers than the letters she'd read in Boston.

Her things were dumped on the sofa on her way upstairs. Once in the room with all the boxes, she gave an annoyed growl. "Of course they're not labeled. That would be too easy," she muttered before she knelt beside a trunk just inside the doorway. She opened it only to blink in surprise as she saw clothes. Extremely vintage clothes, if her guess was anywhere close to accurate. She pulled out a dress that looked like it belonged in the nineteenth century at the latest. It was beautiful, if not anywhere near her style, and in exceptionally good condition. It could be a reproduction of an older style, but after Emma's revelation, she doubted it.

The dress was folded neatly and set on top of another box and the second dress pulled out. This one looked even older, and the colors were a bit faded, but it was still in very good condition. The rest of the items in the trunk were all dresses or gowns, each one older than the last. She carefully repacked them, not sure what to think about the touchable time line of the history of fashion. The trunk was shoved to one side and she moved on. Half a dozen boxes and trunks held similar items, though they weren't all dresses. Hats, gloves, tunics, blouses...And not a single article of clothing looked like it had been made in the last two hundred years.

Expecting the same, she opened one of the smaller chests, only to catch her breath. Laying on top was a picture of Granny and her mom. Not a picture from thirty years ago, either, or even the Polaroids that seemed to have been popular when her mom should have been a kid, but an old black and white photo on thick paper that made Chloe think of the early twentieth century. Their clothing in the photo certainly matched that era, anyway. She carefully pulled the photo out, brushing a finger lightly over her mom's face.

She glanced down into the chest and saw more photographs, varying in size, color, and certainly age. There were some familiar faces—herself, Granny, and her mom, of course—but also quite a few strangers. There was one of her mom with a man who had his arm around her shoulders, both smiling brightly. Another was of Granny holding a baby. Judging by the age of that one, it couldn't have been Chloe herself, so she flipped it over and nearly dropped it. On the back, in Granny's handwriting, it said 'Lydia and Cynthia, August 1883'. If this was to be believed, her mom had been born in 1883, which would have made her over a hundred when she died. Yet none of the photographs showed Cynthia looking any older than her mid-twenties.

Chloe sat back on her heels and took several deep breaths to calm her racing heart. Okay, she could handle this. So her mom and grandmother were supernatural. So was she. So what? Freaking out would accomplish nothing, and this could actually answer some questions. Granny had never spoken about Chloe's father, or her grandfather, for that matter. It was as though only the women of the family existed and hadn't needed men to reproduce. Which was silly, of course, but that line of questioning had always been neatly shot down whenever it was brought up. But maybe there was a photo in one of these boxes that would give her something. A face, a name, anything.

Unfortunately, though she looked through every picture in the box, none were helpfully labeled 'Chloe's dad' or 'Grandpa' or anything similar.

The photos were carefully replaced, and she went through the other boxes and chests. None of the others held photographs, but she did find another trunk with clothes in it. One of the chests held keepsakes, but Chloe had no reference for what any of them meant. Why save that particular shell? Or that specific pressed flower? The smallest of the chests held letters, but Chloe's mind was too full for her to even contemplate reading them. She made a mental note to at least skim through them later to see if they held anything useful.

Her stomach growled and she glanced at her watch, astonished to find she'd been in this room for more than four hours. She stood, groaning as her muscles protested after spending so long kneeling, and went downstairs. She stopped in the kitchen and remembered there was no food in the house. Since it looked like she was going to be staying, at least for a few days, it was time to go get supplies. Including a bottle of whiskey and some Coke to go along with it.

Chapter 5

G iven how small the town of Salus was, it hadn't been hard for Chloe to find a grocery store and a place to buy whiskey. She'd bought enough for a few days before heading back to Granny's, and after picking at what she'd fixed for dinner, she'd heartily indulged in the whiskey and Coke. To her relief, the drink had done its job and temporarily numbed the feelings of grief and utter shock at all the recent revelations.

She avoided going back into the storage room, though her curiosity about the letters she'd found was getting harder to resist. Instead, she turned on the old TV and watched reruns mindlessly until she'd fallen asleep on the couch near midnight.

It was just after dawn when she was awoken by the sound of someone pounding on the front door. She cracked an eye open and managed to draw her arm up far enough to let her see her watch. Quarter to seven. She groaned and draped her arm over her eyes, blocking out the light that streamed in through the window. Her head was pounding, her stomach was doing flips, and her mouth felt like she'd eaten a bucket of sand.

"What do you want?" she tried to yell, but it came out as a low croak. She tried clearing her throat, but her second attempt wasn't any better. When the pounding continued a moment later, she dragged herself off the couch and shuffled to the door. Her clothes were wrinkled, her feet clad only in socks, and her hair was a mess, but she really didn't give a damn right now.

She unlocked the door and threw it open. "What?" she barked before she could even register who was on the other side.

It was Sheriff Adams, and he didn't look at all pleased.

"Can't you come back later? Like after my funeral?" she groaned as she leaned heavily against the doorframe and closed her eyes.

Wesley arched a brow, leaned in, and took a quick sniff. "Hungover, huh? Salus isn't that bad, you know" he said, his tone mildly amused, his lips twitching at her current state. But as quickly as the amusement appeared, it vanished and his eyes narrowed. "Or at least it didn't used to be," he said, his tone mildly accusing.

"Am I supposed to know what you're talking about?" she asked miserably as she squinted at him.

"Perhaps," he said cryptically. "But I also don't think I'm going to get anything out of you until you sober up some. You got a coffee pot in there?"

"Dunno. Maybe? Probably not," she mumbled, falling back to a half-asleep state despite standing up. She had bought coffee the night before but hadn't thought to look for a coffee pot in the kitchen. The one thing that had marred her grandmother's perfection was the fact that she couldn't stand coffee. It was entirely possible there wasn't one in the house.

Wesley sighed and pushed past her, heading for the kitchen. "Shit," she heard him say a minute later. He emerged and walked back over to her. "Okay, put your shoes on. I'm going to take you to the station. You can get your coffee, sober up, then I need to talk to you."

"'Bout what?"

"We'll talk about that when it has a chance of actually reaching your brain," he said dryly as he steered her toward the couch and sat her down.

She stared dumbly at him as he knelt and put her shoes on her feet. For some reason it amused her to see the big, strong sheriff putting her shoes on her like she was a toddler.

He glanced up at her face then made a vague motion toward her head. "You might want to brush your hair or something first."

Some women, Chloe knew, never stepped out of the house without their hair and makeup being perfect. Which was fine, but not her. A quick pat of her hair told her that her ponytail was still intact...sort of, though strands had tugged themselves free and tangled around her face. She sighed and searched for her messenger bag. Spotting it, she managed to make her way over to it to grab a brush out. She pulled the hair tie out and quickly redid the ponytail. It wasn't perfect, but it would do. Next up was to dig out a pair of sunglasses and slip them on her face with a sigh of relief. That done, she slung the bag over her shoulder and turned toward him. "Done. Coffee. Now."

"Yes, ma'am," he said blandly as he helped her out to his cruiser. She didn't balk when he put her in the back seat, which earned her a curious look from Wesley. She figured it might have something to do with the fact that most people didn't like the idea of sitting in the back seat of a police car, whether they were guilty or not. It would probably bother her on a normal day, but right now she felt too wretched to care.

Five minutes later they pulled up to the sheriff's office and he helped her make her way inside. The office wasn't large, with the bulk of that space going to the main room, since it also held three jail cells, all currently unoccupied. The area was spartan, with no personal effects, and was kept tidy. There were three desks, though one was completely bare. A fridge and table were set against one wall, with a microwave and coffee pot set on the latter. Chloe dimly noted three other doors, leading to a bathroom, the evidence room, and a room that was probably used for storage.

Wesley pointed toward the desk with the most paperwork heaped on top of it, or to the chair sitting in front of it, more specifically. "Sit," he instructed as he went to the table and got a pot of coffee brewing. While he waited for it to brew, he grabbed a bottle of water and moved to his desk, opening a drawer and pulling out a bottle of aspirin. He shook a couple pills into his hand, opened the water, and offered both to Chloe. "Take these, they'll help."

Chloe eagerly swallowed the pills before she slumped down in the seat. "You really going to make me wait to find out why I'm at the sheriff's office at seven in the freaking morning? With a hangover?" she asked grumpily.

He perched on the edge of the desk and folded his arms. After studying her face for a moment, he shook his head. "Nope. It's about Jeremy Banner."

"Who?" Chloe asked, genuinely confused.

"Jeremy Banner. He worked at the council building. And he was killed last night, in the woods behind your house."

She sat upright, sharply enough that she winced as her head screamed in pain. "Someone was killed behind my

34

house? Are you shitting me?"

"Really not. Wish I was. We don't get a lot of murders around here, and I tend to prefer it that way."

Chloe struggled to think past the icepicks ramming into her brain. "Are you sure he was killed there? Or was it a body dump?"

He frowned. "I'm sure. Why do you ask that?"

"Because there's a body behind my grandmother's house, which makes me a person of interest." He arched a brow and she continued. "I've got a damn criminal justice degree. I may not be a cop, but I'm not ignorant," she snapped, only to moan when it increased the throbbing of her head. "No, I don't know this…what was it, Jeremy? And I've got no reason to kill anyone."

"Even a man who had a long-standing rivalry with your grandmother?"

Chloe's brow furrowed. "Even if that's true, I still don't know him. And I didn't know about any rivalry." She looked hopefully toward the coffee pot and whimpered when she saw there was probably a cup's worth of dark liquid in it. Before she could get up, Wesley went over, poured a cup, and brought it back to her. Normally she preferred her coffee with plenty of cream, sugar, and a bit of caramel, but right now she needed the jolt only hot, black coffee could provide. She took her first sip, wincing when it scalded her tongue, but took another shortly after. It was horrible, but it was still coffee.

"Hard to prove that, now, isn't it?" Wesley asked, watching her like a hawk.

"Considering you can't really prove a negative? Yep," she grumbled before taking one more drink. "Look, Sheriff…Until two days ago I didn't know Salus existed. Until yesterday I thought I was human. Same for my grandmother. After I found out a whole bunch of shit that my grandmother should have told me years ago, I spent my time freaking out, then getting drunk. I passed out on the couch sometime after eleven thirty and didn't wake up until you so rudely interrupted a very good dream. I don't give a damn about some rivalry or some guy I've never even seen. I just want to find out what else has been kept from me my whole damn life, then go back to my nice, *normal* life. All right?"

His face gave nothing away. She was good at reading people, but she had no idea if he believed her or not. She'd hate to play poker with him.

"You really knew nothing about Salus, or the supernatural, until yesterday?" he asked, his voice not quite so hard anymore.

"That's right. And you can check that part with Emma Mitchell, since she's the one who wrecked my whole view of the world."

He blew out a sharp breath. "I'll have to verify that, but if it's true, then you probably really were drinking yourself into oblivion. You certainly smell like you were, though that wouldn't be admissible in any court outside of Salus or towns like it."

She narrowed her eyes. "You believe me, then? And I can't smell that bad."

Wesley shrugged. "I don't not believe you. And I don't have enough to try and charge you in any case. And yes, you do smell that bad."

Chloe decided to ignore the insult about her current aroma since he probably was right. She'd drank enough that it was probably seeping through her pores right about now. "Of course you can't charge me. There can hardly be evidence I was involved when I wasn't. It's not like anyone here knows me, so why would anyone try to pin it on me?"

"Because you're new and people here distrust outsiders,"

he answered without hesitation.

"Okay, point." She took another drink, relieved when it didn't burn her quite so bad. "You suck at making coffee, by the way, though it does the job on sobering you up."

One corner of his mouth curved upward. "So I've been told. Finish the cup, give me your phone number, and I'll drive you home. And I guess I don't have to tell you not to leave town until my investigation is concluded. Since you've got your degree and all."

"Yeah, I know the drill," she said as she grabbed a pen and notepad off his desk and wrote down her number.

"You work with the police?" he asked curiously.

"Not regularly. Private investigator."

His mouth thinned. "Not sure how I feel about that. Seems to be only two types of those. The sort who don't mind bending, or even breaking the law to get a paycheck, and the much rarer good guys who just want to solve their cases and help people." When she started to speak he held up a hand. "Don't even tell me. If you say you're a good guy, I won't believe it until I see it, and if you're the rule breaker, I don't want to know."

"Fair enough." Chloe drained the last of the coffee and set the mug on the desk. "I'm ready. Though if the diner were closer to Granny's house, I'd just ask you to drop me off there."

"You don't cook?" Wesley asked as they headed out to his car.

"I do, but nothing beats a hangover like the trifecta—coffee, aspirin, and greasy diner food. So far I'm only two for three."

He couldn't argue with that, so nodded and got into the cruiser. "As it happens, I haven't eaten either. I've been in the woods since three, so I could go for some food. And Joel's is the best place for breakfast around here."

"Oh, thank god," she groaned. She hadn't been looking forward to navigating the unfamiliar roads with a hangover. It was better, yes, but still enough to make her mind fuzzy. "Wait, Joel's? I thought we were going to the diner."

"Joel's is the diner. A guy named Joel owns it, and everyone just kept calling it Joel's. Eventually it stuck."

"Gotcha. Okay, enough local history, mama needs some bacon."

Wesley chuckled and pulled out of the lot.

Chapter 6

Though it was a Tuesday, and not even seven-thirty yet, Joel's was about half full. As before, the moment Chloe stepped in the door she was stared at, but since she was accompanied by the sheriff, she supposed it was a little more understandable.

The waitress from the day before, Lexi, was there. She gave Chloe a big grin before she turned back to the customer she was serving.

Chloe was confused by the reaction, unsure why Lexi would be smiling at her like she knew some wicked secret no one else did, but the smell of bacon and pancakes had her stomach growling, so she hurried to a booth and slid into it, with Wesley sitting across from her.

"I didn't realize you knew Lexi," he said as he got settled in.

"I don't, not really. I ate here yesterday. She gave me directions to Emma's house and approved of me telling off everyone who was too busy staring at me to eat anything."

"Ah. Yeah, that sounds like something Lexi would approve of," he said with a nod.

The waitress in question arrived at their table, her pad at the ready, a wide smile on her lips. "Hey there, Wes, Chloe. What are you two doing here so early? Together?" she asked, giving Chloe a knowing and amused look.

Chloe rolled her eyes. "Long story."

"Mmhmm," Lexi said, drawing the sound out and making it sound dirty. "You'll have to tell me sometime. In great detail."

"It wasn't that exciting of a story. And not that sort of story anyway," Wesley said, shaking his head.

"Well, that's a shame. What can I get for you two?"

"You guys have caramel?" Chloe asked.

"Sure do."

"Coffee, loaded up with caramel, hash browns, a whole lot of bacon, and a pancake," she said, hoping that the meal would finish off the worst of her hangover. She hated wearing sunglasses indoors, but no way was she going to risk taking them off just yet.

"Ah. Hangover," Lexi said with an understanding nod as she jotted it down. "And for you, Wes?"

"Actually, I'll have the same, minus the caramel and plus a pancake," he decided. "Thanks, Lex."

"No problem. I'll have the coffee out in a minute," Lexi said, still smiling as she sauntered away.

"You know, I really envy her," Chloe murmured absently as she watched the brunette leave.

"Why's that?" Wesley asked curiously.

"She grew up here, right? So, she's something supernatural, too. But she grew up with all this."

"She is," he verified. "And I suppose that's one way of looking at it. But you've got a perspective she can never have. It's a trade-off."

"True, I guess. Right now, it's hard to see me as getting the better end of the deal, though."

"Why does it have to be better or worse?" he asked, shaking his head. "Yeah, it sounds like you're going through a hell of a rough time right now, but that'll pass. A few weeks, maybe a few months, and things will settle down. You might see things differently then."

"Maybe," she said, unconvinced. "Back at the office, you said something about the murder victim working for the council. You've got a city council around here?"

"What, you thought supernaturals didn't have things like local government, despite sitting across from the sheriff?" Wesley asked, amused.

"Honestly? I never really thought about it," she admitted. "All new, remember? There's a lot I haven't thought about yet. There's a lot I don't even know to ask about yet."

"Point. And yes, we have a council, though I wouldn't call it a city council," he began, pausing when Lexi returned.

"Here you go. Caramel coffee for the hangover victim, and regular for our fearless sheriff. Food will be out in a few," Lexi said with a smile before disappearing again.

While Chloe dumped creamer and sugar into her coffee, Wesley continued. "Instead of a mayor, we've got a council that runs things." He started to add to it, then hesitated. "How much do you know about Salus and the supernatural?"

"Island inhabited by supernatural people, that there are other towns like it. Tidbits about the different races. Elementals, psychics, and—I can't believe I'm saying this—gods." Chloe grimaced. "I still can't quite wrap my head around that."

"Right. Well, the council is made up of five people. Four are from the major supernatural groups that live here—elementals, witches, vampires, and shapeshifters—while the fifth—we call it the omni councilor—can be from any race. All are elected by their particular group, with elections occurring every five years. That way all the races get equally represented, since they all have such vastly different powers and needs."

"Oh. That makes sense. I think." Chloe took a sip of her coffee and gave a soft moan. "Oh yeah, that's good," she murmured, cradling the cup in both hands. "Is it considered rude to ask what someone is?"

He shrugged. "Some people don't care, some do, so it's really a gamble."

She studied him over the rim of her cup. "Good thing I don't mind being rude, then. What are you?"

His lips curved. "I had a feeling you were going to ask that.

I'm a shapeshifter."

"So, you can turn into an animal, right? Like a werewolf?"

Wesley winced. "Yes, though don't reference werewolves too much."

Chloe frowned. "Why not?"

"Okay, there are wolf shifters, they're pretty common actually, but even they don't like to be called werewolves. One, because when you say shifter, every human thinks wolves. But the big reason is the way movies and TV shows tend to show them. Mindless monsters, tied to the moon. Cannibalistic killers. It's not really flattering."

"Oops. Duly noted. You're not a wolf, though?"

"No, I'm a bear."

The mug was set down quickly, a few drops of coffee splashing over the rim, but Chloe didn't notice. "No shit. Like a grizzly bear?"

Wesley let out a surprised bark of laughter. "Actually, yes, though not all bear shifters are grizzlies. Brown, black, polar…they're all out there."

"That is…very freaking cool. At the risk of being rude…again…I'd like to see that sometime." She grinned. "I've always wanted a teddy bear." For a moment he was struck speechless, and the sight of him gaping at her made her laugh. It wasn't until she did that she realized her headache had eased. "Never had anyone call you a teddy bear?"

"Considering I'm almost ten feet tall in that form when I'm standing up, with claws as big as your palm?" He shook his head. "No, I can honestly say they haven't."

"Guess it's that other perspective you were talking about," she said with an innocent smile.

He could only shake his head.

Lexi returned, carrying their plates, and paused, pancakes halfway to the table, when she noticed Wesley's expression. "What'd you do to break the sheriff? I've never seen that look on his face before," she said as she finished setting their food in front of them.

"Said I wanted a teddy bear," Chloe said as she grabbed a

piece of bacon and took a bite, making a sound of pleasure at the taste.

Lexi's eyes widened in gleeful shock. "You did not!"

"No, she did," Wesley confirmed, still sounding disbelieving.

"Hey, give me a break. I don't know the etiquette for all this," Chloe said, using her bacon to make a vague motion. "Not that I've ever been big on etiquette beyond please and thank you."

"Tell me you're sticking around," Lexi begged. "It's been way too dull around here lately, and I have a feeling you're going to stir things up."

"For a little while. I've got to figure out this world, figure myself out, and it seems like Salus is the best place to do it."

"What do you mean figure out this world?"

"Just that. Until yesterday I thought I was human," Chloe answered, trying not to sound as bitter as she felt.

Lexi's pleading expression shifted to a sympathetic one. "If you want some help, I get off work at three and I know where your grandmother's house is," she offered.

For that, Chloe actually held off on gobbling down another piece of bacon. "My grandmother sent me to Emma Mitchell, and she told me a little, but I think I'd like that." She couldn't help but feel that Emma was complicit in keeping the supernatural world a secret, however illogical that feeling might be. And though she knew now that she couldn't base someone's approximate age on their appearance, she got the impression that Lexi was closer in age to her own, which might be easier for her.

"Then I'll be over around four," Lexi said with a smile. "Enjoy," she said, lightly touching Chloe's shoulder before moving to her next customer.

"You could do worse than Lexi for help in figuring things out," Wesley said.

"She seems nice enough," Chloe agreed. "And fun, too."

"There's that, yes, but she's also got a gentle way about her. It doesn't show on the surface, and I won't go into details, but I think she might be the best person on Salus for you to talk to."

"Well, that's not cryptic," she muttered, which made him smile.

"I'm sure she'll tell you this afternoon. For right now, I'd finish your breakfast so you can go home and shower. Then probably a nap once you're feeling more human."

"All very good ideas." A few minutes passed before she asked, "Will you keep me in the loop on the incident behind my house? I mean, my grandmother's house? I know I'm not cleared of suspicion, not completely, and I'm not a cop, but I'm curious." She paused and arched a brow at him. "I might even be some help."

Wesley cocked his head. "I've got a deputy, and we've got people with all sorts of powers to help out, but I'll keep that in mind. And yes, I will let you know what I can, when I can."

"That's all I can ask," she said, trying to convince herself to be satisfied with that. The investigator side of her itched to dive in and do what she did best. No, she'd never investigated a murder before, or not directly, but at the core of it, an investigation was an investigation. Okay, so the supernatural aspect skewed things—a lot—but she'd adjust.

Twenty minutes later Wesley had dropped her off and she took his advice, showering until the water went cold, then crawling into bed for a lengthy nap. Maybe afterward she'd feel human. Or whatever the hell she was now.

Chapter 7

A few minutes after four, Lexi arrived. She knocked and called out, "The party has arrived!"

Chloe smiled as she padded toward the door, wearing a clean pair of jeans and a tee-shirt, her hair pulled up into a neat ponytail once more. "The party, huh? And here I thought you were going to help me figure things out," she said after she opened the door.

"Oh, I am, but wherever I go is a party," Lexi said with a bright grin as she strode into the house. She looked more herself now that she was off work. At Joel's, her hair had been pulled up and she'd worn jeans, a polo shirt, and black apron. Now her chestnut hair fell straight to her hips, and she wore a pair of skinny jeans and a snug sapphire sweater that almost matched her eyes. It suited her.

"Can't argue that," Chloe said, amused, as she followed Lexi into the living room and dropped down onto the couch.

Lexi sat beside her and patted her knee. "Don't worry, you'll learn to love me. Before you know it, I'm going to be your favorite person in Salus."

Chloe laughed. "You kind of already are. You haven't dumped any huge revelations on me, almost accused me of murder, or stared at me like I was some exhibit in a zoo."

"Whoa, back up there," Lexi said, suddenly serious. "Murder? Someone thought you killed Jeremy?"

"Why do you think I was at the diner with the sheriff this morning?"

Lexi snorted and shook her head. "What an idiot. I expected more of that guy. Of course you didn't kill Jeremy."

"I think I convinced him of that," Chloe muttered. "No reason for me to kill him, considering I had just gotten into town, never met the guy, and was busy being passed out right where we're sitting when the guy was killed."

"Damn. Hell of a day you've had, then."

"Not just today. This last week has sucked. My grandmother died, I find out I'm not human, see magic—real magic—and I get accused of murder while I have a hangover." Chloe grimaced. "Hopefully it can only get better from here."

"Well, I'm here, so that's better," Lexi said with a grin. "But let's start with the not human thing. You're *that* new to all this?"

"Mmhmm. Though I have to admit, it's not all bad."

"Oh?"

"Yeah. I mean, finding out the slightly grumpy sheriff turns into a bear was pretty kick ass. And apparently, I'm an elemental, which is…okay, that part's just weird, but the bear thing is cool." She drew her legs up and cocked her head. "Have you ever seen him as a bear?"

"Man, I wish," Lexi said with a sigh. "That man is hot. But shifters don't just shift in the middle of town. It's not a super private thing—at least not in Salus—but they don't tend to just wander around in their animal forms. I have seen a few others shifted, but not him."

"I kind of really want to see it," Chloe admitted. "Emma did this thing where she made water float around, and that sort of cemented the whole magic is real thing for me, but shifting sounds cooler."

"It is pretty damn cool," Lexi agreed. "You'll end up seeing a lot of magic around here. Some people are super casual about it. Plates get levitated at the diner all the time because it's just more convenient."

"Do you do the levitating?"

"Me?" Lexi shook her head. "Nah. I'm a psychic, sure, but my gift isn't telekinesis."

"What is your gift?"

Lexi shifted uncomfortably and sighed as she glanced to a spot over Chloe's shoulder. "Promise not to freak out?"

"Uh, no? Sorry, but I just can't predict what my reaction will be to something unknown. Like when someone promises not to get mad, how do you know? Maybe you'll be royally pissed off. But I can *try* not to freak out?"

"Good enough. I'm a medium." When Chloe just looked blank, she toyed with the ends of her hair. "I see ghosts. Talk to them. Ghosts are my thing." Chloe said nothing for so long Lexi got nervous. "Say something."

"Now I know why the sheriff said you were really empathetic. You'd either have to be really bitter or really sympathetic if you deal with ghosts a lot."

Lexi relaxed back into the couch and smiled. "You're not wrong. Though I have my moments of bitterness. It can be hard seeing ghosts all the time, especially when they know you can see them. They all want help. It's not so bad with supernatural ghosts, because most of them understand the limitations a medium has, but human ghosts? They're demanding."

That made a weird sort of sense to Chloe, so she nodded. "Are there downsides to every supernatural race?"

"Eh," Lexi said, shrugging. "Witches are pretty much downside free, though it all depends on what their powers are. Some are mediums, too, for example. It's actually where people like me get their gifts."

"What do you mean?"

"Psychics are sort of supernatural lite. We don't necessarily have supernatural parents, though there's always one somewhere in our ancestry. In my case, I have a human mom, and my dad's psychic. His dad is a witch, who can see ghosts too, of course. That's where dad and I get our powers."

"Seriously? That's kinda cool. Do you still…" She trailed off, unsure how to ask how long a psychic's lifespan was. There was no tactful way to ask someone how long they were going to live. "I know Emma said supernaturals lived a long time..." she hinted.

Luckily, Lexi caught on and grinned. "Psychics are supernatural in that regard, yes. We just don't have the same versatility in powers, that's all. We generally only have one gift and that's it. Sometimes two, but it's rare."

"Oh. Well, good."

Lexi laughed. "I'm not going to argue. If I was human, I'd have gray hair already and be dealing with wrinkles." She shuddered in disgust. "I am so not ready to deal with wrinkles."

Chloe frowned. "Gray hair? Just how old are you?"

"Sixty-two," Lexi answered, grinning gleefully when Chloe's jaw dropped.

"I don't think that's really sunk in, yet," Chloe admitted. "And it's really messing with my mind. I'm a private investigator, so I deal with people a lot, and judging ages comes in handy. I was good at it, too, but now that's just out the window."

"You'll adjust. You said you just learned about this stuff yesterday, right? Give yourself a break. It'll come. Soon you'll be a Salus island expert," Lexi assured her.

"I don't know about that. And it's not like I'm going to be staying."

Lexi's face fell. "You're not staying?"

"I've got a business in Philadelphia, Lexi. I've got a life there." Though if she thought about it, really thought about it, she didn't have much of one. She'd been too focused on getting her business off the ground she'd stopped socializing much. She hadn't had a date in almost a year, and her friends were all busy getting married and having kids. "There's nothing for me here, though."

"A business? An investigative business?" Lexi asked.

"Yeah. Started it almost two years ago. It's just starting to take off."

"Why don't you just move it here? We're not a big city, but that just means you won't have a lot of competition for business."

Chloe cocked her head. Staying here hadn't really occurred to her before. Until now it had just been a temporary visit to get answers, then she was gone. But really, she didn't have that many clients yet, and it wouldn't be that hard to uproot her life. She rented, and she did have enough money to last her until she got settled. *If* there was enough business. Though her grandmother's house was paid for, so that would be one bill she didn't have to worry about. "What use could people here have for a normal investigator, though? I asked the sheriff to keep me in the loop on the murder, offered to help, but he said there were people with powers that could help more. So why would they need me?"

"Don't get me wrong, there are a lot of times where powers make investigating things easy. Have a stray object at a crime scene? Bring in someone with psychometry to touch it and tell you who it belonged to. Have a murder victim who left a ghost? Which is rare, by the way. You just bring in someone like me and hope the ghost knows something useful. But magic can also be used to obscure a lot of evidence or whatever. And magic can make people lazy about certain things, too. If you could read minds, would you bother to really learn how to read body language?"

"I don't know. Maybe not? Depends on how often you read minds, I guess."

"Exactly. Which is why our sheriff isn't someone with any of those powers, but a bear with a lot of experience and a criminal justice degree." Lexi paused, then added reluctantly, "And a really good sense of smell."

"Why not a wolf, if they wanted a good sense of smell?"

"Bears actually have one of the best senses of smell of any animal, even better than dogs or wolves," Lexi answered, then she grinned. "You learn things like that when you live with animals that can actually talk."

"Huh. That's actually pretty cool. And explains why they're so big on making sure campers keep food in sealed containers."

"Exactly." Lexi kicked her shoes off then drew her legs up to sit cross-legged, facing Chloe. "Now, any other supernatural questions you have for me, or do you want a surprise?"

Intrigued, Chloe shifted to mirror Lexi's pose. "What sort of surprise?"

"Hopefully a good one."

"Let me have it."

Lexi drew in a slow breath. "Your grandmother's here."

That wasn't at all what Chloe was expecting, and just blinked at Lexi. "What?"

"Your grandmother. She's here. Or, well, her ghost is."

Chloe straightened sharply and twisted around but saw no one but Lexi.

"I'm sorry, Chloe. I can't make ghosts visible to anyone who can't see them naturally," Lexi said quietly. "But she can see you, hear you, and I can tell you what she's saying."

Chloe turned back to Lexi, fighting against a surge of emotion. "What's she saying now?"

"She's sorry she never told you about Salus, about your heritage. She says she almost told you a hundred times over the years, but she wanted to make sure you had a normal life, at least for a little while."

"There are hundreds—no, millions—of people who would give a limb to grow up with magical powers. What's so bad about being supernatural that she preferred normal over this?" Chloe whispered.

Lexi winced sympathetically but listened to Lydia's ghost. "She can't tell you, not everything. Apparently, it's dangerous information to have. But she says being an elemental isn't bad. It's wonderful. And being an aether elemental, like you are, opens a lot of possibilities, even if it's not flashy like fire or earth."

"What can be so dangerous about knowing who I am? And I know now, so why can't she tell me why she kept it from me?" Chloe demanded, grief buckling under growing anger.

Poor Lexi, caught between a new friend and the ghost of an old friend, grimaced, but she continued to relay Lydia's words. "She says you'll find out soon enough. That you need to trust in yourself and learn about Salus and your powers. She says she

50

loves you, and that you'll understand before too much longer."

Chloe's eyes closed and she slowly shook her head. "I'm sorry, Granny. I don't know if I can accept that. I...I just can't do this right now. I love you, and I miss you, but this has been way too much in too short a time." It felt like something brushed her shoulder and she opened her eyes, but Lexi hadn't moved. She lifted a hand to her shoulder and frowned at the woman across from her.

"She's touching your shoulder, and she says she understands. That she'll be here for you when you're ready," Lexi said gently.

"Bye, Granny," Chloe said, voice choked and quiet.

"I'm so sorry, Chloe. I didn't know...I just wanted to help give you both a little bit of closure," Lexi said, her face full of remorse.

"It's not your fault, Lexi. You couldn't know." Chloe worked up a shaky smile. "I do appreciate it, though. She died so suddenly, I never got to say good bye or that I loved her."

Lexi leaned over and wrapped her arms around Chloe. That was all it took to have Chloe breaking. Not once since she'd gotten the news about Granny's death had anyone offered her such a simple, and meaningful, gesture as a hug. She pressed her face against Lexi's shoulder and let the tears come, purging the grief, the anger over her grandmother's death.

Chapter 8

Lexi ended up spending the night and crashing on the couch, though they kept topics mild after Chloe had composed herself. When Chloe woke up the next morning Lexi was already gone, leaving a note on the table saying she had to get to work. She'd also added her phone number at the bottom, which Chloe added to her contacts.

Chloe showered and changed before she headed to Joel's. Today she was going to make damn sure she got a coffee pot. Even if she was only staying for a week or so, she couldn't run to the diner every time she wanted coffee, no matter how much she enjoyed Lexi's company.

After she'd gotten breakfast, she sat in her car and debated what to do with her day. First stop would definitely be finding the coffee pot, but that would require finding a place that sold them. Maybe she should spend the day checking out the town. It wasn't quite as small as she'd feared, and now she was curious to see what sort of businesses a town populated by witches and shapeshifters would have. She'd seen some normal places on her first day—the hospital, vet, and diner—but they had to have some unusual businesses. Psychics who were legit, maybe, or stores that sold magic wands or cauldrons or something.

She shut the car off and grabbed her bag before getting out. Yes, she could drive around and see everything easily enough, but walking would allow her to look in windows and wander inside as she liked.

The street Joel's was on was normal as far as she could tell. A boutique, gym, library, and lawyer's office, along with the grocery story she'd stopped at before. She went over a street and passed the library and fire station, before she came across the first business that made her want to giggle. Salus had an apothecary. Not a pharmacy, no, the window clearly said apothecary. Chloe wandered closer to the window and peered inside, delighted to see jars and bottles full of odd materials and bundles of herbs hanging from hooks. She'd never been one to really go for alternative medicine and herbal healing, but she was oddly tempted to go inside and check it out. Maybe there would be some magic hangover cure. She made a note to go in later.

A few hours later she'd finished wandering through the town, disappointed that the only other unusual places she'd seen were a business that helped people with ghosts, and one that offered enchanted objects. That one had been extremely hard to avoid going inside, but part of her was nervous to find out what sort of things enchanted objects could do. Every other building looked annoyingly...normal. A bar, gas station, furniture store, pet store. And a general store which had a coffee maker. She wasted no time in buying one before she made her way back to her car and deposited it in the back seat.

The walk around town had been surprisingly exhausting, so she headed back to Granny's and carried the coffee pot inside and got it set up. It was tempting to go ahead and make a pot, but she made the mistake of glancing out the window to the trees behind her house.

The sheriff hadn't said how far behind her house the murder site had been, but it couldn't be far for him to connect it to her so easily. She was an urbanite, but surely she could make it a few hundred feet into the woods and back without getting lost. And her cell signal had been surprisingly good everywhere on the island so far. Hopefully that would extend into the woods.

Besides, she didn't doubt there was still crime scene tape up, and bright yellow would stand out amongst the greens, browns, and reds.

Unfortunately, she didn't have any gloves, but she found a flashlight and some tweezers. The sheriff probably wouldn't be too happy about her poking around his crime scene, but dammit, it was behind her house and she'd been blamed for the murder. It was unlikely Wesley would actually give her any information, which meant she would have to get it on her own. No doubt the body had already been transported, but it was entirely possible she'd find something.

Chloe moved slowly into the woods, scanning for any sign of the crime scene. A few minutes later she couldn't see any sign of the house but was pretty certain it was still directly behind her. It was another ten minutes before she stumbled upon the yellow she'd been searching for. She doubted she was really all that far from her house, but she'd had to backtrack and find ways around natural obstacles, such as the large patch of briars she'd nearly stumbled into.

As expected, the body had been moved, which was a good thing, as a crow rested in the branches above the crime scene. Even without the crow or police tape, Chloe would have known where the body had lain. Leaves and dirt were disturbed and bloodstained. There was actually quite a bit of blood, but it had pooled rather than splattered. At least she didn't see much in the way of splatter, which limited the potential causes of death. A gunshot, for instance, would have left the trees and surrounding area sprinkled with blood.

Though the sun was shining, she used the flashlight as she searched for anything Wesley may have missed, but saw nothing. She glanced around, then crept closer to the police tape, until she stood only a few feet from the nearest bloodstain.

Suddenly she felt lightheaded. It was bad enough that she stumbled until her shoulder hit a tree, which helped keep her upright. On the heels of that feeling came a tingling sensation across her skin, just like she'd felt when she first arrived on Salus.

Chloe turned so her back was against the tree, and she slowly sat down, struggling to breathe normally and fight against the panic. Twice in three days she'd been overcome by this vertigo, and she still had no idea what the cause was. But now she had a third option to add to sickness and stress—magic.

She dug out her phone and fumbled with it until she could hit the button to call Lexi. It rang so long she was afraid it was going to go to voicemail, but Lexi finally picked up.

"Chloe? I can't really talk right now. Lunch rush is—"

"Something's wrong, Lex," Chloe said, her voice trembling.

Lexi's voice switched from harassed to concerned. "What is it? What's wrong?"

"Keep feeling weird. Lightheaded, bad. And my skin feels like it's crawling," Chloe answered, rubbing her free hand over her arm, but it did nothing to help the odd sensation.

There was a long pause from Lexi. "What were you doing when it happened?"

"First time I was just getting to Salus. This time…" She was reluctant to admit to what was borderline illegal, but she trusted Lexi, even after only a few days. "I'm at the crime scene behind my house."

Lexi made an unhappy noise. "You're an aether, honey," she said gently. "I think you're reacting to magic, but that's just my best guess. I'd tell you to talk to another one, but there hasn't been an aether elemental on Salus since your grandmother left."

"What about an elemental? Someone who might be able to help?" Chloe was desperate. She'd take anything at the moment.

"Actually, yeah. He's not an aether, but he's pretty damn smart, so he might be able to tell you something at least." Lexi pulled the phone away from her mouth to tell someone, "Just hold on a second, okay? You'll survive without your BLT for two minutes." Back to Chloe, she asked, "Do you know where the bookstore is?"

"Yeah. Saw it earlier."

"Good. Go there. Guy named Zane owns it. He's an elemental. See him, tell him I sent you." Her tone turned apologetic. "I'm really sorry, honey, but I've got to go. Talk to Zane, and let me know if you need anything else, okay?"

"I will. Thanks, Lexi." Chloe disconnected but didn't move immediately. The dizziness was still present, though it had receded a little. If Lexi was right and she was reacting to magic, it seemed to be centered on the crime scene. If she put some distance between her and it, maybe she'd feel better. She wasn't quite up for walking, but she forced herself onto all fours and crawled away from the taped off area. The further she got, the better she felt, until she was able to get to her feet.

"That really sucked," she muttered as she stood, put a hand on a tree, and leaned against it, giving herself a minute to make sure she wasn't going to relapse. When she still felt good a few minutes later she sighed with relief. "Now just to find my way back home." She was pretty sure what direction the house was in and started walking.

Twenty minutes later she hadn't found her house or anyone else's, nor did she see anything familiar. "Dammit." She put her hands on her hips and turned in a slow circle but had no idea which way to go.

"Who are you?" came a woman's voice from her left.

Chloe turned and saw a woman a few inches shorter than herself. She looked cute and utterly harmless, which matched her sweet voice, though something about her made Chloe wary. Short, curly red hair, fair skin with freckles, and bright blue eyes really worked for her, but seemed out of place to Chloe in the middle of the woods. Maybe if she had a fawn next to her or a bluebird on her shoulder it would make the picture seem more complete. But something in her demeanor had Chloe watching her closely.

"Chloe Chadwick." And because she knew it would come up, she added, "Lydia Chadwick's granddaughter."

The woman made a noncommittal noise. "What are you doing out here?" she asked, a suspicious gleam in her eyes that was at odds with her voice.

"Honestly? Trying to find my way back to my grandmother's house," Chloe admitted. "Who are you?"

"The woman who knows where she is," came the sarcastic reply before the woman sighed. "I'm Peyton. You want to go that way," she said with some impatience, pointing. "About five minutes, give or take."

"Ah. Thanks." She started to say something else, but Peyton's demeanor didn't really suggest she wanted company. Still, Chloe was curious what the woman was doing out here. She was in jeans and a sweater and carried a burlap bag that looked mostly empty. With nothing more to say she just nodded to Peyton and started walking. She glanced over her shoulder at the redhead, uncertain just why the woman gave her such a weird feeling. Peyton watched her for a moment before she headed deeper into the woods.

"Weird," Chloe murmured, shaking her head before continuing on.

It was a little more than five minutes before she saw her backyard and felt a swell of relief. Wandering around the woods, lost, was not how she wanted to spend the rest of her day. And no way would she have given in and called the sheriff for help. Odds are, he would've given her a lecture, if he didn't try to stick her in a jail cell for interfering with a police investigation.

Inside, she changed, since her clothes had gotten dirty while she was crawling around on the forest floor, then left for the bookstore and, hopefully, answers.

Chapter 9

Chloe parked in front of the bookstore and stared at it for a moment. It didn't look like a business owned by an elemental. Not that she knew what a business owned by an elemental should look like. It was actually a little disappointing how absolutely *normal* everything here looked.

She got out of the car and went into the store, a little bell dinging when she opened the door. The place smelled like books, old and new, and though she'd never been a huge reader, she found the scent comforting. Before this, she'd only been in chain bookstores, and this one didn't resemble one by any stretch of the imagination. It had dark wooden shelves, most of which reached the ceiling, with books stacked here and there. There was a clear organization, yes, but it was less regimented and more homey. Plus, she had never seen some of the sections she saw here in the big chains. None of them would have shelves set aside for alchemy or magical history, no biographies on important supernatural beings or books on how to deal with a familiar. She had to admit, she was tempted to pick up a few of them herself but couldn't let herself get distracted.

"Hello?" she called out as she wandered past shelves and tables. "I'm looking for Zane."

"Second!" There was a low thud, followed by a muttered curse and what sounded like a stack of books falling over.

She winced sympathetically. "You okay? Sound like that hurt."

A man came out of the back, limping a little. "Yeah, I'm okay. Just...tripped," he said, looking sheepish.

He was kind of cute, in a nerdy sort of way, Chloe thought. Tall, slim, with brown hair gone a little shaggy. His eyes were blue behind his glasses, which he pushed up his nose as he studied her in return. "Did I hear you say you were looking for Zane?"

Chloe nodded. "Yeah. My friend Lexi told me he might be able to help me."

He frowned. "She did? With what? Do you need a book or something?" He brightened. "Because I can definitely help you find a book."

"So, you are Zane, then?"

"Oh, yes, I am. Sorry," he answered, cheeks going pink.

Chloe fought not to grin. He really was cute. Adorable, really. She found herself wanting to ruffle his hair or take him home like a puppy. "I'm Chloe Chadwick."

Zane brightened. "Lydia's granddaughter?" When she nodded he moved closer and offered his hand. "Great lady, Lydia. Happy to finally meet her granddaughter. But what is it I can help you with?"

"Well, my grandmother kept all this...supernatural stuff from me, so I just learned it existed. Which means I just learned I was an elemental," she explained. "So, I've got no idea what I can do, or how to do it."

The smile on Zane's face dimmed. "I'm not an aether—"

"I know," she assured him. "Lexi told me my grandmother was the last one to live on the island. But you're an elemental, right? And Lexi said you were really smart. I mean, just because we have different elements or whatever, it doesn't mean you can't help me, does it? And if there aren't any other aether elementals...well, someone has to teach me, right?"

He looked thoughtful. "I can certainly try, though your

element is unique as far as elementals go. The rest of them all have physical manifestations, even if it's just energy like fire or wind. So, there's something…I don't want to say real—tangible works better—to control. You? Your element is magic, life. It's a bit more complicated."

"Exactly why I need some sort of direction. I've been having…issues."

He looked concerned as he led her to a pair of comfortable chairs and sat. "What sort of issues?"

She settled herself and shrugged, feeling both like she was at the doctor's and back in kindergarten. Hell, kids in Salus probably knew more about magic right now than she did. "Lexi thinks I'm sensing magic. I've gotten majorly dizzy twice now, and it's felt like my skin is crawling, or something's crawling over it."

Zane made a thoughtful noise and nodded. "Very possible. Some of us can sense our element, even scry through it, so if you're untrained the feeling would be extremely unfamiliar," he agreed. "I can see it even being unpleasant or frightening, especially with it manifesting how you described. And with you not having grown up with it…"

"Frightening? Yeah, you could say that. I may have had a freak out," she admitted. "So, do you think you could help me? Even just some basics would be good."

He blew out a quiet breath before he nodded. "I can try. But not here. I'm an air elemental, and I'd rather not risk a book tornado. The park would be good, though. Nice, open area. I close at five today, so I can meet you there at five thirty?"

"That sounds good. I think I saw the park earlier when I was exploring the town."

"Wonderful. Then I'll meet you there," Zane said with a warm smile.

"See you there."

Chloe got to the park half an hour early. She liked being outdoors…in a civilized setting, which a park was. She was hoping it would help relax her, which she definitely needed.

She sat on the grass under a tree, leaning against the hard bark. There weren't a lot of people around, but she wasn't alone either. A crow was perched in the branches above her, watching people much like she was. On a large stretch of grass, four boys ran around kicking a ball and laughing while a pair of women sat on a bench, watching and chatting. One of the kids kicked the ball and it went wide, bouncing well away from them. It gave Chloe a jolt when another of the kids gestured and made the ball stop, then fly back toward the group.

It was one thing to know the supernatural existed, to know she was on a supernaturally populated island, another to see people using powers so openly. It also proved that these kids did, in fact, know more about magic than she did, which was mildly depressing.

"Weird," she murmured before she settled in to relax and people watch.

She'd started to doze off when Zane arrived.

"Relaxed is a good way to be when trying to use your powers for the first time," he said as he stood beside her, grinning.

Chloe cracked an eye open. "Half asleep isn't really relaxed, but it'll work, I guess." She stretched and sat up. "Thanks for coming, Zane."

"My pleasure." He lowered his body to the grass beside her. "So, what do you know about aether as an element?"

She shrugged. "It's the essence of magic. And you said life, too?"

"I did," he confirmed. "Aether elementals can affect magic itself. From what I've heard and read, you can possibly affect magical blocks and wards, tweak spells, and, of course, sense magic. Basically, there's the potential to do anything you want with magic itself, though you're limited in what magic you can do on your own."

Curious, Chloe asked, "How do you mean?"

"Okay. All other supernaturals have magic of their own. Or

61

powers, if that makes more sense. Witches can throw fireballs and cast spells. Shifters can change their form. Vampires have magical persuasion. Other elementals can do things like create fire, turn their skin to stone, direct a breeze or the course of a stream. But aethers?" He shook his head. "Most don't have active powers of their own. From what I've read, your active powers are creating a wall or bubble to block magic or sense it, but to do anything else you need someone else to be doing magic first."

"Gotcha. I think. I'm guessing you won't be starting me off with the bubbles, so what are you going to teach me?"

Zane smiled. "First, we'll start with me doing magic, so you can get used to the feeling it generates in you. Then I'll get you to try to affect my magic. To stop it, at first. I think that'll be easier than hijacking it."

Chloe's brows lift. "I can hijack other people's magic?"

He shrugged. "Some can, yes. And that's what I meant by you need someone else to do magic for you to really flex your own powers. But not every member of a race has the exact same powers, so you may or may not be able to." He thought for a moment, then said, "It's just like non-magical talents. Everyone has a different skill set. Taking away magic, you and I are both humans, but I'm sure there are things you're good at that I'm terrible at, and vice versa." When her lips started to tilt downward, he patted her knee comfortingly. "Don't worry. There are a few things every member *can* do. Like all elementals can manipulate their element to some degree, all shifters can transform into their animal. Things like that."

She nodded slowly, and really hoped she didn't get the short end of the magical stick. "Gotcha. Okay. Let's do this."

He smiled. "Close your eyes. It'll help you focus on what you feel rather than what you see." When she complied, he lifted his hand, palm up, and generated a small cyclone that danced atop his hand.

When she said nothing, not even the smallest reaction, he made a gentle throwing gesture and sent the cyclone moving off his hand and onto the grass. There he made it grow, until it had transformed from a few inches high to a whirlwind as tall as he was.

Chloe shivered and rubbed her hands over her arms. "I feel that. It's the same as I mentioned before—the tingling and skin crawling—only not as intense."

"Good. Sensing magic is the first step to manipulating it."

"What is it you're doing?" she asked, opening her eyes. When she saw the tiny twister, which had picked up bits of grass and leaves, she gasped in surprise and delight. "Holy crap."

Zane chuckled. "I started small, but you didn't seem to react to it, so I put more magic into it, basically. Stronger magic, stronger reaction."

"Can you tone it down, now? I know I'm supposed to be getting used to that feeling, but I think doing that gradually would be better."

His brows lowered. "Is the feeling that unsettling?" he asked as he clenched his hand and had the whirlwind disappearing.

"Sort of? It's more that it's a weird feeling and I'm not used to it. The first time it happened I wondered if I was sick." But when he stopped using magic, the sensation dissipated.

"Oh. I'm sorry, I didn't realize it was that bad," Zane said apologetically.

She smiled and shook her head. "No, it's fine. You couldn't have known."

He considered her for a moment. "I know you wanted a break from that feeling, but are you ready to try something yourself? I'll do the small cyclone again, and you can try to stop the magic. So, you'll still have that tingling feeling, but…"

And now she was nervous. Sensing magic was one thing, doing it? Was terrifying. Especially if it came with the skin-crawling. But she wasn't a coward, and she needed to learn, so she straightened her back and nodded. "I am. How do I do it?"

"I only know the basic idea here as it's not something I can do myself," he explained. "But you should be able to sense the magic, reach out with your own power, and shut it off. Some people can absorb it, too, I think. If you're a visual person, you might imagine yourself reaching out slicing through the flow of

63

magic, though. Or something similar. Why don't you just give it a few tries, and if it doesn't work, we'll try something new?"

"Okay. Go for it."

Zane summoned the tiny whirlwind again. "Anytime you're ready. And if you can't focus, try holding my hand. Contact can make magic easier, or stronger," he offered, holding his other hand out to her.

Chloe took a deep breath and nodded, taking his hand. She focused her attention on the spinning air. She couldn't really feel it like she could when it was big, and no matter how she tried to reach it, nothing happened. She thought about shutting it off, snuffing it out, even just nudging it, but it was all just thoughts. Even his visualization suggestion didn't help. It didn't *feel* like she was reaching out in any way.

After several minutes passed, with Zane only watching her patiently, she drew her hand back and made an aggravated noise. "Nothing. I can't even feel it. And I'm not feeling anything else even trying to happen," she admitted, slumping back against the tree.

Zane let the magic fade and frowned. "Hmm. And you said you've never used your power before? Even accidentally?"

She shook her head. "No, never."

"You might have a block on your powers. Something done intentionally so you didn't do something on accident and discover your powers. If it's okay with you, I'd like to call someone who can sense such things, have him come check you out."

"Sure. If I do have some sort of block I'd like to know." Something tickled in the back of her mind, something she knew she should remember, something that was related to her powers. But the harder she tried to grasp at it, the further away it slipped.

Zane nodded and shifted so he could pull out his phone. "Diego? It's Zane. Are you busy? Great. I'm at Olympus Park with Lydia Chadwick's granddaughter. Any chance you could come down here? No, not just to meet her. I think she might have a block on her powers. Okay, great. Yeah, that's fine. We'll be waiting." He hung up and smiled. "Diego will be here as soon as he can. I think you'll like him."

"Who is he?" Chloe asked as she leaned back against the tree.

"A witch. The witch councilor, actually. His specialty is actually pretty close to your powers. Raw magic, essentially. If anyone can tell us what's going on with your powers, it's him."

She wasn't sure how she felt about meeting a member of the council—politicians weren't her favorite sort of people—but she'd take whatever she could get.

It was twenty minutes later when an attractive man in slacks and a button-down shirt walked over to him. Though he was well-groomed, he wasn't slick, which Chloe appreciated. His black hair was neatly trimmed, and he clearly took care of himself. His brown eyes matched the smile on his face when he neared them.

"Hello, Zane," he said, with the faintest hint of an accent. She wasn't sure what it was, not with as subtle as it was. Wherever he was originally from, he hadn't been there in a while.

"Hey Diego. Thanks for coming," Zane said.

"Of course." He turned to Chloe. "And you must be Lydia's granddaughter."

While she was happy so many people fondly remembered Granny, she was getting tired of her identity being just 'Lydia's Granddaughter'. Still, she smiled and nodded. "I am. Name's Chloe. Nice to meet you."

Diego offered his hand to her. When she took it, rather than shake it, he bent and brushed his lips lightly over her knuckles. "The pleasure is all mine." Unconcerned about getting grass stains on his nice pants, he sat beside them. "Zane says you might have a block on your powers? Do you know where it might have come from?"

"His guess is better than mine, so probably? And it was probably my grandmother. She kept the truth of what I was from me," Chloe answered. Suddenly it clicked. "Emma...she was my grandmother's friend. She said something about my powers being bound."

Diego nodded. "That's the same thing as a block. Let's see what we've got." He held both his hands out, palm up. "Touch will—"

"Yeah, Zane explained it makes magic easier," Chloe said with a grin, happy to know *something* about magic.

Diego smiled as she laid her hands in his. "You're learning then. Zane's a good teacher."

"I don't know about that. I've never actually taught someone how to use their powers before," Zane said, scratching the back of his neck.

"It sounds like you're doing fine," Diego promised. "Okay. This might feel a little odd, because I'm basically going to be probing your magic and aura, but just relax. I won't hurt you."

Though she'd only known Zane a few hours longer than Diego, she glanced to him. He smiled and nodded reassuringly, so she nodded. "Okay."

Diego closed his eyes and she felt a slight tingling. She was surprised to feel something so mild, when every other reaction she'd had to magic had been strong. Almost as soon as she had that though, she felt like someone was poking at her, but internally. It wasn't really a pleasant sensation, but it didn't hurt. Her nose wrinkled but she said nothing.

"Zane was right," Diego murmured. "There's a strong block on your powers. It's very well done, actually, but there are cracks in it."

"That's probably why you can sense strong magic but not do anything with it," Zane said.

"Probably," Diego agreed.

"Can you get rid of it? I get the purpose for it—sort of—and I'm sure my grandmother had a good reason for it, but I don't want to have part of myself locked away. Even if it's something I don't understand and am not exactly sure I want," Chloe asked.

Diego's eyes opened. "I can certainly try. If you're sure that's what you want me to do. Once it's down, I don't know of anyone offhand who could recreate it. Not as strong as it is now, in any case."

Was it what she wanted? She could leave it in place and stick to her original plan of going back to her normal life. "What are the chances it'll break on its own if you leave it alone?"

"With the cracks in it? Almost certain. It's just a matter of when. Which would likely be a stressful situation," he warned.

"Then yeah, get rid of it," Chloe confirmed. "Please," she added as an afterthought. She wasn't trying to be rude, but she was reaching her limit on what she could handle at once.

"Okay. This might feel even worse. I can't promise it won't hurt a little," Diego said apologetically. "It sounds like this block has been there for a while, so it might be resistant."

She grimaced but nodded. "I can handle a little pain." She'd handle whatever she had to in order to figure this all out.

"Okay." Diego closed his eyes again and this time Chloe got the strong sensation she was expecting before. Almost immediately it morphed. Instead of feeling like something was crawling across her skin, it started to feel like someone was pulling off a thousand Band-aids, slowly, all at the same time. She grit her teeth but when the pain grew stronger, she couldn't help but whimper. Her hands clamped down on Diego's hands against her will, but she couldn't stop herself. It was that or scream.

"Hold on, Chloe. He'll be done in a minute," Zane said encouragingly, though his face reflected his worry. "You can do this. Just breathe."

She gave a jerky nod and tried to focus on his voice rather than the pain, which continued to get more intense. It came to a climax when she felt something snap, then implode inside her, which sent a bolt of agony through every nerve ending.

Her head fell back and she screamed as whatever had gathered inside her exploded outward, throwing Zane and Diego back twenty feet, and nearly flattening the tree behind her.

Chapter 10

Chloe slumped forward, her cheek against the grass. For a minute she could only lay there and breathe, dimly hearing the sound of children screaming and a strange hoarse cry from somewhere nearby.

It took a great deal of effort, but she was able to lift her head. The kids she'd seen playing earlier were yelling and running toward the women who'd been watching them. It took a moment for her to spot Zane and Diego. They were both sprawled on the grass, unmoving.

"Oh god." She tried to get to her feet, but her limbs simply wouldn't cooperate, so she scrambled clumsily on all fours toward them. She reached Zane first and checked his pulse, relieved when she felt it beating strongly beneath her fingers. Her eyes closed and she fought against a sob. For a second, a terrifying second, she had been afraid she'd killed him. Killed them.

"Diego," she whispered, and managed to move the five feet toward the other man. Like Zane, his pulse was fine, and she could see him breathing, so it looked like they had just been knocked out. She sat back and tried to figure out what to do. Her phone was in her hand when Diego groaned. She dropped the phone in the grass to lean over him. "Diego? Please say something. Please say you're all right."

"I'm all right," Diego said in a low, raspy voice as he slowly opened his eyes. "Zane?"

"He's alive, but still out cold."

Diego started to sit up and she moved to help him. Her arms still weren't fully functional, so she didn't know how much help she actually gave, but she tried.

"What happened?" Zane mumbled as he slowly rolled himself over onto his back. "What was the light?"

Chloe sat down between them, guilt shining on her face, as well as confusion. "Light?"

"When I broke through the barrier containing her power, her magic exploded," Diego explained, rubbing his temples. "Her power was the light you saw."

"Why would it do that?" Zane asked as he slowly pushed himself upright.

Diego shook his head, brow furrowed in confusion. "I'm not sure." But he gave Chloe a very curious look. "What I do know is that you're either the strongest aether I've ever met…or you're something that's not possible."

Something in Chloe's chest went cold. "What do you mean?"

Diego and Zane exchanged a look, with the latter frowning in concern. "When members of different races have children, their children aren't hybrids. You can't have an elemental shifter or a vampire witch. The children are just one thing or the other," Diego began.

"Why not? Seems like it would make sense if they'd have powers from both their parents."

Diego shrugged. "How come when the father has black hair and the mother red, that the child doesn't have a mix of red and black hair? It's just the way things are. My point is, there are no hybrids. But your power? Chloe, have you looked behind you?"

Confused, Chloe twisted around, only to stop breathing for a moment. The tree she'd been using for a perch was half destroyed. Branches had been snapped off and the trunk had cracked, leaning at an unnatural angle. The crow sat on the uppermost branch, staring down at them. In her guilt-stricken state, she imagined the crow looked disapproving.

"I did that?" she whispered.

"Your power did," Diego confirmed. "And while there are people who could do that, if they were trying, it isn't with raw power. It's with focused magic. Telekinetic blasts or an earth elemental intentionally splitting the wood," Diego explained.

Slowly she turned back to the two men. "What does that have to do with hybrids?" she asked, shaken by the clear proof of her power. And how dangerous it could be.

Diego started to answer but paused to carefully study her face. He smiled gently and shook his head. "Most likely nothing. It was just a thought. Probably came from hitting my head," he said, rubbing the back of his head gingerly. "Your power, the depth of it, just surprised me."

Zane cleared his throat softly. "With that much power, though, it's extremely important that you learn how to control it. Away from Salus it might not cause too many problems, as there are fewer supernaturals in one place, but you could cause a lot of trouble with other people's magic. And even off the island…well, if you accidentally use your powers and your eyes change color, it could be extremely awkward."

Chloe blinked in surprise. "What? My eyes changed colors?" she asked, searching for her phone with every intention of checking. She snatched it up but stopped when Diego chuckled.

"They're fine now," he assured her. "I didn't see it, but yes, your eyes probably changed colors. For shifters, vampires, and elementals, whenever they're feeling a strong emotion or using a lot of power, their eyes change colors."

"Oh." It was weird, no doubt about that, but also kind of cool. But now she was curious what color her eyes would change. "Um…are you still willing to help me, Zane? I get it if you're a little freaked out since I just blasted you guys."

Zane gave her a crooked grin. "Are you kidding? I mean, sure, I want a long, hot shower and something for the aches, but that was cool. I can't wait to see what you can do when you have full control."

"I, too, would like to see that," Diego agreed. "I'll leave you to it, then," he said, starting to stand, but halfway up his leg buckled and he sat back down abruptly. Embarrassment colored his cheeks lightly and he cleared his throat. "Or maybe I'll stay for a bit."

Concerned, Chloe asked, "Are you sure you're okay? I know you guys are trying not to freak me out or whatever, but if I hurt you, I need to know."

"It's nothing serious, Chloe," Diego assured her. "I'm a little shaky and a little battered, but it's nothing a shower and a good night's sleep won't cure."

Zane nodded his agreement. "If it were something serious, we'd let you know." He grinned. "I would, at least. I'm not too macho to yell for a healer if I need one."

"Okay, but if it gets worse, I want you two to tell me. And I am sorry for hurting you," Chloe told them earnestly. She wasn't against violence toward someone if they deserved it, but hurting people for no reason? Especially people who were trying to help her? It made her lunch sour in her gut.

"It's not your fault," Diego insisted. "You had no idea what would happen. Just let us help you learn how to control it."

"I'm completely on board with learning control, but I think it should wait for another time."

"No reason for that," Zane said, shaking his head. "You'll be the one doing all the work, really. The little cyclone like I used before is easy enough I could do it in my sleep."

"And I'm happy to help as well," Diego offered. "If I'm staying anyway, I might as well be useful," he added with a smile.

Chloe started to ask if they were sure, but the stubborn, eager looks on their faces gave her answer enough. She sighed and nodded. "All right. But only for a little bit. Then you guys are letting me buy you dinner," she said firmly.

Zane only grinned and nodded, while Diego chuckled. "I'll never say no to a beautiful woman buying me dinner. Shall we get started, then?"

Chloe felt her cheeks heat at the compliment, but she ignored it and nodded. "Yeah."

71

The cyclone was summoned back to Zane's hand. "Do you remember what to do?" he asked.

"I think so." He gave her an encouraging nod and she glanced from him to Diego before she took a deep breath and focused on the cyclone. It was then she realized the magic felt different this time. She didn't feel dizzy, and while there was a sensation against her skin, it wasn't unpleasant like it had been before. Now it just felt like she had a breeze brushing lightly against her, gentle enough that she could ignore it if she chose to. "I think the block was affecting how I sensed magic."

Diego leaned forward. "How so?"

"It was weird as hell before, and not in a good way. Now it just feels like air against my skin. It's more subtle, too."

"Interesting. I'm going to test something." It was Diego's turn to lift a hand, but instead of a cyclone, he manifested a small ball of water. "How does that feel?"

Chloe's head tilted. "Wet, like I'm in the water with it lapping against my skin, but it's still a barely there sort of feeling. A little bit of the tingling from before, too, but it's not as strong as the water."

He nodded and let the water dissipate, replacing it with a fireball. "Now?"

Her lips curved in a half-smile. "Warm. Like I'm sitting in front of a campfire. A small one."

Diego's hand clenched and extinguished the fireball. "One more, then I'm done," he promised as he gestured at one of the branches she'd broken and had it lifting a foot off the ground.

Chloe frowned. "It feels more like how it did before. Just the tingling all over my skin, but it's bearable now."

He nodded and set the branch back down. "So, you have an easier time sensing elemental magics. Or identifying them, I should say. Very curious, and very handy."

"Curious? Is that not how most people sense magic?"

"Oh no. Most just feel that there's magic around, not what sort it is," Diego told her, shaking his head. "But you should get back to Zane's cyclone."

"Oh, yeah. Sorry Zane," she told him with a sheepish smile.

"It's okay. That's important to know, so I don't mind waiting," Zane promised her. "Now, try to reach out and cut off the flow of magic." He paused a moment then added, "Gently."

"Definitely gently," Chloe agreed as her focused settled on the cyclone again. With her attention on it she could feel it more clearly. What was really weird was she that could almost see it in her mind, like a bright spot in the darkness. Her head tilted and instinct had her reaching out with her mind to brush it. The light 'popped' like a balloon hit with a pin. The cyclone disappeared, and along with it went the feel of air against her skin.

When she realized what she'd done, she straightened and a look of pure delight crossed her face. "That was me, right? I mean, you didn't stop it?"

Zane's brows lifted but a grin curved his lips. "No, that wasn't me. It was all you. You did it, Chloe!"

"Congratulations," Diego said with a pleased smile. "Would you like to try again, with something larger this time?"

Excitement warred with caution and she gulped. "Not too much bigger. The bigger the magic, the bigger the risk, right?"

"True," Diego allowed, "but you did that easily enough. And I won't do anything too dangerous."

Excitement won out and she nodded. "Okay then."

He made a lifting gesture with both hands, and small twigs and leaves that had fallen or been broken off the tree started to levitate and dance around them, forming a moving ring that circled them at a distance. The crow in the tree squawked, annoyed, and flew off, but she barely noticed, too focused on the display of magic. "Anytime you're ready," he told her.

First, she concentrated on the way the magic felt. It was the tingling feeling, but stronger now, which she assumed was because he was using stronger magic. This time she deliberately looked for the light that was Diego's magic. It was brighter than it had been for Zane, which she also attributed to the strength of the magic. Again, she brushed her mind against the magic, and she felt it vibrate and thin, but it didn't snap.

"He's putting more power into it than I was," Zane told her when she frowned. "It may take more effort on your part to stop

73

it."

That made sense. "Oh. Right." Chloe nodded and reached out again, this time jabbing at the magic. It shattered and all the pieces of wood fell to the ground, but during that, she saw Diego flinch slightly. "Shit. Did that hurt you?"

Diego shook his head. "No, it didn't hurt, but it felt uncomfortable. Stopping magic like that, the more effort you have to use, the more the caster will feel. If you were to stop a very powerful spell using that method, I imagine the caster would suffer for it. Potentially be knocked unconscious, even."

Chloe's eyes narrowed. Her years as an investigator didn't leave her without skills, and she knew he was holding back. "Uh huh. And?"

Diego arched one dark brow, but he didn't pretend to misunderstand her. "A strong enough spell, with enough force from you? It could potentially kill them. But it would have to be an *extremely* powerful spell, Chloe, so don't think it's something you'll be coming up against frequently."

"God. I hope not. I don't want to kill anyone. For that matter, I don't want to be running around killing magic."

"I don't imagine you will. This is just to learn control," Diego said with a shrug.

"Which you're doing really great in so far," Zane assured her. "Though maybe we'll call it a day here? I know we haven't been out here long, but you actually accomplished a lot. You got your powers unblocked, learned more about sensing magic, and learned how to stop magic once it's been cast."

She glanced at her watch and noted they'd been there for an hour, and almost half of that had been waiting for Diego. But now that he mentioned it, she was feeling tired, drained. "That does sound like a good idea. Though I would like to learn more."

"Sure thing. I can't do anything tomorrow, but Friday, maybe?"

"Friday sounds good. But thank you, both of you, for helping. Especially since it wasn't without risk," Chloe told them.

"It was my pleasure. And if you need any more help from me, please let me know," Diego said as he pulled out his phone.

"What's your number? I'll send you a text so you can contact me." She told him and a moment later her phone dinged. A few seconds after that, it dinged again, and she saw Zane had used the opportunity to give her his number as well.

"All right. I believe I promised you guys dinner?" she said as she got to her feet.

"You did, but I think I'm going to take a rain check on that," Diego said as he stood. "But I will certainly take you up on that another night, I promise you," he added with a flirtatious smile. "Take care of yourself, Chloe, and I'll see you soon."

Chloe smiled. "I will. And you do the same. Don't go breaking anymore blocks without a net," she joked.

Diego chuckled. "I won't." He nodded to Chloe, then Zane, before he walked away.

"I think I'm going to have to do the same," Zane told her apologetically. "I really don't want to, but I think I need a shower and a nap before I go out in public." He paused and glanced around the very public park. "Err, anywhere public that serves food. They'd probably kick me out right now."

Chloe laughed. "Fair enough. But seriously, Zane. Thank you. I'll drop by sometime. Saw some interesting books in your shop."

"Come by anytime. I'd love the company."

"Sounds good. Take care," she told him before heading for her car, then for home.

Chapter 11

The next day Chloe decided to swing by the sheriff's office. No, Wesley wouldn't be happy she'd gone out to his crime scene, but she had information that he might not have. She couldn't, in good conscience, keep that to herself. Not when there was a murderer on the loose. Not when she was a suspect.

To her relief, a cruiser—she assumed his—was there when she pulled in, and she went inside to see him sitting at his desk, frowning at a file he had open.

"Sheriff?"

Wesley looked up, but his frown didn't disappear. Instead, he leaned back and tilted his head. "Miss Chadwick. What can I do for you?"

"Not yell at me," Chloe muttered under her breath as she started over to him. She didn't count on him having such good hearing, though.

His brows lifted. "Did you do something I should yell at you for?"

She sighed, shrugged, and dropped down into the visitor's chair. "Depends on how you look at it. Personally, I don't think you should yell at me, but I might be biased."

Lips twitched, but he nodded. "Fair enough. Why don't you tell me what you've done, and we'll see if I need to yell at you or not."

Rather than draw things out, Chloe cut right to the chase. "I visited the crime scene."

Immediately, his gray eyes darkened and he leaned forward. "What do you mean you went to the crime scene?" he growled, and she thought she heard a hint of his bear in it. Probably just her being fanciful, but it was still an intimidating sound. Good thing she wasn't easily intimidated.

"Exactly that. But before you really start yelling, I didn't pass the crime scene tape. Didn't even touch it. Or anything else for that matter," she said defensively.

His eyes narrowed, then he surprised her by smiling. It was a good smile. An understanding smile. But she didn't trust it, or what he said next. "You know…you're right."

She automatically started to defend herself before his words penetrated. Suspiciously, she asked, "I am?"

He nodded. "Mmhmm. You are. You're biased. Because I absolutely should yell at you! What sort of school did you go to that they teach you it's okay to go tromping around crime scenes?" he shouted. "Just because I've transported the body doesn't mean all the evidence has been found, you idiot! I swear, if you—"

"I told you I didn't touch anything!" Chloe shouted back, actually managing to get enough volume to be heard over him. "If any evidence has been taken or tampered with, it was. Not. Me!" She lowered her voice, though it was still loud, still sharp. "And you can't tell me you wouldn't have done the same damn thing if our positions were reversed."

He looked surprised that she'd yelled back, almost impressed, actually, then he looked thoughtful. "You might have a point there," he slowly agreed. "I'm not saying I like it, I'm definitely not saying I approve, and if I find out you've done it again, I'll toss you in a cell, but you have a point. Of course, that point means nothing if you actually *are* the one who killed Jeremy."

Chloe gave an annoyed growl. "I thought we were past this.

Besides, if I had killed him, do you think I'd be in your office telling you I was at the scene of the crime? How stupid do you think I am?"

"Jury's still out on that one," he drawled. "I'm guessing you have a reason for telling me this? Or did you just want to see if riling me up would make me shift? Because let me tell you, angry grizzlies don't make good teddy bears."

She rolled her eyes. "Of course I have a reason. And no, it's not to make you shift." But now the thought was on her mind. "Though if you do want to shift, I'm more than happy to watch." She'd seen witches, psychics, and elementals in action. She was dying to see a shifter, too. And a vampire, she supposed, but she didn't actually want to get bitten. Or at least she didn't think she did. Maybe it did feel good like a lot of TV shows and movies made it out to be, but she wasn't counting on it. And she wasn't a fan of sharp things, either, especially near her throat.

"Get to the point," he said blandly.

"Spoilsport," she muttered. "I don't know if you're aware that I'm an aether elemental?"

"I am."

"Well, I can sense magic. It's, uh, why I was blocking traffic the day I got here, though I didn't know it at the time. It was the first time it'd ever happened."

Understanding lit his eyes and he nodded. "That makes sense. You did look pale and freaked out that morning. I'm almost sorry I had to move you along."

She shrugged. "It's not like either of us knew at the time. But it happened again when I went to the crime scene. And it was…bad. Really bad. Like I had to crawl away to put some distance between it and me before I could stand."

She saw his eyes harden as he transformed from mildly interested man into on-duty officer of the law. "Could you identify the type of magic?" he asked, reaching for his notepad.

"Unfortunately, no," Chloe said. "I might be able to now, though, if you wanted me to go back there. Or look at the body."

He frowned. "What do you mean? What's changed?"

"I had a block on my powers. It was affecting how I sensed magic. Diego—the councilor, but I don't know his last name—took care of the block for me, so I'm sensing stuff more...clearly, I guess? I could tell the difference between a few different types of magic they were doing."

"They?"

"Oh, sorry. Zane. Him and Diego were helping me figure out how to use my powers," she explained.

Wesley grimaced. "Hell, I thought this was an ordinary murder," he admitted, running a hand through his hair. He stared at her for so long it became a little uncomfortable, but she said nothing, sensing he was debating with himself about something. Finally, he got to his feet. "Come with me," he said, his long legs carrying him quickly toward the door.

"Where are we going?" she asked, scrambling to keep up with him.

"The morgue. I could ask Diego—it's Councilor Sanchez, by the way—since he's really good with sensing magic. I probably still will, actually, but you've got the criminal justice background, and he doesn't." He looked at her over the roof of his cruiser. "Just so you know, the only reason I'm allowing this is because I ran you when I thought you might have killed Jeremy."

Chloe had a clean record, she knew. No criminal history, and she'd done damn good in school. Top of her class, actually. And she'd done good work as an investigator, both solo and as part of a firm. She gave him a hard look, daring him to try to say something negative about her past. "And?"

His expression softened and he opened his door. "I'm taking you to see the body, aren't I?" he asked before he got in and slammed the door.

Wesley drove her to the hospital, then led her to the basement where the morgue was located. Before he opened the door, he paused and gave her a serious look.

"Have you ever seen a body before?"

Chloe actually hadn't, but she didn't want to admit it. "I'm guessing you don't count those in coffins at funerals?"

"No."

She sighed. "Then no. But by this point I'm sure the ME has done the autopsy and cleaned the body up, right? So, it's not as bad as it could be."

"It's always bad when someone dies before their time," Wesley said coldly before he shoved the door open and motioned for her to go first.

Well, shit. She hadn't meant to piss him off, but she'd definitely done just that. Still, she couldn't back down, not now, and she stepped into the sterile room beyond the door. It looked precisely how she'd expected it to, though it was a bit smaller. But Salus was a small town, not a big city, and with the longevity of supernaturals she supposed there weren't as many deaths by natural causes either. "Where is he?" she asked Wesley at the sight of the clean, empty tables.

He folded his arms over his chest and just stared at her. For a second, she thought his eyes were yellow, but he blinked and they were gray again.

"Did your eyes just…?"

"Stop stalling. If you could sense magic that strongly, and it was used on him, then I'm sure you can figure out which drawer he's in," Wesley told her.

Oh yeah. Still pissed. It made her wonder if Jeremy had been his friend, but she wasn't about to ask right now. Or tell him how uncertain she was that she could do what he expected. These new skills were too untested, but she had to try.

"Fine," she murmured and turned her back to him. Remembering what Zane had said about blocking out distractions, she closed her eyes and felt for the part of her that reacted to the presence of magic. Seconds ticked past as she steadied herself and gently coaxed her power to the surface. Her breath caught in a soft gasp as she was hit by two competing sensations.

The stronger of the two came from behind her and tickled

across her skin like coarse fur. The temptation to step closer to Wesley and see if the feeling would grow more intense was hard to resist, because it wasn't hard to tell it was coming from him. She forced herself to stay put, while part of her brain wondered why she hadn't felt Zane or Diego, just their magic.

The more subtle of the sensations came from the right side of the wall and was harder to pin down. The feeling of fur overshadowed it, and she was too inexperienced to easily separate the two.

"Can't do it?" came the rumble of Wesley's voice. "It's been five minutes."

Shocked it had been so long, she turned and opened her eyes. "Are you kidding me?" At the negative shake of his head, she sighed. "Well, it would be easier if you'd tone it down a little."

"Tone what down? I'm not doing anything," he said with a frown.

"No? Well, I can sure as hell feel you, which is making this a little like hearing a whisper at a concert." An exaggeration, but he was starting to annoy her. It was partially her fault, she knew, but she preferred not to get angry at herself when she could avoid it.

His eyes narrowed, but after a moment he seemed to accept her words as true and closed his eyes. A few seconds later, the brush of fur subsided, leaving her with the single sensation.

"Thank you," Chloe said and turned back to the drawers. This time she was able to focus on the magic from within the drawer. It was easy to tell it was there, but it felt like...nothing, which baffled her. How could she sense nothing? Her eyes popped open and she stomped over to the drawer, opening it without hesitation. She saw Wesley shift in surprise when it was the correct drawer. Annoyed, she snapped, "If you didn't think I could do it, why bring me here?"

"To see what you'd say. The lies a person tells, to themselves or others, can tell a lot about them," Wesley answered as he moved closer. "What do you sense?"

"Nothing," she said flatly.

"Then how did you find the right drawer?"

Chloe shook her head. "No, I mean, I sense nothing. I can

tell there's magic here, but it's like it's a void. Or hiding. I'm not really sure." She looked down to the sheet-covered body. "How did he die?"

Wesley didn't answer, just drew the sheet down to show a clean, almost fake looking cut in Jeremy's chest, right where his heart would be.

She frowned. "If he died from being stabbed in the heart, I don't understand the magic. What was it for? Why is it still here?" She looked up at Wesley. "Wouldn't magic dissipate? Like a scent or something?"

He nodded. "It would, and normally does. Which means either this magic you're sensing was exceptionally strong to begin with—"

"Or it's still active and doing something," Chloe finished. New she may be to magic, but she wasn't a stranger to common sense and leaps of logic.

"Exactly." And he didn't sound happy about that.

He started to cover the body up, but Chloe grabbed his wrist. She'd just gotten a look at Jeremy's face. "Wait a second."

He arched a brow. "Excuse me?"

"His face…I…" She recognized it. Not how he might think, but from one of the pictures she'd seen in Granny's house. Specifically, one of him with his arm around her mom. She debated on whether to mention it, but it didn't seem particularly relevant. And for all she knew, Wesley would just take it as more reason to be suspicious of her.

"Yes?"

She shook her head and released his wrist. "Nothing. Thought I saw something," she said, but it was clear he didn't really believe her.

He pulled the sheet up and pushed the tray back into the drawer. "Uh huh. Come on. I'll take you back to your car."

"What are you going to do now?" she asked as she followed him out of the morgue.

"Call the councilor and see if he understands this better than we do."

Chloe nodded but didn't speak until they were in the cruiser.

"I can help on this. You know I can. Yes, I'm new to investigating murders and using my powers, but I've already given you something you didn't have before."

"You did," he grudgingly agreed. "And I'll consider it. But I meant it about the crime scene. Don't go poking around another one unless I'm there. Understand?"

"Perfectly."

"Good."

Chapter 12

Chloe felt restless after the trip to the morgue. She couldn't bring herself to go back to the house and driving around the island wasn't doing it for her, so she headed back to town. When she passed a twenty-four-hour gym, she slowed and considered. It would be a good way to burn off some stress, and she didn't want to get out of shape.

After a quick trip to Granny's to change into workout clothes, she headed back to the gym and stepped inside.

It was impressive. She didn't know how much membership was, but it wouldn't surprise her if it was a lot. This gym had it all. From reception, she could see a large room full of weights and other workout equipment. Another was empty of equipment and currently held what looked like a yoga class, judging by the twisted positions of the people in there. A hallway led further into the gym, but all she could see from her current vantage point was a rock climbing wall.

With no one currently at the reception desk, she wandered over and picked up a pamphlet. "Holy crap," she muttered as she saw the gym also boasted a pool, indoor track, obstacle course, juice bar, personal trainers, massage, and a sauna. And membership was nowhere what she'd expect of a place with all that.

"Can I help you?"

Chloe glanced up and almost swallowed her tongue. The man was *built*, with strong arms showcased by his tank top, a face created for modeling, and hair just long enough to run her fingers through.

"Ah…I was wondering if you did short-term memberships? I'm only in town for a little while, but I don't want to get out of shape while I'm here," she explained, trying to keep her eyes on his face.

He looked amused for some reason but nodded. "We don't normally, but I think we can make an exception. You're Lydia's granddaughter, right?"

"I am. How did you know?" she asked, surprised.

"I was at your grandmother's funeral," he explained, his faint smile fading. "I thought I recognized you. She was a nice lady, your grandmother."

Chloe smiled sadly and nodded. "She really was. It seems like a lot of people here have good memories of her. It helps, a little."

"I'm glad." He stepped closer and offered his hand. "I'm Garrett, by the way."

"Chloe," she answered as she took his, unsurprised when she found it strong and calloused.

"I know," he said with a grin. "Now, how short-term were you thinking?"

She blew out a short breath. "I don't really know. A few weeks, maybe? I'm just staying until I figure a few things out, so I can't really say for sure."

He nodded. "Okay. We do offer a two week trial. I can get you set up with that, so you can use all the facilities, anytime you want."

Chloe smiled. "That sounds great. Thanks, Garrett."

"My pleasure."

A few minutes later and she was good to go and heading toward the indoor track. She took her time stretching and watching the three people who were already running at various paces—a woman with black hair and dusky skin, a slender man with buzzed blonde hair, and a dark-haired man. The woman and dark-haired guy both had good forms, though the younger blond looked like he was struggling a little. Someone trying to get into shape, she assumed, and she wished him well at it.

Soon enough she was on the track with them, and it didn't take long for her to find a steady rhythm that warmed her muscles and let her clear her mind. For the first time since she heard of Granny's death she wasn't thinking, wasn't stressing about something. It was exactly what she needed.

She'd made several laps when she noticed she had someone keeping pace beside her. She glanced over and saw the dark-haired man smiling at her. He was tall, a couple inches above six feet, with dark brown hair, blue eyes, and a body that proved he visited the gym regularly. And he was handsome. Maybe not as striking as some of the men she'd met, but it definitely wasn't a hardship to look at him.

"Don't mind if I join you, do you?" he asked.

Chloe shook her head. "Not at all. I like having a running partner. I'm Chloe."

The man chuckled and nodded. "I know. Everyone in Salus is talking about you."

She grimaced and shook her head. "I'm not surprised, though I can't say I'm happy about it."

He shrugged. "It'll pass. We don't get too many new people here, so newcomers always get a bit of attention for the first week or so. People will eventually find something else to talk about. They always do."

"I hope you're right," she said on a sigh. "So, if everyone knows who I am, don't you think I deserve to at least have your name?" she asked playfully.

"I guess that would be fair. I'm Erick Jensen."

She worked up a grin. "Any important tidbits you'd care to share since everyone knows my business?"

Erick laughed softly. "Sorry, not that much to say about me. I've been on Salus for a few decades and got elected to the council a few years back. Omni councilor."

"Ah. I'm two for five, then," Chloe said with a nod. "Omni...that's the spot that can be any type of supernatural, right?"

"Right," he confirmed. "In my case I'm a psychic."

"You're not a medium, are you?"

He gave her an odd look but shook his head. "No, I'm not. I'm a clairvoyant." At her confused look he added, "I know things without any logical way of knowing them."

"Ah. Handy for a councilor."

He grinned. "It can be. I can't say I can avoid learning anything about you without your permission, but I can promise not to intentionally look."

"That's a relief. And I mean that sincerely," she told him as she began to slow her pace to cool down.

"Mmm. Feeling a little overwhelmed?"

"Oh yeah. I think I'm one revelation shy of the loony bin," she admitted.

"Sounds like you need to let off some steam."

"Why do you think I'm here?"

He laughed. "The gym, huh? How about a night of relaxation?"

She arched a brow and glanced at him. "What'd you have in mind?"

"Dinner? There's one really nice restaurant here on the island. And a benefit of living in a small town is it's never super crowded."

Her lips twitched. "Are you asking me on a date, Erick?"

"Hmm. Yes, I think I am. Are you accepting?"

It would be nice to get out of the house and socialize for a while. Lexi's visit had been nice, but a date might be just the thing she needed to unwind. It didn't hurt that Erick was pretty damn nice to look at. On the other hand, she did have a lot going on. "I don't know. I am kind of busy with everything. My grandmother only had me, so I have to handle all of the details."

"All the more reason to give yourself a break," he replied smoothly. "It's just an hour or so. And it sounds like you need the time away from serious things." He smiled. "And this will be completely casual, I promise."

"All good points." But she still mulled it over for another moment and decided what the hell, it was just a date. She wasn't marrying the guy. It could be good for her sanity. "What time?"

"Say, seven? The restaurant's pretty easy to find. Banquet, off Main Street."

"I should be able to find it. And seven works."

He flashed her a brilliant smile. "Great. Then I'll see you there."

"See you," Chloe echoed as he jogged off toward the showers.

Unfortunately, Chloe hadn't brought much in the way of nice clothes. Her travel bag was full of jeans, tee-shirts, and a couple hoodies. She'd included one nice sweater, and, paired with her best jeans, she hoped it would be good enough for the restaurant Erick had mentioned.

She arrived a few minutes early and went inside, relieved to see the dress code ranged from fancy, but not quite tuxes and gowns, to clothes not unlike what she was wearing. Benefit of a small town, maybe? Whatever the style of clothing, it smelled absolutely amazing, and she felt her stomach growl.

"Hi. Can I help you?" the hostess asked with a smile as Chloe approached.

"I'm meeting someone for dinner."

"Name?"

"Erick Jensen."

"Ah, yes, he's already been seated. This way, please," the hostess said, leading Chloe to a table for two set near the back in dim lighting.

Erick stood, dressed in slacks and a nice shirt, though he'd gone without a jacket or tie, which she appreciated. "Chloe," he said with a smile, coming around to pull out her chair for her. "Did you find the place all right?"

Chloe smiled and nodded as she accepted the seat. "I did, yes. But then, I'm used to navigating big cities. Next to that, Salus is a breeze. Though my road rage is going to be rusty when I go home," she joked.

His brows lifted as he retook his seat. "You're not staying then?"

There was something about the way he spoke that had her focusing more intently on him. He didn't want her to leave, and despite his smile, she didn't think it was because he was attracted to her. Or not strictly because of that. "Well, I have a home and a life in Philadelphia. I'm only here to clear out my grandmother's house and settle her affairs," she explained, unwilling to go into more detail or explain that the idea of staying was stuck in the back of her mind. She had just met him, after all.

There was a flash of something unpleasant in his eyes, gone so quickly that if she hadn't been watching him so closely, she would have missed it. Even watching him she wasn't entirely certain of what she'd seen. "That's a shame. I'm sure Salus will be a little darker once you go," he said smoothly. "I suppose that means I should make the most of tonight, then, hmm?"

She made herself smile and nod. "I suppose so," she agreed. "Though I'm not leaving tomorrow. It *is* a nice place, and I've only seen a little of the island. Mostly the town, my grandmother's house, and her friend's house."

Erick grinned. "Which friend? Your grandmother had quite a few. They were all very surprised when she moved away. Right after you were born, if I remember right. I recall a few women talking about Lydia taking a baby with her."

That surprised her. "I was on Salus as a baby?" She thought she'd been born in Boston. Hell, it was what her birth certificate said, and she'd never had a reason to question it before.

He arched a brow. "You didn't know?"

She shook her head. "I had no idea. I grew up in Boston, went to college there. It's still where I think of as home, even if I'm not living there anymore."

"I'm so sorry then. I didn't mean to surprise you," Erick said, and he sounded sincere, though she wasn't sure she believed him. "Revelations about yourself shouldn't come from someone you hardly know. Perhaps you should ask some of your family about those years of your life."

Chloe didn't have any family left, not unless she counted Granny's ghost, but something had her holding that back. "I'll have to do that."

"If you can't get in touch with them, this friend of your grandmother's might be able to help, too," he added as he lifted his glass to his lips.

The waitress arrived before she could answer, and the next few minutes were spent ordering. It took her a minute to figure out what she wanted, because it all sounded delicious. To her surprise there wasn't just one type of cuisine on the menu, either. She saw Italian, French, Chinese, Greek...Maybe when there was only one big restaurant in town you had to branch out or risk people leaving the island for some variety.

After they'd ordered, Erick said, "I'd be happy to give you the names of a few people who might be able to help you if you want. I arrived on Salus around the same time your grandmother left, but I hear things."

Chloe smiled. "That'd be great. I've met a few people who knew her, which seems to be most everyone I meet. But please, enough about my grandmother. It's still...raw."

Immediately he looked contrite. "You're right. I'm so sorry. I should be focusing on you, in any case. What is it you do back in what I'm sure you consider the real world?"

"Real world?"

Erick smiled. "We're isolated here. In our own little bubble, of sorts. We don't operate under the same laws and rules as most of the rest of the world. If you're not used to it, I'm sure it seems unreal."

"Ah. You're not wrong," she had to admit. "It's the first time I've been on an island, too—at least that I remember—so that has to be taken into account, too. But I like it here. Maybe not enough to decide to live here, but I like it. It'd be hard not to, unless someone was afraid of the outdoors."

Conversation shifted to more neutral topics when their food arrived, and Chloe had to admit the fish she ordered was probably the best thing she'd ever put in her mouth. It may not be her beloved caramel coffee, but it was damn good. She was mourning the fact that licking her plate was the height of bad manners when a pale, dark-haired man walked up. He was slender and looked like he hadn't seen in the sun in a year or two, but he was dressed in a well-fitted, dark gray suit and had a pleasant look on his face.

"Hello Councilor, mademoiselle. How was your meal tonight?" he asked with a faint French accent, nodding to Erick before he offered Chloe a smile. It seemed to her it didn't reach his eyes, though.

"It was delicious, as usual," Erick said after he dabbed at his mouth with his napkin.

Chloe wasn't quite so proper in her answer. "It was amazing. I think it's the best thing I've ever eaten." She grinned. "Aside from a really good chocolate cake, but nothing tops that."

The man chuckled. "I'm happy to hear that, mademoiselle. You would be Miss Chadwick, would you not?"

She smiled wryly. "You guys really don't get a lot of strangers here, huh? Everyone's known who I am so far. But yeah, I'm Chloe Chadwick." She glanced at Erick and saw a hint of annoyance in his eyes, at least until he saw her looking and smiled again. She turned back to the stranger. "Is this your place?" she asked.

"Ah, I've been rude. Yes, this is my place. I'm Francois. And we happen to have some chocolate cake, if you would care for some dessert," he offered.

She considered it, she really did, but sighed. Not only was she certain she'd pop if she ate another bite, she was also not quite comfortable with Erick. It almost seemed like this date had been nothing more than an excuse for him to dig for information. About what, she wasn't entirely certain, but it didn't make her happy. "I'm afraid I'm going to have to say no. If the fish hadn't been so good, I might have had room for the cake," she told him.

That made him grin, and Chloe was startled to see his canines were longer than they should be. If he was human, anyway. Before she could stop herself, she blurted out, "Holy crap, you're a vampire!"

Francois blinked at her for a moment before he laughed. No discreet chuckle, no, this was a deep laugh right from the belly. "Yes, yes I am," he agreed a minute later, his grin even wider than before. "And I don't think I've ever had quite that reaction before. For the laugh, I'm going to send a slice of our cake home with you, on the house."

Chloe was blushing at her outburst, but when he didn't seem offended, she tentatively smiled. "Sorry. You're the first vampire I've met." She paused, considered. "I think, anyway. I'm not going to turn down the cake, either. Thank you."

He gave a half bow. "My pleasure. I'll have the cake out in a minute." He straightened and inclined his head to Erick. "Councilor," he said in parting before he returned to the kitchen.

"You've never met a vampire before?" Erick asked when they were alone again.

She shook her head. "Nope. But now I've met all the big types of supernaturals. Well, aside from gods, but I think I'm okay with that."

"You don't want to meet a god?" he asked, surprised.

"Nope. Knowing my luck, I'd get smited or smote or whatever it is, and that would be no fun for anyone," she said, one hundred percent serious.

"Interesting," Erick murmured.

Francois returned with a box and offered it to her with a smile. "Your cake. I hope you enjoy, and that you come back and see us sometime."

"Oh, that is definitely going to happen," Chloe assured him with a grin, but she noticed that he didn't look at Erick on this trip to their table. Odd.

"I should get going. It's been a long few days," she said to Erick when Francois was gone.

"Of course. Let me escort you to your car," he said, rising and moving around to pull out her chair.

Though she'd like to refuse, she just forced a smile and stood. He walked with her out of the restaurant, his hand lightly resting on her lower back until they reached her car.

"This is me," she told him, unlocking it and turning to face him.

"I hope you had a good night. I'll see you soon?" Erick asked, brushing a thumb lightly over her arm.

"I'm sure you will. Small town and all," Chloe joked while she fought not to tense up. What was it about this guy that was giving her the heebie-jeebies?

He smiled. "Very true." He leaned closer and her breath caught. While she tried to figure out if she should turn her head or just step back, his lips brushed hers in a light, chaste kiss before he withdrew. "Have a nice night," he told her before returning to the restaurant.

Chloe managed to fight the urge to rub the back of her hand over her mouth, but only until she was out of sight of the restaurant.

Chapter 13

Chloe was a responsible, rational adult. She also had chocolate cake for breakfast. It was the one good thing that had come of her date. Well, meeting Francois wasn't bad, but the cake? She had to admit, it was even better than dinner had been.

After she'd showered and changed into a pair of jeans and a tee-shirt, she got out her laptop. She may not officially be on the case, but that didn't mean she wasn't going to approach it like she was. For the next hour she made a list of people who might be involved, what she knew about them, and what they knew about the murder. Unfortunately, it wasn't as much as she would have liked. It was unsurprising, but frustrating. She made a new file and started inputting what she knew about Salus and supernaturals. That, too, was a shorter file than she wanted, but it wasn't as vital.

Chloe sat back and frowned as she sipped at her coffee. Except, it *was* just as important. Magic had been used in Jeremy's death, and not the sort of magic that was seen every day, even on Salus, so it did narrow down the suspect list. To whom she wasn't sure, but it was a factor. And magic had been used to discover that, too.

She lifted one of her hands and stared at it like it was a loaded gun. So far, she'd been able to sense magic, strongly sense it, and had been able to stop it. What else could she do? She wished Granny was still around to ask. Zane was knowledgeable, yes, but even he admitted his familiarity with aether powers was lacking. And she was curious why her power had been visible when Diego removed the block. Zane had said he saw a light, but there hadn't been any light when they practiced. It made her curious and confused, but that was her default state this last week.

Maybe she was going about this the wrong way. She shouldn't be focusing on the unique aspect of the town, but the victim. A new file was created, this one for information about Jeremy. Unfortunately, she didn't have much to go on, so it was bare, but that would change. Surely there were plenty of people on Salus who knew Jeremy and could give her information.

A knock on her door made her close the laptop before she went to answer it.

"Surprise!" Lexi called happily the moment she saw Chloe's face. "It's my day off, so I thought I'd come by, see how you were holding up, or if you had any more questions that only the amazing Lexi could answer."

Chloe laughed and waved Lexi inside. "As it turns out, I do. And I'm holding up…okay. I'm waiting for that last revelation that's going to push me over into insanity, though."

"Pfft. What's the fun in life if you're not a little insane?" Lexi asked, dropping her purse on a chair before she flopped down onto the couch.

"True, but I'm not talking a little insane. I'm meaning full on, rubber room, self-hugging jacket insane," Chloe corrected, holding her arms in a strait jacket pose.

"Uh oh. What happened to get you to that point?" Lexi smiled slyly. "Would it have anything to do with the fact that I heard a certain newcomer was seen on a date with a certain hot councilor?"

Chloe grimaced. "That didn't help matters, but no."

Lexi looked surprised. "You didn't have a good time? Erick is yummy and definitely has some moves on him. Not that he's ever used them on me, but I've heard."

Chloe sighed and sank down onto the other end of the couch. "He is hot," she conceded, "and I can't deny he's got that charming thing going on, but there was just something…off. And not just the fact that I felt like he was just pumping me for information the whole time."

Frowning, Lexi asked, "About the murder?"

"No, though that would have made sense. Or more sense, anyway. He seemed super interested in my grandmother and childhood, which was…weird."

Lexi wrinkled her nose. "Yeah, it is. Who goes on a first date and focuses on that? First dates are to make sure you're not going to jump in bed with crazy."

Chloe laughed a little. "Yeah. So…weird. There's not going to be a second date. Though I'm absolutely going back to that restaurant."

"Oh yeah, the food is to die for," Lexi agreed. "But if the date isn't what's driving you crazy, what is?"

Afraid she'd sound like some scared little kid, Chloe procrastinated, toying with the hem of her jeans. She didn't speak until Lexi reached over and flicked her in the forehead. "Hey!"

Lexi smiled sweetly. "Start talking or I'll flick you again."

Chloe sighed. "I talked to Zane like you suggested."

"And? Did he help you learn to access your powers?"

"After a fashion. Turned out my powers had some sort of block on them, thanks to my grandmother. He called Diego, the councilor—"

Lexi let out a low wolf whistle. "Another hottie. Get him to whisper sweet nothings in your ear in Spanish," she said, fanning herself. "But again, nothing I've experienced firsthand."

Chloe fought a smile and nodded. "I'll keep that in mind. Anyway, Diego confirmed the whole block thing and got rid of it except…I blasted them both and half-destroyed the tree I was sitting by. Freaked me out."

"I can see how blasting them would freak you out," Lexi

agreed with a somber nod.

"It wasn't just that. I mean, yeah, I didn't want to hurt them, and I'm glad they were okay, but it was the tree that's been stuck in my mind. A week ago, I was powerless, and now I'm a supernatural who should just be able to affect magic, right? So how the hell did I do that?"

Lexi frowned and took a moment before answering. "That…is a good question. Unfortunately, I don't have a good answer. I've never heard of an aether doing that. It doesn't mean one hasn't, though. I'm not really a magical historian or anything like that. You'd be better off talking to Zane about that, or Daphne."

"Who's she?"

"Elemental councilor. She's got some years on her, so she might have heard something."

Chloe nodded slowly and mentally noted the name down. "On another note, since I'm all wrapped up in this whole murder thing…I know nothing about the guy who was killed except his name was Jeremy and he and my grandmother didn't get along."

"Not a whole lot to tell, really," Lexi said apologetically. "He kept to himself, at least as far as I know. Could be he used to be a wild party guy, but that was before my time. I know he worked at the council building and wasn't super well liked. Not hated, but people wouldn't go out of their way to say hi or anything."

"So, you don't know about this whatever between him and my grandmother?"

Lexi thought for a moment before she shook her head slowly. "I can't think of anything. I want to say I heard something about him dating Lydia's daughter at some point, but that's the only thing I can think of."

"Damn," Chloe murmured, grabbing a throw pillow and hugging it to her chest as she slumped down. Then she frowned and straightened abruptly. "Wait. I'm dumb. Lydia's daughter? As in, he dated my mom?" That would explain the picture of them.

"Uh, yeah, actually. I hadn't thought of it that way, but yeah," Lexi confirmed.

That had Chloe's head spinning with possibilities. Jeremy had dated her mom. He'd also not gotten along with her grandmother. Maybe the two facts were connected. Granny had also always refused to talk about Chloe's dad when the subject came up. Could that be related to the other two facts? Could he have been her father?

Interrupting Chloe's musings, Lexi shifted over until she could press against Chloe's side and rest her head on the younger woman's shoulder. "Hey, you'll figure it out. There are people here who've been around since the town was founded."

Filing away her thoughts to look into later, Chloe asked, "When was it founded? I know nothing about the town, really. It's not on Google, which is really annoying."

"Mmm. Early sixteen hundreds, but I couldn't tell you exactly what year," Lexi answered.

"Oh wow. So, it's really damn old then. Any big surprises I should know about? There's not some mysterious cave with some elder god you guys feed sacrifices to every five years or anything, is there?"

Lexi bust out laughing. "No elder god, no. We don't see too many gods here, of any sort."

Chloe gaped at her. "Are you serious? You get gods here? Like, actual gods?"

"I thought you said you knew about the different races?" Lexi asked, frowning.

"Yeah, but I thought it was just…I don't know what I thought. It didn't really compute, you know?"

"Oh. Yeah, I get it. But occasionally we do get gods visiting. It's a rare occurrence, but it happens. Last time was…fifteen years ago, maybe? Hecate showed up around Halloween. And twenty, thirty years ago? Apollo showed up for the summer solstice. Before that it'd been decades since we'd seen any of the gods."

Chloe shook her head, trying to wrap her head around the concept of gods visiting mortals, even supernatural mortals. "Anything else? Emma said no unicorns, but what about, I don't know, dragons or whatever?"

Lexi laughed and shook her head. "Sorry, no dragons, though that would be freaking awesome. We do have familiars, though?"

"Like witches with black cats?"

That got her an elbow in the side. "Hey now, no stereotypes. Have you seen anyone in a pointy hat, carrying a broom, or wearing robes?" Lexi chided her. "Though some familiars are black cats, yes," she had to admit. "But no, a familiar can be any animal that can come in contact with a person. So, cats, dogs, mice, deer, whatever, but not so much sharks or jellyfish, if that makes sense."

"It does. But what *are* familiars?"

"Animals with a little something extra. They can choose to bond with a supernatural—not just the witches—and they've got a link. Familiars can help their chosen person, communicate with them, and some can help with magic. And they always know where their person is, and vice versa."

"Huh. That sounds cooler than just having a black cat that looks spooky. How do you get a familiar?" Chloe asked. One of these days it might be nice to have someone else around, and she wasn't anywhere close to ready to live with a person. But a dog or something that she could actually communicate with? That might be nice.

"It varies," Lexi answered, "but most get found by chance. Or, well, fate more than chance, I guess. Walking through the woods, finding a stray in an alley, things like that. Which is kind of weird since they're just as smart as you or me."

"So, any stray animal I find could be a familiar? And I could just…take them home and have a familiar?"

"Yes and no," Lexi said with a shake of her head. "Familiars aren't super common, but yeah, any stray animal you find *could* be one. But you can't just decide to take them as your familiar. The familiar has to agree, or they'll take off. If they're in bad shape they might hang around until they're better, but you can't force a familiar bond. It's got to be mutual. It's kind of like marriage, except there's no divorce. You're stuck together until one of you dies."

"That sounds…" A little terrifying. She'd never formed a

commitment that lasted more than a year, but maybe boyfriends were just higher maintenance than familiars? "I don't know. Maybe kind of cool."

"It can be," Lexi agreed. "Now, off the serious subjects. It's my day off. Let's have some fun!"

Chapter 14

Hours later, after Lexi had left, Chloe grabbed a hoodie and went to meet Zane. He'd texted her earlier asking if they could meet at his place, which was fine by her. She wasn't ready to see the tree she'd almost destroyed.

She hadn't even reached the town when it became hard to steer. Lights flashed angrily on the dash a moment before her car died. She had enough momentum to coast to the side of the road so she wasn't blocking traffic, but she couldn't get the car to start again.

"Dammit!" She smacked the steering wheel then pulled out her phone. She felt bad calling Lexi for help yet again, but she didn't know anyone else quite so well yet.

"Damn girl. I just left. You can't be missing me already, can you?" Lexi asked cheerfully.

"Always, but that's not why I'm calling. Since I can't just do a net search for mechanics…who would I call for a tow if I'm stranded on the side of the road?"

"Oh damn. You're just not having good luck this week. But yeah, I know a guy. I'll text you the number."

"Okay, thanks."

"No problem. Stay safe."

Chloe got the number a moment later and called the mechanic, whose name, according to Lexi, was Cole the Grumpy Hottie. But Lexi seemed to think every guy in town was hot, so Chloe would wait and see for herself. Not that it really mattered so long as he could fix her car.

The phone rang and rang until it just disconnected, no voicemail or anything. She frowned at the phone, checked to make sure she called the right number, then hit redial. For a minute she thought it was going to disconnect again, but then a grumpy voice answered.

"Total."

Well, he didn't sound happy. "Uh...I'm broken down and need a tow."

"You don't sound too sure of that," the man said sarcastically.

Chloe bit off a retort. "I'm sure, since my car died and won't start again."

"You're not on empty, are you?"

She rolled her eyes. "I'm not that dumb. I've got half a tank of gas. My last tune up and oil change was only two weeks ago, and it hadn't been making any funny sounds before it died. Now, can you come look at my car?"

He gave an annoyed sound. "Yeah, yeah. Where are you at?" She gave him her basic location. "I'll be there in five."

It was more like ten when he rolled up in a tow truck. By then she'd texted Zane that she was going to be late and had gotten out and was leaning against her car, arms folded over her chest.

He got out and Chloe had to admit Lexi was right. Yes, he was wearing a standard mechanic's 'uniform' of dark blue work pants and a button-down shirt with the name 'Cole' embroidered on his left breast. And sure, he had grease on his hands and a smudge of it on his cheek, but the hotness was definitely there. His dark blond hair was kept short, and his eyes were a pretty blend of green and brown. There was no doubt his work kept him fit, either.

"Hi. Pop the hood," Cole said.

Chloe narrowed her eyes. "Hi, I'm Chloe. I'm assuming

you're the oh so pleasant guy I spoke to ten minutes ago? Not five, by the way, but ten."

He didn't look the least bit fazed by her sarcasm. "That'd be me. Now, you wanna pop the hood, or you wanna keep wasting my time?"

"Fine." She popped the hood and gestured toward it. "Have a look."

"Thanks." He lifted the hood, and it was only ten seconds later that he closed it again. "Need a new serpentine belt. Yours snapped. Nothing's going to run without it. I'll tow you back to the shop and have you out in ten. Think I've got a belt for it in stock."

Chloe took a single slow, deep breath before she nodded. "That's great. Thanks."

He unbent enough to say, "You're welcome," before he got her car hooked up. The drive to the shop was made in silence, and after he showed her to the tiny waiting area, disappeared into the shop. He showed one virtue by being quick to replace the belt and came back in only ten minutes. "You're good to go. I had to give you a jump, so you'll probably need to replace the battery, soon. It's good for now, though, and I gave you a break on the tow, so it'll be eighty bucks."

It wasn't as much as she'd been afraid it would be, but it still stung. Hopefully the lawyer would get in touch with her soon. It would certainly help. She paid and he handed over the keys. "Thanks for the help."

"No problem." It looked like it pained him, but he added, "Sorry I was an ass earlier. Just been busy."

"I get it. I'll let you get back to it."

"Thanks," he said, before escaping back into the shop.

"Grumpy hottie indeed," she murmured before leaving.

Just after six, Chloe found parking in front of the bookstore and went inside, passing a customer as they were leaving.

"Everything okay?" Zane called from the other side of the store.

"Yeah. Broken belt on my car," she explained as she crossed to him.

Zane straightened abruptly, his eyes sharp and alert on hers. "Did you call Cole?"

His reaction hit every one of her curiosity buttons and she slowly nodded. "I did. Why?"

"No reason," he said quickly. "He fix it for you?"

"Yeah, though he's not the most pleasant person. Actually, he's the first not pleasant person I've met on Salus." She paused, then added, "Aside from that guy at the ferry, and only at first." Well, then there was Peyton, and Erick's weirdness, but she didn't see any reason to bring that up.

"Oh, yeah, he can be a little…"

"Dickish?" Chloe asked with a smile.

"Sometimes," he agreed, deflating a little. "But he's really a nice guy," he insisted.

"I'm sure he is. You need more time down here or are you ready to teach a baby aether how to do magic?"

Zane smiled. "No, I'm good. Just let me lock up. I thought we'd work up in the loft today. It's not brand new to you now, so we should be good. And the books are all down here anyway," he said, flipping the open sign over then locking the front door. "Come on."

Chloe was curious to see what Zane's space looked like and didn't hesitate to follow. Her first glimpse at his loft made her lips twitch. It was an open room with the exception of the bathroom, with the living area flowing into the kitchen and the bedroom hidden behind a screen. While the bathroom and living room were kept neat and tidy, what she could see of his bedroom was anything but. Twisted sheets, a pair of jeans on the floor, a single shoe laying on its side. And he may have said all the books were downstairs, but she saw a few dozen scattered on various flat surfaces. What caught her attention though was a tree branch that had been sanded smooth and stood upright, attached to a heavy base, but she didn't get a chance to ask about it before he spoke.

"Have you been practicing since the park?" Zane asked as he sat down on the couch.

"Not like I did with you and Diego," Chloe admitted, "but I did use my magic to...help the sheriff out." She trusted Zane, to an extent, but she wasn't about to share police business with a man she'd only met once before. A good judge of character she may be, but she wasn't infallible.

"You did?" he asked curiously, pushing the glasses up his nose. "Well, good. That you're using your powers, I mean. Why don't we start with some of the same? Just get you more familiar with dispelling magic?" She must have gotten a confused look on her face because he added, "Stopping magic is called dispelling it."

"Oh, gotcha. Yeah, that works."

For the first few minutes he conjured small cyclones and breezes, to get her comfortable with using her power again. Then he grinned mischievously. "Ready to try something a little bigger?"

A thrill of excitement ran through Chloe, and she nodded eagerly. "Oh yeah."

He smiled and lifted his hands, palms up. A light breeze began to swirl around the room, circling around them and growing in strength. When it grew in intensity she saw it pick up objects from around the room—a book, a crystal paperweight, a remote—and spin them around. Though the wind didn't touch her directly, it was powerful enough to tease her ponytail and have it twitching.

She laughed in delight at the display before she looked back to Zane, the sound ending abruptly. His eyes, normally a pretty blue, were solid white aside from his pupils, which remained black.

"What's wrong?" he asked, the wind starting to lessen.

"Don't stop. Your eyes...they surprised me," she explained, though she vaguely remembered them saying something about elemental's eyes changing color when they used a lot of power. "Keep going."

105

He nodded and ramped up the intensity of his magic once more. This time she focused on the magic, that brush she felt tickling her skin, and reached out with her own. She broke the magic, which was a lot easier than she'd expected from such a strong display, and all the things the wind had picked up fell to the floor.

The loud thud of the paperweight hitting the wood floor made her wince. "Oops. Sorry."

Zane chuckled and shook his head. "You're fine. It was bound to pick stuff up, and it's not the first time that hunk of rock has been dropped," he assured her. "You did well, too. That was a lot of power for you to stop. Was that the first time you'd seen someone's eyes change, though?"

Chloe nodded. "Yeah. It just threw me off. Especially the white. I had a flash of you being a zombie."

He laughed. "That's a new one. Now I know how to improve on my Halloween costume next year, though."

"You're going to just keep wind going indefinitely instead of putting in contacts?" she teased.

"Good point. You ready to try absorbing magic?"

"Depends. I know what it sounds like, but what is it really?"

"Well, keep in mind that not all aethers can absorb magic, so it might be nothing," he warned. "But basically, you'll take the power I'm pumping into the magic and take it into yourself. It'll end the magic, though maybe not right away, and you'll get a boost."

Chloe's eyes sharpened. "So, I can spend a little bit of power to sort of recharge my batteries?" She paused a beat. "Do I have batteries?"

He couldn't help but chuckle. "In a manner of speaking, yes, actually. Magical energy is just like physical energy. You can exhaust it just like you can exhaust your body, just exchange running a marathon for using a lot of magic."

"That makes sense. And doing this is like drinking really potent coffee?"

"Essentially, yes."

"Okay, this sounds much cooler now. How do I do it?"

106

"How do you dispel magic? Specifically, how does it feel in your head?"

"I can see this sort of light, and I just reach out and pop or break it."

Zane nodded. "Then instead I would suggest instead of breaking it, you grab hold of it and let the magic flow into you. Maybe drag it into you. But you might have to try a few things, to see what works for you."

"Got it. I'm ready."

"Okay, we're going to start small again." The miniature cyclone appeared on his palm, and he nodded for her to begin.

The connection between him and the magic was easy to find, and it would be so easy to just break it, so she had to go slow and careful when she reached out. The first time she accidentally dispelled the magic rather than absorbing it. "Damn."

"That's okay. It takes practice," Zane told her reassuringly and brought the magic back.

The next two times she got closer, but still dispelled rather than absorbed. The third time she grabbed hold a little too strongly, and though she felt a minute surge of power, the connection ended almost immediately.

"That was closer. I felt your draw on my magic that time," he said with a proud smile. "Once more."

It was hard controlling something so firmly when it was all in her head, like trying to pluck a single harp string while wearing fluffy mittens. But she took hold of the flow of magic and held it tight, careful not to break it. She felt the magic trickling into her, making her feel like she'd just injected pure caffeine into her bloodstream. Her eyes half-closed with pleasure at the sensation, and she saw the cyclone shrink, then finally disappear. Dimly she realized she was still feeling that trickle of magic.

"Chloe…Chloe, you need to stop," Zane said, sounding like someone who was getting worried, but trying very hard not to be.

"Hmm?"

"You're still pulling on my magic. Pull back. Break the connection."

107

"Oh!" Being so startled at his words helped her draw back and the sensation ended. "I'm sorry. I just…"

He shook his head. "It's all right. It was your first time, and you didn't take too much."

"I didn't know I'd keep taking your magic once the cyclone was gone," she explained, her brow furrowed with worry.

"Neither did I," he admitted with a wry smile. "But it's a good skill for you to know. If you're ever attacked—which I don't imagine you will be—you can not only end whatever magic your attacker is using, but drain them to make them less of a threat."

"But I also need to be careful if I ever need to dispel magic a friend is doing," she added.

"True. But this is still a very good thing for you. Don't be scared of it, just learn how to use it. It's a tool, so it's only dangerous if you don't know how to use it."

That made sense to her. It was very much like a gun in that sense. "Can we try again? I'll be more careful this time."

He considered for a moment before nodding. "Of course. As soon as you see the cyclone disappear, pull back."

"I will."

It was easier this time, since she wasn't surprised by how good it felt to draw someone's magic into herself, and was able to stop when the magic ended. But it occurred to her that it had been too easy, and she said as much.

"I don't know if it will always be so easy," Zane said thoughtfully. "I'm not exactly one of the strongest people in town. Diego, for example, might be a lot harder for you."

Chloe's lips split into a grin. "Harder for me, huh?" she teased.

He blushed a little. "He *was* flirting with you, but you know what I meant. He's more powerful so it's probably going to be harder for you to absorb his magic."

She laughed and nodded, bumping his knee with hers. "I know. You're just cute when you're flustered."

"You've been hanging out with Lexi too much," he muttered, and she could only shrug. "I think you've got the hang of it, though it wouldn't hurt for you to see how you do with other people. Especially people who aren't elementals. For all I know, it's simpler with me because we're both elementals. You might find it near impossible to stop a shifter from turning."

"Could be." And she smiled, slowly, wickedly. "I wonder if I can talk the sheriff into shifting so I can give it a try. I've never seen a shifter, well, shift." And there was still the whole teddy bear debate. Could a grizzly be cuddly in any way, shape, or form?

"If you get him to agree, I want to hear all about it. He's not the most serious person on Salus, but he is a little…"

"Uptight? Has a stick up his ass?"

Zane grinned. "Sometimes."

"I'll let you know how it goes. Now, can I buy you dinner to thank you for helping me?"

"I'd like that."

Chapter 15

They went to the only pizza place on town, which made Chloe happy. What sane person didn't like pizza, after all? And it was the perfect way to relax and just enjoy herself for a bit. Even if she did intend to do some work while they were there.

The place was twice the size of the diner, and more than half full, but they were able to find a booth easily enough. Chloe was distracted at first, as she watched a group of teens in another booth. One was making a flame appear and disappear on the tip of his finger, while another was pelting a third with rolled up bits of paper propelled by magic. It was fascinating, and proof that her world had definitely changed.

After they'd ordered a large pepperoni and some drinks, Chloe went serious. "Did you know Jeremy?"

Zane looked surprised by the question but nodded. "I did. Not as well as some, but well enough to talk to. Why?"

"Well, with everything going on, I wanted to learn more about him. Especially if he and my grandmother had this feud or rivalry or whatever it was going on between them."

He frowned. "I honestly don't know anything about that. He never mentioned your grandmother to me, or vice versa. I know they were friendly at some point, and then they weren't, but I don't know what caused the change."

Chloe was disappointed, but not surprised. "Okay. Do you know anything about him that doesn't have to do with my grandmother? Wesley said he worked at the council building, but that's pretty much the extent of what I know about the guy."

Zane slowly nodded. "He did work there, yes. He was an admin. He basically did odd jobs for the council members."

"All of them?"

"Mmhmm. There isn't enough work for each councilor to have their own admin, so they share. It seems to work well enough for everyone."

"And what was he? No one's mentioned that." And if he was something formidable, maybe it would help prove her innocence.

"Psychic."

There went that hope. "And no spouse? Girlfriend? Boyfriend?"

"Not that I know of. He may have had one in the past, but not since I've known him, and none that he ever mentioned to me." He cocked his head. "Why do you want to know all this?"

She smiled faintly and shrugged as she sipped on her Coke. "I'm the only suspect in his murder. I'm also a trained investigator, so it's ingrained in me to want to find out the truth. Except being on Salus has taken away a lot of my normal tools."

"What do you mean?"

"The internet, for one. Most people have something that can be found online, whether it's social media or government records that would show up in a background check," she explained. "You can look at work histories or family members. Salus is way too private for any of that to work. Not to mention the whole longevity thing, which means people change names over the years. Or I assume they do if they're not on Salus."

"Oh. Yeah, I suppose that would make your job rather difficult," he agreed.

"Until I adjust to it and find alternative methods, yeah. So...I have to settle for asking people questions. And since most people here don't know me..."

111

"They're not willing to talk freely."

"Bingo."

Their server returned, placing the hot pizza between them, and only when the smell hit her did Chloe realize just how hungry she was. She lifted a slice and had just taken a bite, searing the roof of her mouth, when she heard a kind voice say, "Hello, Zane. Chloe."

Chloe tried to ignore the heat of the pizza and swallow as quickly as possible as she glanced up at Emma, who had a pizza box in hand.

Zane smiled at the witch. "Hi, Emma. How are you doing?"

"Oh, I'm doing okay," Emma said, smiling warmly. "And you? Is everything going okay at the bookstore?"

"Rolling along. Not a lot of highs or lows, really."

Emma nodded, hesitated, then turned to Chloe. Her smile wavered a bit but didn't disappear. "And you, Chloe? Are you starting to…settle in?"

Chloe felt her cheeks heat as she recalled how she'd run out of Emma's house. "I am. Zane's actually been helping me learn to use my powers. And several people have been…educating me on things."

The smile firmed and Emma seemed genuinely happy. "That's wonderful. I'm happy to hear that. Well, I can't stay, but you two have a good evening."

"Bye, Emma," Zane said.

"Bye," Chloe echoed as Emma left. "I was such an asshole to her," she muttered, picking at the pepperoni on her pizza, her appetite gone.

"What do you mean?"

She sighed and slumped back in the booth. "She told me I was an elemental, and I didn't believe her. At first. Then I sort of got pissed and ended up storming out."

"That's kind of understandable," Zane told her gently. "It was a big thing, especially since it involved changing what you thought you were. Changing your identity."

"Yeah, but I could have handled it better. A lot better." And she felt sick at how she'd treated the one woman her grandmother had trusted enough to tell Chloe the truth.

He smiled and shook his head. "Don't be so hard on yourself. Like I said, it was a huge thing. And she's a very forgiving woman."

Chloe slowly nodded. She was going to have to apologize to Emma, and soon.

Zane nudged her foot with his own. "Come on. Cheer up. You're learning magic, making new friends, and you'll make it right with Emma. Just enjoy the rest of the evening."

She made herself smile. "Thanks, Zane."

He grinned. "Anytime."

The next morning Chloe drove into town. Though it was November, and chilly, the sun was bright. It was the perfect morning, so she sang happily as she followed the road that wove through the trees. When the trees opened to reveal the town, she slammed on the brakes.

Someone was lying half in the road.

She put the car in park and shoved the car door open, rushing over to the person. Kneeling, she checked for a pulse but couldn't find one. Nor did she see any visible wounds. It was as if he'd just dropped dead while trying to cross the street.

"Help! Someone help!" Chloe yelled, lifting her head to look for someone, anyone, who could help. Instead, her blood ran cold as she saw another figure lying prone on the sidewalk. She stood and ran but slowed halfway there. Even with his face turned away from her she recognized the still figure. It was Zane. "No," she breathed and fell to her knees beside him. Like the first man, there was no pulse, no wound. Tears stung her eyes and she couldn't stop herself from shaking him. "Zane. Zane! Wake up. Please, wake up. This isn't funny. It's not—"

All the breath caught in her lungs when she caught sight of a familiar brunette lying in front of the diner. "Lexi," she sobbed. Tears flowed freely down her cheeks, but she couldn't make her

113

suddenly petrified muscles move.

She shook her head, unable to believe that two people who had become important to her were dead. But it wasn't just them. Everywhere she looked she saw someone else sprawled out with the limpness that could never be truly mistaken for sleep. Men, women, children...they were everywhere. Some were still in their cars, which had run into lampposts, buildings, other cars.

Chloe stumbled to her feet, though her legs weren't fully cooperating. "Hello?" she yelled as loud as she could. "Anyone?" she called, voice cracking, as she stumbled to the nearest building. It had a large window in the front so she could see inside, but everyone there was just as dead as those in the street. The next shop was the same and she felt her heart beating harder, faster, than it ever had.

She wanted to hope that there was someone, anyone, who was still alive, but it was getting harder to hold onto that tiny tendril. Then she saw two bodies lying next to each other, like they'd been talking when they'd died. Diego and Wesley. If she'd though it was hard to see Lexi and Zane lying there, dead, it was nothing compared to this sight. Her legs buckled and her knees stung as they hit the concrete, but she barely felt it.

What had happened here? Why was everyone here dead but her? What had killed them?

The perfect sunshine began to fade, everything darkening around her. Even more confused she looked around. When she saw behind her, the trees she'd emerged from, she scrambled backward until her head hit brick.

A mass of black, thicker, darker than any cloud, a mass that looked somehow wet and alive, rolled through and above the trees. Whatever it touched rotted instantly, the tall trees losing their leaves, turning black and decaying to almost nothing in a matter of seconds. And the blackness wasn't stopping. It plowed over everything as it made its way to the town.

Chloe knew she needed to get out of the way of that rot-inducing veil of darkness. If it touched her, she'd be as dead as the trees, as the people who were sprawled all around her. She knew that, but she couldn't force her body to move. All she

114

could do was sit there with her back against the building, trembling in icy terror.

The blackness came closer and closer, engulfing everything, until it rolled over her. For a single instant she thought she was safe, but then every cell in her body was attacked, causing more pain than she could have ever imagined. She screamed as her body rotted in seconds, until her entire world was pain.

Her scream echoed in her bedroom as her mind forced her out of the nightmare and into reality. It was still dark out and her body throbbed with an echo of the pain she'd felt. She laid there for several minutes as she worked to get her breathing under control, waited for her heart rate to return to normal.

She'd had realistic dreams before, even a few nightmares that had chased her into consciousness, but none that had come close to the intensity of this one. For that matter, no nightmare she'd ever had was as terrifying as that one had been. Worse, all the others, they'd begun to fade as soon as she woke. This one? She knew she'd never forget this one.

Knowing she wasn't going to get back to sleep anytime soon, she got up and into the shower, hoping the water would help wash away the memory of the pain.

Chapter 16

The shower did little to help, and she felt strangely jittery. Though she attributed most of that to the nightmare, she thought the magic she'd absorbed from Zane wasn't helping. It really had felt like a couple good jolts of espresso, after all. She tried to work for a little while but couldn't focus. Instead, she pulled her hair up and went to the diner for breakfast.

Lexi was working and gave her a quick grin before bringing over a cup of coffee. With caramel, Chloe discovered after a single sip.

"Lexi? I love you."

The woman in question laughed as she topped off another customer's coffee. "Oh, I know. Everyone does." She winked at the man she was serving. "Isn't that right?" she asked, grinning when the tips of his ears turned pink and he hid behind his mug. "See? He loves me," she said with a fond smile for the man. "What can I get you this morning, Chloe?"

"Eggs, bacon, and toast, please," Chloe said between sips of coffee.

"That sounds good. Can I have the same?" a woman asked as she took the seat next to Chloe.

She looked like an elementary school teacher. Long skirt, sweater, her brown hair secured at the nape of her neck, her brown eyes warm, with little laugh lines at the corners.

"Sure thing," Lexi said, smiling at them both before slipping off to give the cook the orders.

The woman smiled at Chloe. "I hope you don't mind me sitting here. I've heard so much about you lately, I wanted to meet you," she explained. "I'm Gina."

"Doesn't bother me." And the distraction of a new person might help the memory of the nightmare fade a bit more. "And does everyone in Salus really know who I am?"

"Pretty much," Gina admitted with a smile. "Though your grandmother told me some about you, so I haven't only heard about you through gossip."

Chloe sighed. "That's something, anyway. Though I think even people who heard about me from my grandmother are still gossiping."

Gina smiled sympathetically. "You're not wrong, and I can't say I'm entirely innocent there myself. It's not often—"

"You get a new person here," Chloe interrupted, but she smiled to take the sting out of it. "Believe me, I know. Haven't seen you here before, though. The diner, I mean."

"I'm here most every morning, but the library opens later on Saturdays," Gina explained. "If you ever want a quiet place to go to get away from people, you're more than welcome to come by. It's not your typical library."

Chloe cocked her head. "Kind of like how Zane's bookstore isn't a typical bookstore?"

"Basically, yes. Though I have more town history than he does, I think. But we both have books regular libraries—or bookstores—would put in the fantasy section, if they carried them at all."

"I might stop by sometime, then. Thanks."

Gina smiled warmly. "Of course. Besides, I always enjoy the company." She sighed. "So many people, even here on Salus, have gone digital. Makes me sad sometimes."

Not sure what to say to that, Chloe just nodded

sympathetically and took a drink of her coffee. Luckily, Lexi delivered their food then, which gave her an excuse to focus elsewhere. Gina seemed nice, but Chloe was one of those people who had gone digital, when she even read at all. It was just so much more convenient, but she didn't want to make the librarian feel any worse.

"Everything going smoothly, Chloe? Tell me you've managed not to have anything major happen since yesterday," Lexi said a few minutes later when she got a chance to stop and breathe.

Chloe snorted softly. Just the most terrifying nightmare ever, but she didn't want to bring down Lexi's chipper mood. "No, nothing major. Car trouble, grumpy mechanic, learning from Zane. Which was actually a lot of fun," she admitted.

"Oh, so you're getting all settled in, huh? You starting to like Salus? Thinking you might stay and be a productive aether?" Lexi teased.

"I don't know if I'd go that far," Chloe said slowly. "I'll admit, the whole aether thing *is* kind of badass, and the guys…"

"They are pretty easy on the eyes," Gina chimed up with a shy smile.

"That they are," Lexi agreed. "And lucky me, I've got a date with one of them tonight. But I'll tell you all about that tomorrow," she added with a wink. "I'm telling you though, you really should seriously consider staying."

"I guess I'm just worried about there being enough work for me here, and…I don't know, the differences between Salus and nor—other towns? They're pretty major."

"Not really," Gina disagreed with a shake of her head. "I mean, yes, you'll see magic around, and we're run by a council instead of a mayor, and yes, we're secretive, but other than that? It's a normal town."

"She's right," Lexi said with a nod. "Plus, here on Salus? You don't have to hide what you are. You don't have to worry about accidentally displaying your power to humans."

Chloe frowned. "What would happen if I did?"

Lexi and Gina exchanged a look before Lexi spoke. "Depends on how bad it is. If it's one person? It's manageable.

Their memory would be wiped and you'd get in some trouble. If it was bigger than that, but not so bad that you completely outed supernaturals to the rest of the world? More complicated. If you did out us? You'd never see the light of day again."

Chloe paled, her eyes widening. "Holy crap. They take that seriously, don't they?"

"Oh yeah. Just think of how humans would react if they knew we existed," Lexi pointed out.

"Look at how they reacted when they just suspected," Gina added. "No actual supernaturals were killed during the witch trials or Inquisition, but they still hunted for us. And now? We'd be imprisoned and studied."

"And if we weren't, we'd still be feared," Lexi said on a sigh.

"And supernaturals still choose to live outside of protected towns like this?" Chloe asked in astonishment.

Lexi laughed and shrugged. "Well, yeah. There are limitations to a town like this. Jobs, the number of people you can interact with. And some like moving around. There's nothing saying you can't live anywhere you want, you just have to be discreet if you don't live someplace like Salus."

"Maybe I should stay until I'm sure I've got my powers under control then," Chloe said, grimacing.

Lexi beamed. "I wouldn't argue. Would you argue?" she asked Gina.

The librarian smiled and shook her head. "I don't think I would, no. But take your time in thinking things through and remember that no choice you make has to be permanent."

Instantly Chloe felt better. She could choose to stay for now and move whenever she wanted. No pressure. "Thanks, both of you."

"No problem," Lexi replied while Gina just smiled.

"I should get going though," Chloe said as she stood and fished out the money for her breakfast. "Got some things to take care of today."

Lexi grinned. "Sure thing. See you around."

Chloe was becoming entirely too familiar with the sheriff's office, especially since she hadn't even been in Salus a week. Which meant she was surprised when she found a vehicle in the small lot other than Wesley's cruiser. More specifically, a newer pickup.

Curious she went inside, and saw Wesley sitting at his desk, a tall blonde man standing by the coffeepot. He was pouring a cup while he talked to the sheriff. "We've just got to do something soon. I can't believe we're no closer to finding out who did this," the man said, his voice rough, almost a snarl.

"You know I'm doing everything I can, Colin. I just—" Wesley broke off, eyes narrowing when he saw Chloe. "Don't you know it's rude to eavesdrop?"

Chloe smiled brightly as she crossed the room. "It's not eavesdropping if I don't try and hide," she pointed out cheerfully.

The unknown man turned to face her, and she could see he was tanned, sturdy, and had a rugged look to him. His hazel eyes were tired, but she had a feeling he missed little. She certainly didn't miss the sensation of fur she felt as those eyes raked over her. It wasn't quite the same as she'd felt from Wesley, but similar enough that she pegged him as a shifter. Being able to do so gave her a spurt of pride in her growing abilities and knowledge.

"Hi, I'm Chloe," she offered, but she stood equidistant from both men, careful to keep Wesley in her peripheral vision. She didn't think he'd hurt her, but she knew he wasn't entirely happy with her either.

"Yes, I know," the stranger said with the faintest hint of amusement. "I don't think you need to introduce yourself to anyone on Salus at this point."

She grimaced and nodded. "True." Her lips slowly curved. "Of course, everyone else still has to introduce themselves."

The man glanced to Wesley. "She always like this?"

"Unfortunately," Wesley said, shaking his head. "Chloe, this is Colin Baker, one of the council members."

"Ah! That makes three then. All I'm missing are the elemental and vampire councilmen," Chloe said with a nod.

Colin cocked his head. "You've heard of me?"

"No. Well, I was told about the council, but you weren't mentioned specifically. Why?"

He grunted softly. "I'd forgotten how annoying it could be when an aether was around," he muttered to Wesley. Chloe frowned as he turned back to her. "It's nice to meet you, I suppose, but what exactly are you doing here?" he asked.

She glanced between the two men before focusing on the councilman. "I don't know if he told you, but I was able to tell him that there was magic hiding…something. I was just curious if he'd found anything else out about that."

Colin frowned at Wesley. "Should she be getting involved in this? Especially since she's a suspect?"

"Technically no," Wesley said, sighing. "But she was the one who pointed out that there was magic on the body. Without that I wouldn't have had any reason to call in Diego." He turned to Chloe. "Who's coming in to see the body tomorrow, by the way."

"Good. I hope he finds something," she told him. "But I thought I wasn't a suspect? Just a person of interest?"

Wesley nodded. "True, you aren't officially a suspect, but if this were a normal case in a normal sheriff's office, you wouldn't be getting a single detail that wasn't necessary to question you with."

Colin scowled. "Sometimes I hate that this isn't a normal sheriff's office," he muttered. "Just make sure you're careful," he told Wesley. "I'm heading out for now."

Chloe's lips twitched and she rolled her eyes. She watched him hurry out the door and yelled after him, "Nice to meet you, too!" Grinning, she turned back to Wesley. "He's a cheerful guy."

"Yeah, well, no one's at their best when someone they know has been murdered," Wesley pointed out dryly.

"Good point," she admitted as she dropped down into the visitor's chair. "Since Diego hasn't looked at the body yet, I'm guessing there's nothing new?"

Wesley shook his head. "Unfortunately, no. But you should know murder investigations are rarely quick."

"I know." TV shows always made it seem like crimes were solved in no time, but she knew it took hours upon hours of work to collect enough evidence to not only find the killer but get a warrant.

She sat there thinking so long Wesley arched a brow. "Was there something else you needed?"

"Hmm? Oh! Yes, sorry. Actually, there was. I told you Diego and Zane, mostly Zane, have been helping me with my powers, right?"

He nodded. "Sure."

"Zane suggested I see if I could find a shifter who would help me, too."

Wesley frowned. "Help you how? I don't know anything about using actual magic. I don't know that any shifter does. We change shape and occasionally can talk to or control animals. We don't do magic like the witches or elementals, or even some vampires."

Chloe shook her head. "He wasn't talking about magic like that. He's been teaching me how to stop—dispel—magic, and how to absorb it. Zane says that the way each type of supernatural uses magic is different, so just because I can dispel his magic doesn't mean I could, for example, stop a shifter from shifting."

A look of acute disgust flashed over his face before it cleared and he gave her blank face. "You want me to start to shift and let you stop me? In the middle of the process?"

His reaction made her frown. That was exactly what she wanted, sure, but from the way he made it sound, it was an unpleasant process. She wanted to learn, but not if it hurt anyone. It was bad enough that she'd drained from Zane beyond what she'd needed to. He'd said he was fine, that it hadn't hurt him, but she still felt guilty about her loss of control. "I'm sorry,

I didn't know it was…painful or whatever."

He gave her a suspicious look. "It's not painful, or it doesn't have to be, but I've heard it can be…uncomfortable."

"Oh. Yeah, Zane didn't say that. He just said I should give it a try. And since I wanted to see you shift anyway, I figured it would be a win win." She shrugged. "But if it's that bad, don't worry about it."

"It's not horrible, and like I said, it shouldn't be painful, but let me think about it, okay? Shifting in front of someone, outside of an emergency, isn't really something we do casually. But I'll consider it."

Chloe smiled and nodded. "Sure. I'm taking this whole thing slow in any case. It's so new I don't want to screw up or anything, you know?"

"Is that likely?" he asked dryly.

She had to laugh. "I haven't killed anyone yet, so there's that?"

"Good to know. I should get back to work, but I'll let you know what I decide."

"Of course," Chloe said, getting to her feet. "And thanks, Wesley, whatever you decide."

She had just started her car when her cell rang. It was Miles Saxon, her grandmother's lawyer. The check they'd talked about had been cut and he just needed to know where to send it. The question should have been simple, but since Salus didn't exist to the outside world, it made normally easy answers such as a mailing address complicated. She told him she was out of town and would call him right back with an address, then she went back inside the sheriff's office.

Wesley looked up, a mildly annoyed look on his face. "What is it now?"

"Sorry, but I need to have something mailed here, from a human, and not sure how to go about that," Chloe answered.

His expression cleared fractionally. "Oh, easy answer there. There's a bed and breakfast just on the mainland called Salus B and B. It's run by a supernatural. We have all our mail and deliveries sent there and they get sent out here. It's the standard practice."

"Wait, a bed and breakfast? I saw that when I first heard about Salus and was hitting the internet to try to find information about it."

He nodded. "It's a cover if anyone overhears someone saying they're visiting Salus. Just use that address and you'll be fine."

"Okay, thanks again."

"No problem."

She went back outside and found the bed and breakfast online, got the address, and relayed it back to the lawyer, who assured her she'd have the check in a few days. Though she hadn't wanted the money at first, with everything going on, it would be nice to have that buffer. And one less thing to worry about.

Chapter 17

There was one more thing Chloe wanted to do today. It wasn't going to be super pleasant, but it needed done. She needed to see Emma and apologize for freaking out. Plus, Emma had known the supernatural side of her grandmother, and Chloe wanted to hear about that. And maybe Emma would know about the deal between Granny and Jeremy. Maybe she'd even know if Jeremy was her dad.

She knew Emma owned a boutique and decided to start there. It took a good deal of driving around before she found a boutique, but considering it was named, unimaginatively, Emma's Boutique, she was pretty sure she was in the right place.

Chloe parked and went inside but found a teenage girl rather than the woman she'd expected.

The girl was about sixteen, with a slim build, brown hair and a bright smile. "Hi! Can I help you find something?"

"Uh, yeah. I'm looking for Emma?"

"Oh, man, I'm sorry. She's not here today," the girl answered. "She called me this morning and said she couldn't come in, asked me to open the shop for her."

"Oh. That's fine, I'll just swing by her house. Thanks though," Chloe said with a quick smile before she left. This was probably better anyway. Who knew what they'd end up talking about, and someplace private was better than a public place, even one Emma owned.

Chloe drove out to Emma's, and it struck her at how much less nervous she was this time. She knew the big secret, so all her anxiety now was about apologizing. Not knowing what sort of woman Emma was, she didn't know how easily her apology would be accepted. Emma hadn't seemed to hold a grudge at the pizza place, but Chloe was aware of how deceiving looks could be.

She knocked and waited, but there was no answer. She knocked again, but even after a few minutes there were no sounds from within the house. Maybe Emma had called in because she was sick, and if that was the case, she'd probably be sleeping. Hoping Emma would feel better soon, she went back to her car and headed back to town. She only had one more thing she needed to do, so she decided to explore some more, maybe do some shopping. She'd left Philadelphia with only enough for a weekend, and her earlier shopping trip for groceries had been for just a few days, so she needed some supplies.

It surprised her when she had fun on her outing. She returned to the boutique and grabbed a few outfits, including a dress. She didn't think she'd be going on another date anytime soon, but it never hurt to be prepared, and she couldn't resist the silver and black dress when she saw it. She wasn't really a dress sort of girl, but it was cute and looked good on her without being too fancy.

Next, she hit the bookstore, disappointed when she learned Zane wasn't there, but she picked up a few books on elementals and Salus. It was great learning from people, but people weren't perfect. They tended to forget details, and in this case, they'd probably not mention something because it was just so commonplace to them. Books wouldn't have that problem. Or she hoped they wouldn't, anyway.

Before she realized it, it was nearly dark, so she hit the market and got enough groceries for another week.

It had been a productive day, despite not being able to see Emma, so she was singing softly to herself as she carried the bags out to the car. She'd just unlocked her door when she felt magic start to build nearby, rapidly. It wasn't the feel of fur or elements on her skin, or even the tingling she'd gotten from Diego, but more the feeling of vertigo she'd gotten from Jeremy's body and from arriving on Salus. Strong, powerful. Dangerous.

Chloe only had a second to react, but dispelling magic wasn't yet second nature to her, and this wasn't in a safe setting with a friend. Her attempt to break the spell was more like trying to slap at a bullet. She partially blocked it, but still got hit by the magic. The bags of groceries hit the ground and she staggered, slamming into the car. She fumbled in her bag for her pistol as she looked around for some sign of the person who attacked her.

Nothing, just the growing darkness. The insects starting to awaken as the day passed into night. But no other people. Still, it was several minutes later when she felt like she could put the gun away. She picked up her groceries. The eggs were goners, a can of Coke had exploded, and a bottle of ketchup had broken open, but the rest was salvageable, even if the containers did need wiped off.

She got in the car and drove home, though she was still feeling shaky. The dizziness had passed, but now she felt like she was getting sick. Once back at the house she got everything inside and put away. Upstairs she took her shoes off then climbed into bed, too exhausted to even change into her pajamas.

Chloe woke in the morning with the sun streaming in the window, warming her face. She yawned and ran her hands through her hair as she went downstairs, desperately craving a cup of coffee. The craving was bad enough she could almost smell it. When she stepped in the kitchen, she realized it wasn't her mind toying with her, she was actually smelling coffee.

And there was a man sitting at her table.

No, there was a perfect man sitting at her table. He looked like a surfer, with sun-bleached hair, bright blue eyes, and a tan, but he was literally perfect. Symmetrical features, hair just the right length to look shaggy but not messy, and well-built. He didn't look real.

Despite that perfection, she stopped and stared, annoyed. "Who the hell are you? And why are you in my kitchen?"

The man chuckled and pushed a steaming cup of coffee across the table so it sat in front of an empty seat. "I'm here to talk to you. And I brought a peace offering," he said, gesturing at the cup. "Why don't you sit, and I'll tell you why I'm here?" he suggested, not at all put off by the annoyance in her tone. "I promise I'm not here to harm you. My intentions are absolutely pure."

Something made her trust him, but she was still cautious as she walked toward the table and sat down slowly. She kept her eyes on him as she lifted the cup, sniffed it. It smelled like coffee. Actually, it smelled like heaven. She took a wary, testing sip and nearly whimpered. It was exactly right. The sugar, the cream, the caramel. It was ambrosia.

Her reaction drew another low laugh from the man, but he said nothing until she'd drank half the cup and woken up a little more. Once the fog of sleep had cleared, she narrowed her eyes at him. "So, who are you?"

The man looked apologetic. "I'm sorry, but I can't tell you that. I want to, I really do, but it wouldn't be safe. I know they say knowledge is power, and it can be, but in some cases, knowledge puts you at risk. Knowing who I am would put you at great risk."

Chloe made a frustrated sound and set the cup down a little too hard. "You sneak into my kitchen, make me coffee, but won't tell me your name? Then why are you here?"

He smiled sadly. "To see you, for one. But more importantly, to warn you."

She frowned and cocked her head. "Warn me?"

"You were attacked last night, weren't you?"

Surprised, she slowly nodded. "Yes, but…how did you know?

I didn't tell anyone. I didn't even *see* anyone after that. I came home and pretty much went right to bed."

"I know quite a lot, Chloe, but not enough. Not nearly enough." He sighed and sat back, his shoulders slumped in defeat.

She found herself wanting to comfort him, the urge stronger than she'd like, but she forced herself to remain in her seat. "What do you know, then?"

"I know that last night's attack won't be the end of it. I know there are people who are looking for you, they just don't know it's you, not specifically."

"That makes no sense. If they're looking for me, how could they not know it's me?"

"They're looking for someone fitting a description, and not a complete one at that, but they don't know your name. It's like if I told you to look for a tall man in his thirties with brown hair. You could go after every man who fit that description, but you'd have a lot of men to sort through," he explained.

"But *why* do they want me? Why do they want to hurt me?"

"Unfortunately, I can't tell you that either. What I can tell you is that Salus isn't entirely safe for you."

"You're suggesting I leave?" That would be a first. She kept hearing how she should stay.

But he shook his head. "No, I'm not. It's not safe, but Philadelphia wouldn't be safe either. It might be worse, in fact. I just want you to be on your guard, Chloe." He sat forward, resting his arms on the table, his expression dire. "I mean it. Be very careful about who you trust. You have good instincts, but they're not infallible."

He straightened and looked annoyed for the first time since Chloe saw him. "And I'm afraid our time is up, but you'll remember all this. Tell no one what I've said, but don't forget to be careful."

"What? What do you mean? Why wouldn't I remember?" She made a low sound of frustration. "You can't just leave now!" Chloe said, standing so quickly her chair wobbled, almost tipping over. She heard a sound, but it was faint, like a memory in the back of her mind.

"I'm sorry, Chloe."

The sound repeated, louder now, and she recognized it as knocking.

The man stood and walked around the table. "It's time to wake up now," he said gently before he reached out and touched the tip of a finger to her forehead.

Chloe bolted upright in her bed. "No!" she cried out, even before her eyes had fully opened. But she couldn't deny the reality. She was in her bed. The man in her kitchen had just been a dream. Probably her subconscious being paranoid about the attack outside the market, she figured. But it was still weird. Her dreams normally faded quickly once she woke up, no matter how hard she tried to cling to them, but this one was as vivid as the room around her. At least it wasn't as terrible as the nightmare she'd had.

Worse than the disorientation from the dream was the way she physically felt. After the attack she'd been shaky and weak, but she'd attributed that to adrenaline. Since she was still feeling that way, she had to wonder if the magic that had hit her had done something to her.

She heard knocking and sighed, remembering the sound intruding into her dream. Though she wanted nothing more than to fall back asleep, she dragged herself out of bed. A groan tore from her lips as the movement revealed aches through her whole body. Some, she was sure, were from hitting her car. She'd check later, and she was betting her hip was probably bruised. But there was no time for that, since whoever was knocking at her door was getting impatient, judging by the strength of the knocks now. She managed to shuffle downstairs and open the door. When she saw Wesley there, she groaned. "Whatever it is, Wes, can it please wait?"

"Tell me you're not hungover again," Wesley said, though

there was no humor in his voice.

"No, but you did just wake me up. I take it this can't wait?"

"No, it really can't."

She sighed and waved him inside. "All right, but whatever it is, you need to say it in the kitchen, because I need coffee." She expected some quip, but Wesley followed her into the kitchen in silence and waited until she got coffee going. While the coffee brewed, she leaned against the counter and crossed her arms over her chest. "Okay, what's up?"

Wesley didn't answer immediately, and her anxiety began to build. "There was another murder last night," he said quietly.

Her arms dropped. "Oh god, no. Who?"

His jaw clenched. "Emma Mitchell."

"What? No!" she exclaimed, her eyes widening. She barely knew Emma, but it hit her hard. Emma had seemed nice and had been her last living link to her grandmother. She leaned more heavily against the counter and rubbed her chest. She'd felt bad when she'd been told about Jeremy, but she didn't know him. She'd met Emma, and she mourned the loss of such a sweet woman. The woman who'd introduced her to her true self. "What happened?"

"I spoke to Christie, a girl who works at her shop," he said instead of answering. "She said that you were there yesterday, looking for Emma, and when she wasn't there, you said you were going to go by her house?"

"I did, but she didn't answer. I figured she was sick and probably sleeping it off, especially since the girl at the boutique said she'd called in," Chloe answered. "I saw her the night before at the pizza place, but only for a few minutes." There was something on his face that had her straightening. "You...don't think I killed her, do you?"

Again, he asked his own question rather than answering hers. "Do you own a gun, Chloe?"

Her eyes closed, his non-answer telling her all she needed to know. He did suspect her. Or at least had what he believed to be evidence pointing to her. "I do," she whispered.

"What caliber?"

"Nine millimeter."

"I'm sorry, Chloe, but I'm going to need to take it in for testing," Wesley said, still all business.

Her eyes opened and met his, and she thought she saw a crack in his composure. "Of course." She'd left her bag on the table when she got home, so she didn't even have to leave the room. She opened it and pulled the pistol out, offering it to him, grip first.

Wesley pulled out an evidence bag and held it out, open, until she dropped the gun inside. "Where were you last night between eleven and one?" he asked as he sealed the bag and marked it.

"Here. Sleeping. By myself, so no alibi, unfortunately," Chloe said, rubbing her temple in an attempt to lessen the headache building behind her eyes. "But there is something you should know, though I doubt there's any way of confirming it, and I'm sure it's going to come off as an attempt to deflect your focus off of me."

"What's that?"

"I was attacked last night. With magic."

Wesley frowned, and she could tell he was fighting between concern and suspicion. "Where? What sort of magic?"

The coffee pot chirped at her and she poured a cup while explaining. "I was coming out of the market, was nearly at my car. As to what sort of magic? That's harder." She added the cream, sugar, and caramel to her coffee. "I know it wasn't a shifter, and it wasn't elemental magic. It felt more like what I felt when I first got to Salus, or first saw the crime scene in the woods. I dispelled it, at least some of it, but I got hit. I've felt sick since then. Sort of like I've got the flu. Maybe it's not connected. Maybe it's just someone who doesn't like outsiders and is trying to get me to leave, I don't know, but it felt powerful."

"Why didn't you report this last night?"

"Because I came home, put my groceries away, then passed out until you knocked on my door." Chloe smiled weakly. "You keep waking me up, but it's never under good circumstances. Sheriff."

"True, but we hadn't had a murder in decades until you arrived, Chloe. That's something to keep in mind," he pointed out. "I'm going to get going, but you really can't leave town now, not until this is settled. And do *not* go to the crime scene. I mean that. Don't even go near Emma's house."

"I won't. But I didn't kill anyone. I think some part of you knows that."

There was a pause, long enough to make her hope she was right about that. "I'll look into the attack. Let me know if anything else happens. I'll let myself out," Wesley said, heading for the door without a single glance back at her.

Chapter 18

Her coffee sat on the table, untouched but for a single sip. She was trying to process the fact that Emma was dead. At her house, judging by the warning Wesley had given her. He had asked for an alibi for two hours the night before, after Chloe had been to Emma's house, but for all she knew, Emma had been inside, held hostage by her killer. The thought made her shudder. Worse, the timing made her wonder. Chloe wasn't a big believer in coincidences, and since learning magic existed, she'd started to doubt them even more. So, could it really be a coincidence that she and Emma were both attacked on the same day? Somehow, she doubted it. But what was the connection? Emma had been killed, while Chloe had only dealt with a single attack that had left her bruised and feeling sick.

Another thought occurred to her. The attack had made her tired, so much that she went to sleep immediately after coming home. That took away any chance at an alibi. Emma had been shot, apparently, and she doubted too many people on Salus had guns, given they were all armed with magic. Had the attack been some elaborate attempt to frame her for Emma's murder? It was a little out there, but it made more sense than her being the murderer.

She got out her laptop and brought up the files she'd created. She updated Jeremy's first, including her theory about him being her father. Then she started a new file for Emma. Creating it made a cold knot form in her belly. So much had happened in the past few weeks. Her grandmother dying, a man who could be her father being murdered, and now the woman who'd been her grandmother's best friend had been murdered. She knew they said bad things happened in threes, but something inside her said she wasn't done with unpleasant events. More, it felt like all three events were connected somehow. She had no idea what that connection was, but she was determined to discover it. Not just because it would be proving her innocence, or even because she had an insatiable curiosity, but because it felt important. And, no matter how egotistical it sounded, it felt like she was involved beyond being a convenient scapegoat.

Thinking so hard with her head already hurting made the headache worse. Ignoring the coffee, she went upstairs to grab some aspirin then took a shower. It made her feel better, though still not a hundred percent. She'd only just gotten dressed and put her hair in its usual ponytail when someone knocked at the door.

"I swear, if that's Wesley telling me I'm under suspicion for another murder, I'm going to scream," she muttered as she stomped downstairs. Except it wasn't the sheriff on the other side this time.

A small, short woman with dark blue hair framing her face stood there, arching a brow when Chloe just looked at her. "Are you...Chloe Chadwick?" she asked uncertainly.

"Yes, sorry. I just expected...never mind. You've got to be the only person not to recognize me on sight, though," Chloe answered. "Can I help you?"

"It's the other way around, actually. I'm Daphne Carver, I'm the elemental councilor."

Chloe frowned. "It's nice to meet you, but...I'm not sure why you're here. Help me how?"

Daphne sighed. "Wesley didn't tell you I was coming?" Her voice dropped to a mutter when she said, "Idiot."

"Uh…no? Why would he?" she asked, confusion pushing the fear of her current situation to the back of her mind.

"Town law. When someone's in serious trouble—I don't mean minor things like traffic tickets or public intoxication—their councilor is notified. Since you're an elemental, that's me."

It seemed like every day Chloe learned something new about this town. "Okay…I can see why you'd want to know if a member of your race was in major trouble, but I don't get why you're here, as in at my door."

"The reason the councilors are notified is first, so we know what's going on, and second, so we can help. Think of me like your rep. Not a lawyer, but someone who's got your back," Daphne explained.

"Oh. That's…handy. Though I really hope I'm not going to need a rep or a lawyer," Chloe said. "Come on in."

"Thanks," Daphne said as she stepped inside and into the living room. "You haven't changed anything."

"No, but I've only been here a week. And since I'm not sure if I'm going to stay, it seems stupid to redecorate," Chloe answered with a shrug as she followed Daphne.

"Logical," Daphne said with a nod as she sat down. "I know you're under suspicion for Emma Mitchell's murder, and the sheriff also said you were a person of interest in Jeremy Banner's death. He also mentioned that you had a pistol he's taken in to test to see if it's the same one used to kill Emma."

"That's what he told me, too," Chloe said, a trace of bitterness in her tone. "There's no way it's going to be a match though, because I didn't kill Emma."

Daphne nodded. "Okay. Why did you try to see Emma yesterday, then?"

Her dream came back to her, and the mystery's man warning to be careful who she trusted. Still, she had to trust *someone*, though she would have felt better if she'd known to be expecting the councilor. On the heel of that thought came another—what if this wasn't town law? Since she couldn't prove or disprove it without being rude, she decided to err on the side of caution.

"Emma was friends with my grandmother," she began.

Daphne nodded. "Quite a few people were, but those two were especially close. I was sorry to hear about her death, by the way."

Chloe had a hard time knowing what to say to that, so she went with, "Thanks." She took a slow breath then continued. "Anyway, my grandmother told me in a letter to come here and talk to Emma. I did, on the day I arrived. Emma's the one who told me about supernaturals and everything. I...didn't take it well. I freaked out, really. Since then, I've adjusted and started accepting it. I wanted to apologize for freaking out on her. That's all." There was no need to mention Jeremy. It sure as hell wouldn't help make her look any more innocent.

Daphne looked disappointed, like she'd expected a different story, maybe a more exciting one, but she nodded. "But no way to prove it?"

"Not really. I mean, Emma may have told someone about how I reacted, and I mentioned it to Wesley and Lexi from the diner, but that's the best I can do," Chloe answered.

"Okay. And why did you have the gun?"

"I'm a private investigator. Back in Philadelphia, I mean. Occasionally I have to go to some rough locations, so it's safer to go armed. I have a permit and the gun's registered. In Philly, I don't leave the house without it, most of the time, so it's habit to just take it everywhere with me."

Daphne made a thoughtful sound and nodded. "Okay," she said again. "I think that's all for now, unless there's something else I should know about the situation?"

Chloe considered, then shook her head. "Not that I can think of. Other than the fact that I'm innocent."

For the first time Daphne cracked a smile. "Good to know." She stood and pulled a business card from her pocket, offering it to Chloe. "My number and email are on there. If you think of anything, or if you need anything, give me a call. My job is to help take care of this town in general, and the elementals specifically, so that means you."

Chloe took the card and hesitated. "Actually, if you have a couple more minutes, there is something. It's not about the

137

murders, though."

Curious, Daphne retook her seat. "Of course. What's the problem?"

"It's...me."

Daphne frowned. "What do you mean?"

"I'm an aether elemental. Which, let me tell you, is kind of a disappointment."

The councilor's brows shot up. "It's a disappointment to be the rarest sort of elemental? The one who can affect magic itself?" she asked dryly.

Chloe grinned. "Well, when you put it that way...But I've seen some other elemental magic and it's just more..."

"Flashy?"

"Yeah, and more useful in day-to-day stuff," Chloe agreed with a nod. "But that's not the problem. Zane, from the bookstore, has been helping me learn how to use my powers. I didn't know about the supernatural until Emma told me, so I had no idea how to do anything. And he's been great," she was quick to point out, "but even he's admitted that he doesn't know a whole lot about aethers. He can just tell me about the stuff everyone knows, and some theories from books."

"And you were hoping I knew more?"

Chloe nodded.

Daphne smiled. "Considering I knew your mom and grandmother, yes, I probably do. I won't say we were as close as Lydia and Emma were, but we were friendly enough. Was there something specific you were wanting to know?"

Chloe chewed on her lower lip as she considered. "What all can we do? I know about dispelling and absorbing magic, and Zane said there were a few other things some aethers might be able to do, but..."

"There are, yes," Daphne agreed. "And of course, it varies from elemental to elemental. Like I'm a water elemental, but my powers aren't going to be identical to another water elemental. One of us might be able to conjure water from nothing while the other can turn their bodies into water."

"I get that," Chloe confirmed with a nod. "I'm not asking you to tell me what I, specifically, can do, just what powers I might have."

Daphne nodded slowly. "Well, theoretically, an aether can affect or control any magic in any way they like, they just can't create a spell themselves. Or most can't."

"And by control, you mean..." Chloe prompted.

Daphne grinned. "You already mentioned dispelling and absorbing, and I'm sure you've sensed magic at some point. I've also heard of aethers who could take control of someone else's magic. Like if I were lifting water from a lake, an aether could potentially take control of my magic and put the water back, or hit me with the water, or whatever they like."

"Handy, though I can guess people aren't super fond of that particular power."

Daphne laughed softly. "No, not unless it's being used in their favor," she agreed.

"And what'd you mean when you said most can't create a spell themselves?"

"I never saw it myself, so I can't confirm it, but I heard that your grandmother was able to create wards. Ones that could block magic," Daphne answered after a brief pause.

Chloe blinked, then realized she already kind of knew that. She'd had one of those wards on her. Everyone was just calling them blocks. Zane had also called them bubbles, when they weren't containing a person's powers. "Are powers passed down genetically?"

Daphne sighed. "That's not an easy question. Yes and no. If your parents are both fire elementals, you'll be one, too. If your parents are a fire elemental and a water elemental, you'll be one or the other. But just because your parent has a specific power, that doesn't mean you'll necessarily inherit that power. And a child can absolutely manifest a power that neither parent has." She smiled wryly. "Genetics are tricky enough on their own, but when you add in magic, things can get...Weird."

"So, I may not be able to create wards."

"Right. But you might also have powers that neither your mom or grandmother had."

"Huh. Okay, well, thank you. You've given me a lot to think about."

Daphne smiled and rose. "I'm just happy I could help. And as I said, if you need anything, you have my number now."

"I do. And thank you. Hopefully this will get cleared up and we'll both have less to worry about."

"I hope so, too," Daphne said, and Chloe thought she sounded sincere, but she was getting paranoid after that dream.

She showed the councilor out, then leaned against the door once it was shut. "Damn. Anything else?" she asked to the ceiling. "How much can we fit into one day? This week wasn't bad enough?" She trudged back upstairs to get her phone and shot a text to Lexi. *Emma's been killed. I'm a suspect. Wes took my gun for testing. Met Daphne.*

It only took a minute before she got a reply back. *Oh hell no. I don't work until tonight. I'll be over in twenty.*

Lexi leaping so quickly into her defense made Chloe smile. And seeing a friendly face would be good for her. Now all she had to do was wait.

Chapter 19

Lexi was clearly becoming comfortable at Chloe's house—and with Chloe herself—because she didn't even bother to knock when she arrived, but let herself in, followed by a more hesitant Zane. She immediately spotted Chloe sitting on the couch and hurried over to her. After dropping down beside Chloe, she engulfed the other woman in a tight hug. "This is total bullshit! There is no way in hell you killed anyone. Especially not Emma!"

"I happen to agree with you, but somehow I have to prove it," Chloe said dryly.

"Wouldn't it be more accurate to say the sheriff would have to prove you did for you to be arrested?" Zane asked, hovering nearby, looking apologetic and uncomfortable. "Though I agree with Lexi. Especially with as bad as you felt about how you reacted when she told you about being an elemental."

Lexi drew back and shook her head. "You've been living on Salus too long, Zane. They may say innocent until proven guilty, but it doesn't always work that way."

"She's right. And doesn't take into account stuff like political pressure or frame jobs," Chloe added. "But don't just stand there, Zane. You are allowed to sit, you know."

He did, but the chair he chose was meant for someone at least four inches shorter than him, so he continued to look uncomfortable. "What exactly happened? Lexi just showed up, told me Emma had been killed, that you had met Daphne, and dragged me over here." He paused, then added quickly, "Not that I wouldn't have come, of course. You're my friend and I want to support you."

Chloe's lips twitched despite the situation. "I know, and thank you. But I don't know much more than that. I know Emma was killed, apparently shot, and they think I might have done it because I was looking for her yesterday and own a pistol. Then Daphne showed up." She shifted so she could look between the two of them. "Is that seriously town law? Councilors showing up to be a rep or whatever?"

They both nodded, but it was Lexi who spoke. "Yep. Just a way to make sure one race doesn't get railroaded because of ignorance or whatever, I guess," she said with a shrug. "I didn't think they usually showed up so quick, though."

"They don't, but we don't normally have murders occurring here either," Zane pointed out. "I would guess that it was a combination of that and her being new that got Daphne out here so fast."

"What can you guys tell me about her? I don't really feel super comfortable putting my life in the hands of a woman I met for five minutes," Chloe said. "She seemed nice enough, I guess, but…" Again, the memory of her dream surged to the front of her mind, and though she trusted these two, she kept it to herself. "I just don't know if I want to go on how she seems rather than how she is."

"I've never really socialized with her or anything. I've seen her around, of course, and I know who she is because she's part of the council, but that's about it," Lexi said apologetically. "I've never heard anything bad about her though, which is a good sign. People like to bitch in diners, you know?"

"I know her a little bit," Zane added, "but then, she is my councilor. She's always been nice to me. A bit distant, but she's usually busy with council business. I trust her, but it's more in the sense that she hasn't given me any reason not to."

Chloe sighed and slumped down. "Great. Here's hoping I don't actually end up *needing* her help." She saw Lexi wince and shook her head. "I'm sorry, that was bitchy. I didn't mean it like that. I do appreciate you guys being here."

Lexi rubbed her shoulder and nodded. "We know. It's a hard situation. Anyone would be bitchy. Right Zane?"

"I don't know if I'd be bitchy," he mused, scratching the back of his neck. "I might be an asshole, though."

Chloe let out a short laugh. "That's okay. If you were, we'd forgive you. And it's not like we…can…" She straightened and looked at Lexi. "Jeremy."

Lexi frowned in confusion. "What about him?"

"You're a medium. Can't you talk to him and ask him to tell you who killed him? Hell, I don't know why all places like Salus don't have a medium on staff. Think about how quick they'd solve their murders!"

Confusion shifted to apology on Lexi's face. "Because it doesn't work that way. Or it doesn't always work that way."

"What do you mean?"

"Not everyone leaves ghosts, to begin with, remember? There doesn't seem to be any real pattern there either. It's not just supernaturals, or people who died in certain ways, or anything else that links all ghosts together. It isn't even people with unfinished business, like TV and books say. Some ghosts are just sort of hanging around, waiting to move on. And I told you that a lot of murder victims don't leave ghosts."

"Oh." She did remember that conversation. "So, Jeremy might not have stayed around. Damn. Still, we could check, couldn't we?" Chloe asked hopefully. She hadn't forgotten her promise to avoid visiting crime scenes, but Wesley wasn't getting anywhere, as far as she knew, and she was tired of being a suspect.

Lexi slowly shook her head. "Even if he is a ghost, and we do find him, he might not be any help. A lot of ghosts don't remember their deaths. Some don't realize at first that they're dead. But there is a chance he'd remember, yes, it's just not common enough for supernatural cops to keep mediums on staff." Seeing the disappointment on Chloe's face she worked up a smile. "I'm happy to take a field trip and see what we can do, though. Zane, what do you say? Up for a short hike?" She frowned. "It is a short hike, isn't it?"

"Um...yes? If you don't get lost like I did, anyway," Chloe answered, watching Zane for his answer.

"Sure, I'll go. But I don't know what help I'll be," Zane answered.

"We might need a big, strong man for something," Lexi said with a grin. "Like reaching tall things."

"It's nice to be needed," he said dryly.

After Chloe had put shoes on and grabbed her bag, she led the way into the woods. It struck her as funny, given how lost she'd gotten last time, but she was the only one of them who'd been to the crime scene. Along the way, she glanced at them and said casually, "There's something else you guys should know..."

"Oh no. What is it now? Isn't Emma's murder bad enough?" Zane protested.

"I'm with tall, dark, and nerdy on this one," Lexi agreed.

"It's nothing that bad," Chloe assured them. "Well, maybe. Not to that extent, at least. But I was attacked last night. In the middle of town."

Lexi grabbed Chloe's arm and pulled her to a stop. "Are you serious? Are you okay? What happened?" she asked, looking Chloe over from head to toe.

Zane said nothing, but he, too, studied Chloe for signs of injury.

"I'm okay. I just felt someone starting to use magic, like throwing it at me. I tried to dispel it, but I wasn't quick enough," Chloe explained.

Zane's frown deepened. "Do you know what sort of magic it was?"

Chloe shrugged a little. "Nothing elemental, and it didn't feel like a shifter either. It felt like when I first checked out the crime scene, to be honest, which was weird. I thought it just felt like that because of the block."

"Hmm. Maybe the block was just making it hard for you to sense magic unless it was powerful? Though if that was the case, then it sounds like the same sort of magic was involved in both Jeremy's death and your attack."

"But I felt the same sort of thing when I first got to Salus," she pointed out. "What sort of magic could be involved in all three?"

"That's really weird," Lexi said, shaking her head. "But maybe we'll find out in a few minutes. If we're lucky, Jeremy will be there, and will be able to point a finger—hopefully his middle one—at the person doing all this."

Chloe was never that lucky, but she nodded.

A few minutes later Zane caught the first glimpse of bright yellow tape, which was good since it was far off to their left. Chloe made a note to invest in a compass if she decided to stay on Salus.

Lexi glanced at Chloe. "You're in luck. There's definitely a ghost there."

Even before Lexi had spoken Chloe had known that. Sort of. She could feel the presence like an itch at the nape of her neck. It was faint, but insistent enough for her to rub her hand over it. What she didn't know was why she was feeling it. She sensed magic, not ghosts. "Is it Jeremy?" She had mixed feelings about this outing. A large part of her desperately wanted Jeremy to be here, to help them figure out who had actually killed him. A smaller part was terrified he would be here and would bring more of her world crashing down upon her.

The medium didn't answer until they were almost at the tape. "It is." She gave a sad smile. "Hi, Jeremy. Yeah, I know. It's been a week. Everyone knows."

Zane leaned in to whisper in Chloe's ear. "It's always really weird listening to her talking to the dead."

Chloe responded just as quietly. "I know. It sounds like she's talking to herself."

"And *she* can hear you," Lexi said as she glanced over her shoulder at them. "So can Jeremy." Her voice softened. "He knows he's gone."

"I'm so sorry, Jeremy. No one deserves this. You certainly didn't," Zane said, eyes flicking around the empty space inside the crime scene tape.

Lexi's lips twitched. "He agrees." She turned back to the ghost. "I know this is hard, Jeremy, and I really hate to ask...Yeah, we need to know. Chloe's under suspicion for your murder and...Emma was killed last night." She went silent, her brow furrowing as she listened to the ghost. "It's blurry. He doesn't remember who killed him, but he says he remembers coming across two people arguing, and one of them killed him." Her expression went grim as she turned to Chloe. "He doesn't remember much about it, but he knows they were arguing about your grandmother."

"What? But...why? If this happened the night he died, then she was already gone," Chloe said, confused and trying hard to connect the dots. The problem was she was missing more than a few dots.

"He doesn't know, but he's positive about what night it was."

Chloe nodded slowly. "Okay. Thanks, Jeremy. I've heard you and my grandmother didn't get along, but I do appreciate the help." Something was better than nothing, especially when murder was involved. She almost asked him if he was her father but chickened out. She hadn't mentioned her theory to anyone yet, and if she was wrong, she'd end up looking like an idiot in front of her two best friends and a ghost. Not the image she wanted.

Lexi let out a surprised burst of laughter. "He said you're welcome and he wants all of us to get the hell out of here. He likes his solitude."

Zane smiled. "He always did. Good bye, Jeremy."

The others murmured goodbyes before they turned back toward Chloe's house. Chloe paused just for a moment as she saw a crow sitting on a branch nearby, just watching them. When it saw her watching, it cocked its head, but didn't make a sound. Chalking it up to even Salus wildlife being odd, she shook her head and continued walking.

"You need to tell Wesley what Jeremy said," Chloe told Lexi when they'd reached her house.

"What? Oh no," Lexi said with an emphatic shake of her head. "I am so not pissing that bear off."

"Come on Lexi, it's important. He needs to know it wasn't just one person involved," Chloe insisted. "What if Jeremy's death is connected to Emma's? That means the same people have killed twice. If the sheriff is going to catch the killer, then he needs all the facts."

"She's right, Lexi," Zane said gently. "Two people being involved changes a lot in how he might look at the evidence."

Lexi kicked a pine cone and scowled at the ground. "Fine. But you both owe me. I expect ice cream and alcohol. But not at the same time."

Chloe slung an arm around Lexi and gave her a tight hug. "Consider it done. And thanks, Lex."

"Yeah, yeah," Lexi muttered, though she returned the hug.

When they reached the house Lexi sighed. "I'm going to get this over with before I go into work. Zane, you want a ride?"

Zane considered Chloe before he shook his head. "No, I'll stay for a bit. Assuming you want the company, Chloe, and can drop me off at the bookstore later?"

"I'd freaking love the company," Chloe admitted. "And thanks, both of you. Not just for the ghost thing, but for coming over," she said, giving them both proper hugs. Lexi accepted hers warmly, while Zane was a bit awkward, and his cheeks were a little pink after he'd drawn back.

Lexi got into her car and left before Chloe cocked her head and looked to Zane. "Can dreams be real?"

"Real?" he asked.

"Like not just my subconscious making shit up," she explained.

"Oh. Yes, dreams can be real. Some have dreams which are prophetic, or they can visit other people's dreams. Some, I've heard, can sort of astral project. They're asleep, but they can visit real places and people who are awake. I think that would be kind of dreamlike for the one traveling. Why do you ask?"

"Just curious. Trying to figure out what's real and what's just stories humans tell our—themselves," she corrected. "And speaking of figuring stuff out...since you're here, and given the whole attack thing...would you be willing to help me practice some before we head into town later?"

"Of course," Zane said without hesitation.

Some of the worry Chloe had been holding onto lifted. "Great. Before that, though, have you had breakfast? I know it's early, and don't—"

The sound of wings cut her off and she looked up, baffled at the idea of a bird coming close enough for her to hear the sound that clearly. Her jaw nearly dropped when she saw a cream and brown owl land neatly on Zane's shoulder before nipping lightly at his ear. "Um...You've got a..." She made a vague motion to his shoulder.

Zane grinned and stroked fingers lightly over the owl's chest. "I do," he agreed. "This is Nostradamus. I take it no one's told you about familiars yet?"

"No, Lexi mentioned it, I just hadn't seen one before. So, this is..."

"Mmhmm. My familiar. He was hanging out nearby, but then you mentioned breakfast, and, well, he likes to eat." The owl hooted and Zane chuckled. "He loves to eat, which is why he's on my shoulder instead of napping in a tree like a sane owl would be."

"Uh...huh. Okay, well, he's welcome, too." Chloe just hoped familiars were better behaved than normal animals, because while she didn't know much about birds, she did know they pooped. A lot. "I've got bacon and eggs." She frowned. "Or are eggs a no no because of the whole bird thing?" Aspects of life on Salus just got more and more complicated.

Amused, Zane shook his head. "Eggs are fine, especially since they're chicken eggs. He'll probably just steal my bacon, anyway."

"Oh, well, good then. I think." Bemused, she made her way into the house, glancing back at the owl sitting so tamely on the tall elemental's shoulder, and she had to wonder if the day could get any weirder.

It certainly wasn't normal watching an owl eat bacon off a plate, but the summoning and dispelling of cyclones that followed had started to become commonplace. Zane started summoning them without giving her warning, so she could practice with dispelling on the fly. If she'd been a little quicker the night before she might not still be feeling achy. And if she had to practice this every single day until it became habit, that's what she would do. She wouldn't be caught off guard again.

Chapter 20

Chloe felt better the next day. Some of the aches lingered, and no amount of aspirin or hot showers seemed to get rid of them entirely, but she felt good enough to get to work. There was no way she was going to sit around doing nothing while people suspected her of murder. She trusted the sheriff, to an extent, but she didn't know how good he was at his job. Not yet, at least. And while she may not have years of experience in investigating murders, she knew how to ask questions and gather information.

Her first stop was the diner, but from the moment she stepped inside she knew she wasn't going to get much here. Lexi was working and gave her a smile, but it had a hint of apology in it. When Chloe saw some of the other customers giving her suspicious looks, she understood the cause for that smile. It wasn't really unexpected. She was new and the timing was perfect for people to think she really was guilty. But she wasn't one to crumble under a little pressure and just lifted her chin as she walked to the counter.

"Hi, Lexi," she said as she took a seat. "Can I get my usual?" she asked, surprised to feel a thrill at having a usual. Maybe Salus really was starting to grow on her.

"Sure thing. I'll have your coffee over in a minute," Lexi called. After sitting the cup down in front of Chloe, she dropped her voice. "I'm so sorry. Somehow it got out that you were a suspect, and people have been talking about you all day." She raised her voice and looked pointedly at a pair of men who were whispering not so discreetly in a booth. "Despite the fact that I've told them repeatedly that you're innocent and it's stupid to blame you just because you're new."

Chloe glanced back and saw one of the men flush, while the other gave Lexi an angry look. Shaking her head, she turned back to Lexi. "It doesn't matter. I *am* innocent, and it'll come out one way or another. Besides, everyone here is suspicious of new people. Eventually I won't be new anymore," she says, shrugging, though it honestly did bother her.

"True. Does that mean you've decided to stay around, then?" Lexi asked hopefully.

"I don't know. I'm thinking about it," Chloe answered before taking a drink. "Did you get a chance to talk to the sheriff yesterday?"

Lexi made a face and nodded. "Yeah, and he wasn't too happy. He yelled at me, yelled about you, then said he'd look into it. I'd avoid him for a couple days if you can," she suggested.

"Somehow I doubt that's going to be possible," Chloe said dryly. "For one, he has my gun, remember? If nothing else, I'll be hearing from him once he finishes the ballistics testing on it. And it doesn't sound like he has any other suspects, in either case, which means I can expect to be questioned. Have you heard anything though? About Emma or Jeremy?"

"Emma's salesgirl, Christie, has apparently been telling *everyone* that you were looking for Emma and said you were going to her house. I think that's why so many people are jumping on the Chloe-is-guilty bandwagon."

"Are you kidding me? I know teenagers gossip, but telling everyone? That's a little overboard."

Lexi shrugged. "It's a small town, and she's minorly connected to some of the biggest news we've had in decades."

Chloe made an annoyed noise. "Great. You do realize you

just put a big check mark in the con category of my list, right?"

"List?"

"My list of the pros and cons of living in Salus."

"Hey, that's not just Salus, that's any small town," Lexi protested. "And any town, big or small, is going to have cons."

Which was true, but Chloe just moved on. "Did Emma have a boyfriend? Any family? Anyone closer to her than an employee? And what about Jeremy?"

Lexi thought for a moment as she retrieved Chloe's food and set it in front of her. "No family, or none on the island, anyway. I'm honestly not sure if she has any still alive. I want to say she was married, but that was before my time. She's been single my whole life." She frowned. "Though I want to say I remember something about a guy she was seeing, but that was...I don't know, forty years ago, give or take? And I really have no idea on Jeremy."

Emma's death wasn't likely to be a crime of passion, then. Those usually were committed by the nearest and dearest. "What about guns? They can't be common, right? Not when most people have built in weaponry or defense in the form of magic?" Chloe asked as she started eating. She wasn't really hungry—the murder had killed her appetite—but she had a busy day ahead of her and needed the fuel.

Lexi grinned. "True, when you can toss someone around with your mind or cover them with ice, a gun seems a little unnecessary." The grin dimmed but didn't disappear completely. "But not everyone has a built-in weapon. Like me, for instance. Yeah, I can see and talk to ghosts, and some ghosts can affect the living, but I'm as helpless as a human. I'm not alone, either. A lot of psychics are in the same boat. Beyond that, just because an elemental or witch or whoever has powers doesn't mean they're powerful."

Chloe frowned in confusion. "What do you mean?"

"Some people don't have a lot of power, or don't have a lot of control over the power they do have," Lexi explained with a shrug. "Met a fire elemental once who couldn't manage more than the occasional spark. It was great for lighting very dry things on fire or startling someone, but that was it. And there's a witch I know who can't do any magic aside from healing. She's a fantastic healer, don't get me wrong, but healing isn't going to keep someone from killing you."

Now she felt dumb. Everything Lexi had just said made sense, and Zane had even said he wasn't super powerful, but for some reason Chloe had been imagining everyone in Salus as being able to do huge, amazing things. Rather than dwell on it, she said, "So guns aren't as rare as I thought they'd be, then?"

"Probably pretty close, actually," Lexi admitted. "Some people think of guns as cheating, but you do have a few people on the island who own at least one. I couldn't tell you how many since it doesn't come up often. We do kind of rely on magic more than guns or knives."

"It's weird that you say that. I honestly expected to see more magic around town," Chloe confessed. "But other than a couple of kids, and my practice in the park with Zane and Diego, I haven't really seen any public displays."

Lexi grinned. "That's because you need to get out more. You'll see them, promise."

Picking up the last slice of bacon, Chloe laughed. "I hope so. I was kind of looking forward to it." She paid for her meal before getting to her feet. "I need to run. Lots of things to do. And I'll be out and about while I do them," she promised with a teasing smile.

"Good. Just stay out of trouble, will you?"

"I make no promises," Chloe said as she headed out the door.

Chloe made a few stops, hitting the market, park, and salon, but found no one who could—or maybe just who would—give her any information on Jeremy or Emma. She fared a little better at the bookstore, but only in that there was a couple who was willing to talk to her. Unfortunately, they didn't have anything more than she'd already learned. Afterward, she stopped at the gym next, hoping to strike up some conversations while working out, but found herself completely shunned by everyone but Garrett.

She stood to one side of the track, hands on her hips, frowning at the back of the woman who had just called her a murderer then took off to continue on her run.

"Not the work out you were hoping for?" Garrett asked as he walked up.

Chloe sighed and shook her head. "Not even a little. I expected suspicion, even if I'm not really okay with it, but that woman took it from suspicious to full on bitchy," she said bitterly. "People here *do* know I haven't been charged with murder, right? I'm not exactly wearing ugly metal bracelets everywhere."

Garrett gave her a crooked smile. "You do know you're not in a town like the ones you're used to, right?" he shot back, though his voice was light rather than condemning.

"Considering I've seen miniature tornadoes form from nothing, watched a woman have a conversation with a ghost, and seen someone's eyes change colors? Yeah, I've gotten the memo," she said dryly.

"I don't just mean the magic," he said, shaking his head. "That's more a symptom than a cause."

"Huh?"

He grinned and she felt her heart thump in her chest. He had a *really* nice smile. "Being able to use magic does change a person, sure, but not as much as our lifespan does. You've got people here who are over a thousand years old. They *really* don't like change, and lucky for them, Salus doesn't really change much. We also don't have much crime here."

"Until I arrived."

Garrett nodded. "Until you arrived," he agreed. "The crime we usually have is the more…tame variety. People—not just kids—playing pranks, some petty theft or vandalism, people getting drunk and dumb, the occasional fight. But we don't usually have the more serious crimes. No murder, no armed robbery, no kidnapping. Things have changed and people need

154

someone to blame. It's easier on people to blame you, an outsider they don't know, than to consider, even for a minute, that someone they know, someone they've known for decades, or even centuries, did this."

He was right. And it made the looks and whispers she'd been dealing with a little more understandable. Maybe not any more bearable, but she got it. "That's a good point. And you're right, Salus is more different than I realized." She shook her head. "Even knowing how long you guys—we—lived for, I didn't see past the magic to how it would affect someone's perspective."

"Most don't. But then, a lot of people on Salus can't understand your perspective either. Quite a few people on the island have never left, or only left for short trips. They don't understand living in a big city or dealing with a lifespan that probably won't reach the one century mark." He leaned in to bump her shoulder with his. "You get a chance only a few people on the island really have. A chance to see things, to experience them, from both perspectives."

Now that did make Chloe feel a little better. "And here I thought you were just a jock," she joked, returning the shoulder bump.

His smile now was small and sad. "You're not the only one."

And just like that, her improved mood was gone, replaced by guilt. "I'm sorry, Garrett, I didn't mean it like that."

He shook his head. "It's okay. I should get back to work, though. I hope I helped a little."

"You helped a lot," she told him earnestly. "Seriously."

He smiled, but it was half-hearted at best. "Good. Take care of yourself, Chloe."

"I will," Chloe murmured as she watched him leave. She no longer felt like working out or trying to get information from the others at the gym. Garrett had given her a valuable insight, and in return she'd hurt his feelings.

She headed to the locker room and grabbed her things, not bothering to change. She was just going to head straight home. Besides, she'd only been on the track for a minute before she'd been called a murderer. She tossed a hoodie on over her shirt and was headed toward her car when her phone rang. She fished it out and answered. "Hello?"

"Chloe, it's Sheriff Adams."

Crap. Not Wesley, no, he used his formal title. Worse, he was using his serious voice. That couldn't be good. "Sheriff. What can I do for you?" she asked, pleased her voice didn't betray her sudden nerves.

"I need you to come to the office."

"Ah, I can be there in five. I'm just at the gym."

"Great. I'll see you in five," he said before hanging up.

"Shit," she muttered, tossing her stuff into the back seat before heading toward the sheriff's office.

Chapter 21

When Chloe got to the sheriff's office she didn't immediately get out of her car. Though she knew for a fact she hadn't killed anyone, she was worried the sheriff was going to arrest her. It made no sense, logically, since no one ever asked a suspect to come to them in order to arrest them, but the worry was there in the back of her head.

She forced herself out of the car and stepped inside to find Wesley sitting behind his desk, his brow furrowed as he read something on his computer screen. He looked up when she shut the door and leaned back in his chair. "Thanks for coming so quickly," he said, his voice and face unreadable. He had a hell of a poker face, and, under any other circumstances, she'd be impressed. Right now, it just caused a cold pit to form in her belly.

"Not going to say no problem until I know why you wanted me to come here," Chloe said bluntly as she crossed the office and stood in front of the visitor's chair.

One corner of Wesley's mouth tipped up. "Nothing that will prevent you from going home when we're done, so why don't you go ahead and take a seat?"

Still wary, she sat. "So...what's up?"

He opened a drawer and pulled out her gun, still in the evidence bag, and set it on the desk, pushing it across to her. "First, I can tell you that the bullet doesn't match. It's the same caliber, of course, and it's actually really close, but this gun didn't fire the shot that killed Emma Mitchell."

"I could've told you that. In fact, I did," Chloe said with relief as she took the pistol and slid it into her messenger bag. Later she'd have to clean it, since she wasn't sure if there was residue from any sort of oil or fingerprint powder left on it. With the way things were going, she didn't need a malfunctioning weapon.

"You know I had to test it," Wesley said, a touch of apology in his voice.

"I know. Doesn't mean I had to like it, though. I had a woman call me a murderer, to my face, not even half an hour ago."

His face darkened. "That's going entirely too far. Even if they had your name—"

"They do," Chloe interrupted. "Have my name, I mean. The girl at Emma's shop, the one you talked to? Apparently, she's telling everyone who will listen that I'm a suspect."

"Damn. I told her to keep her mouth shut," he muttered.

"She's a teenager, Wes—Sheriff Adams. Did you honestly expect her to do anything different? Teenagers love to gossip, and they love to get attention. You gave her a way to do both at once." The explanation didn't appease him, so she changed the subject. "Lexi said she talked to you yesterday?"

It was the wrong thing to say, since he went from simmering to pissed. "What have I told you about messing with crime scenes, Chloe? And then you not only go to one—again—you take other people with you? What the hell were you thinking?"

"If I'd brought the ghost thing to you, what would you have done?" she retorted.

"Done things by the book!"

"But would you have taken Lexi, or any another medium, to the crime scene?" she pressed.

He glared at her for a moment. "Probably. I'm not going to turn down real evidence." She suddenly grinned, which only made him angrier. "What in the hell is so funny?"

Chloe shook her head and forced the grin off her face. "Sorry, no. It's not funny. It just struck me that only in Salus would the testimony of a ghost be considered evidence."

Some of his ire faded. "Not just Salus, but close enough," he agreed. "But I'm serious, Chloe. Do not even think about going near any other crime scenes unless I'm there with you. Especially if people are calling you a murderer."

She sighed. "I guess it doesn't look too good, does it? Especially if you're looking at it from an already biased point of view."

"It really doesn't. And just because your gun wasn't the murder weapon doesn't mean you're innocent—not as far as the evidence is concerned, I mean. We've got two deaths, yes, but they have next to nothing in common. Different locations, different methods, different weapons. They only link I can find is your grandmother. So being cleared of one doesn't clear you of the other."

"Well, you know Granny didn't do it," Chloe said blandly.

"No, she didn't," he agreed easily. "But it's not a big step from Lydia to you, if you're looking hard enough for a connection. And a lot of people are."

"I know. And I get it." She actually did, now, thanks to Garrett. She was going to have to find some way to apologize to him. He'd really helped her out and she'd accidentally kicked him emotionally. Unfortunately, she didn't know him well enough to know what would be the best way to go about it. Or if he'd even listen.

Wesley's desk phone rang and he gave a long-suffering sigh as he answered it. "Sheriff Adams. You are? Good. What? She's here, actually," he said, and had Chloe's brows shooting up. "No. It's not procedure, she's still…Fine." He frowned darkly and hit a button, glaring at the phone. "Fine, you're on speaker," he said, his voice annoyed.

A man's voice filled the room. "Hi, Chloe."

It took her a second, but she placed the voice. "Diego? Hi. What's going on?" she asked, confused.

"I'm at the morgue, checking Jeremy's body for magic, and you were right. There *is* some magic being hidden, but I don't know what. It's powerful enough that I can tell something's there, but I can't see through it, much less break it. But I'm curious as hell now as to what this ward is hiding."

Wesley's jaw clenched so tightly Chloe was surprised she couldn't hear his teeth grinding together. "Is there anyone who can?" he asked, and it looked like his eyes briefly flashed yellow. This time Chloe was clearly looking at him and knew it couldn't just be a trick of the light. But then, Zane had said shifter's eyes changed, too, so maybe bear eyes were yellow?

There was a long pause. "Actually, I can think of one person who might be able to."

"Who? Let's get them down there, find out what's really on the body," Wesley said, leaning forward. "This is the closest thing we have to a lead so far."

"I'm so happy to hear you say that, Wesley," Diego said, his voice silky and dark. Instantly Chloe frowned, wondering what he was up to.

"Why?" Wesley asked, just as suspicious.

"Because the person I'm thinking of is Chloe."

"You want me to bring my only suspect in either of these murders to magically tamper with a body?" Wesley asked through gritted teeth.

"You already had her examine the body, Wesley, and we both know she didn't do it," Diego answered. "Besides, I'll be here. I may not be able to break this ward, but I promise you that I'll be able to tell if she tries to do anything other than remove the magic."

"No."

"Wesley—"

"I said no," Wesley growled. "There's already too much negative attention focused on her. If people find out about this, they—"

"They're not going to find out." Diego's voice went hard. "Bring her, Sheriff Adams, if you want to find out what's going on."

Chloe delicately cleared her throat. "Isn't anyone going to ask me what I think about this?" she asked, her voice even, though her emotions were anything but. They were arguing about what she would or wouldn't do, each just assuming that she'd go along with them if they won. She'd already had enough choices taken out of her hands lately, she wasn't going to let them take another one from her control.

Both men went quiet, and Wesley looked at her. His eyes widened fractionally, though she didn't understand why. It wasn't as though she'd ever acted shy or meek around him.

"Of course, Chloe," Diego said apologetically. "Could I persuade you to come to the morgue and remove the shield on the body?"

"You say that like it's a given that I can, and I'm not so sure," Chloe answered.

"I've felt your power. I assure you, I have no doubts that you can do this."

Wesley sat back and considered her before he gave in. "And if you can't do it, there shouldn't be any harm done. You already heard Diego say he tried, and the body is still intact." His gaze flicked to the phone and narrowed. "It is still intact, isn't it?"

"Of course," Diego answered smoothly. "So, will you come, Chloe? Please?"

Chloe sighed. It would be good practice, and could potentially give them some useful information, but she did have one concern. "Wesley was right about one thing. People finding out. I've already had some...trouble. Can you two guarantee this will stay just between the three of us?"

"Absolutely," Diego said without hesitation.

"I don't report to anyone but the council, and since this is a councilor's idea, I'm not saying a single damn word to anyone," Wesley said.

Chloe caved. "Fine, but you might have to coach me through it, Diego, since it's so new."

"That isn't a problem. I'll be waiting for you both," Diego said before he disconnected.

"You sure you're ready for this?" Wesley asked in a low voice.

"No," she answered honestly, "but I want to try. I owe it to them to try." And best case scenario, they'd find something that pointed right to the real murderer and Chloe would be completely off the hook.

He nodded and stood, putting his hat on. "Then let's go. I'll drive you. I know something like this might leave you weak afterward."

She grimaced. "I won't argue. But I really should be getting a favor in return for this," she said slyly as they headed out to his cruiser.

"Oh? And what favor do you want?"

"Well, have you thought about shifting for me? For my target practice?" she asked, tossing a grin at him over the top of the car.

He groaned. "Fine. But don't blame me if you blush like a schoolgirl when you see me in the buff."

Chloe smirked. "I haven't blushed in years, Sheriff."

Wesley grinned. "Maybe, but you haven't seen me naked yet, either."

There was such confidence in his voice and in his gray eyes that she wondered if he wouldn't end up being right.

Chapter 22

The drive to the hospital was made in silence. When they reached their destination, Wesley shut off the car and started to get out, but Chloe hadn't even undone her seatbelt.

"Everything okay?" he asked with a frown as she stared at the door.

"I'm nervous," Chloe admitted.

He shut his door. "About what?"

She drew in a slow breath before answering, still not looking at him. "I've never done something like this before. Something big, something important, I mean. Especially nothing this important that deals with magic. All I've done so far is practice, really. The attack doesn't count, not really. I fumbled with that, and it was spur of the moment, anyway. It wasn't something I had time to think about. And even then, I screwed it up."

"Chloe, look at me." When she didn't, he reached out and gently turned her face toward him. "I haven't seen you do this before, true, but Diego isn't one to sugarcoat things." A corner of his mouth lifted slightly. "Not unless he's flirting with a beautiful woman, anyway. But magic? He's always serious about that. So, if he says he thinks you can do this, he genuinely believes that you can do this. And you say you screwed up? I say bullshit." She arched a brow, but he just kept speaking. "You've been on Salus for a week, right? You've known about magic for a week? I don't know anyone who could have handled a magical attack perfectly in that time frame. And maybe you weren't perfect, but so what? You're alive, aren't you? You have to give yourself credit for that."

Chloe frowned and studied his face as she rolled his words around in her head. "You didn't think I could do it the last time we were here," she pointed out.

Wesley shrugged. "So? That was days ago, and I was still pissed you'd gone stomping around a crime scene. I'm still pissed, especially since you did it again, but the situation has changed. We've got another dead body, and this time you've got a council member vouching for you. So, what do you say we go in there, you kick some magical ass, and we see if we can't catch a killer?"

"Keep this up and I'm going to be demanding you offer me a job if I decide to stay," she joked as she smiled faintly.

He chuckled. "You'd have to decide to stay, first. But I don't know if you follow the rules well enough to be a deputy," he said before getting out of the car.

"I follow rules just fine," she retorted as she followed. "My own rules, at least."

"That's what I'm afraid of," he said dryly as they wound through the small hospital to the basement morgue. To Chloe's relief Emma's body wasn't sitting on a table. She felt enough guilt regarding the woman without seeing her with a bullet hole. Jeremy's body had been pulled out, however, and Diego stood beside it, a serious look on his face. He turned when the door opened. "Thank you for coming, Chloe. I know this wasn't how you intended to spend your day," Diego said with a small smile.

"I don't think this was how anyone intended to spend their day, but it is what it is," Chloe answered with a shrug as she walked over to him. She could feel the magic coming off Jeremy, but there was a lingering hint of it coming from Diego. That light tingling against her skin, but she had to focus to feel it, since it was just a remnant, not anything he was actively doing.

"Very true. But this shouldn't take long."

"You say that, but Wesley said it took me five minutes just to find the magic last time I was here."

Diego smiled. "You are still new to this, so yes, it may take you longer than it would an experienced aether, but I'm going to help you. Zane told me you can absorb magic, not just dispel it. Is that right?"

"Yeah. You want me to absorb this whatever it is?" She wasn't sure she liked the sound of that.

"It might be easier on you. If you can drain enough of the magic from it, I can do the actual dispelling," he explained. "And that way you're boosting yourself rather than draining, because I promise you, dispelling this *will* tire you out. This is a great deal stronger than the magic you've been practicing with."

"Great way to make me less nervous," she said sarcastically, and she heard Wesley laugh softly behind her.

Diego grinned. "It should have worked, since I'm showing just how much confidence I have in your abilities."

"Now you're just full of shit," Chloe said, but she did smile. It was short-lived, however. "One thing, though."

"Yes?"

She thought for a moment about how to phrase it without sounding like a scared little idiot, but there was something that was bugging her. "Absorbing magic…"

It took so long for her to continue that Diego had to prompt her to continue. "Yes? What about it?"

"Are there downsides? I don't mean being tired from using magic, but more like…if I absorb bad magic, can it infect me or poison me or anything like that?"

Diego frowned and thought about that for a minute. "I don't recall hearing about anything like that," he began slowly. "I won't say it's impossible, especially with stronger magics, or magic from inherently dark sources, but overall?" He shook his head. "I don't believe it's likely. You absorb magic, not a spell."

It was Chloe's turn to frown. "There's a difference? And isn't whatever is on Jeremy's body just a spell?"

He smiled a bit. "There is a difference, yes. A spell is magic that's been directed to do some specific task, while magic itself is just energy. It's sort of like the difference between electricity and a computer program." He glanced to Jeremy's body. "And yes, I believe it's a ward of some sort on Jeremy's body, which—you're right—is a spell, but to use the computer program analogy, you're absorbing the electricity, not the program. But without the electricity, the program can't run."

She wasn't completely reassured, and it showed on her face. "I don't know…"

"I can't say I blame you," Wesley said from a few feet away, his arms folded as he gazed consideringly at the body.

Diego's lips tightened but he slowly nodded. "It is an understandable concern," he agreed. "I can't promise anything, but as I said, I've never heard of anyone absorbing the negativity of a spell when absorbing magic. And I can promise to keep a close eye on you while you do it. If you're still willing to try," he added quickly.

Chloe considered for a long moment before she nodded. "Okay, let's get this done before I lose my nerve."

Diego nodded and motioned for her to stand beside him. "Whenever you're ready. I'll give you a minute, then try to break the shield."

"And I'm right here, just in case," Wesley said, standing on her other side. "So don't worry about a thing."

Chloe glanced from one man to the other, suddenly feeling flushed. It wasn't nerves now, it was just being surrounded by extremely hot men, both trying to look out for her. Normally she'd say she didn't need anyone, especially not a man, to look out for her, but in this case, it was nice. It took her a moment to focus on the task at hand and nod. "Okay. Here we go."

Her eyes closed so she could find that brightness in her mind's eye. It was almost as hard to find as it had been the first time, except now she knew it was there, knew what to look for. It didn't appear as a light in her head, but as a spot that was darker than the rest, which was what had made her think of it as a void. "Found it," she murmured absently as she slowly reached out to it.

"Go slowly. There's no rush here. Take as long as you need," Diego murmured, but it sounded like he was far away, rather than right beside her.

The magic was slippery, somehow. It was hard for her to latch onto it, and she frowned as she fought with the elusive power. When she finally got a hold on it, she felt a jolt of power so strong she gasped and her body jerked forward. Strong hands grabbed her from both sides, keeping her upright.

"Chloe! Are you okay?" came Wesley's voice from her right, his bear peeking out and adding a growl to his deep timbre.

"Fine," she answered breathlessly. "I'm fine. It's…Just touching it was…a rush. Like espresso and sex all rolled into one."

The sheriff didn't answer, but she felt the brush of fur that signaled to her that he was doing *something*. She would also bet money that his eyes were yellow right now.

"Stop that," she whispered. "It makes it hard to concentrate."

"Stop what?" Diego asked, still holding onto her on her left.

Chloe just shook her head and dove back into her task. She'd been so surprised by her reaction to touching the magic that she'd lost contact with it, and it took her a minute to regain that lost ground. This time she stiffened but the men continued to support her so she didn't lose her grasp of the ward. Slowly, she began to pull the magic from that void into her, sipping at it cautiously. There didn't seem to be any other surprises, no feeling of magical poison, just the magic draining into her and setting every sense on high alert. Though she tried to keep it slow like Diego had suggested, the magic started to pour into her faster and faster, until she was panting and clinging to the arms supporting her.

"Break it," she heard growled, but it was background noise, nothing more.

"Wes—"

"I said break it. Look at her! Do it now or I drag her out of here."

"That would do…fine."

167

The magic kept rushing into her, filling her full to bursting, until what remained in the void fractured, then exploded. She got hit by one last blast of power, before everything went dark.

Chapter 23

When Chloe woke, the first thing she noticed was that she was lying on something cold. The second thing was that Diego and Wesley were arguing. Loudly. When she managed to open her eyes, she saw they were in each other's faces, though Wesley seemed to be doing most of the shouting. And jabbing Diego in the chest.

"This was irresponsible and beyond stupid!" Wesley yelled.

"It was not, it was a necessary and logical step," Diego retorted, trying to keep his cool, but his composure was quickly dissipating.

"Logical my ass. I thought you said she could handle it. How? She's a baby to all this. You should never have asked her to do this!"

"She's a baby with potentially more power than anyone else on Salus!"

Wesley snorted. "That isn't helping you in the slightest, *Councilor,*" he said mockingly. "You don't give a baby a gun and expect it to be a sharpshooter on day one. And you don't ask an aether who's new to her powers to risk her life!"

"She didn't risk her life! She just got overloaded with power! It's like a food coma, except she ate magic, not turkey."

"Food comas aren't usually literal though, now are they?" Wesley asked with a sneer. "And she's passed the fuck out because you didn't want to find an alternative!"

The argument was starting to make Chloe's head pound, and she groaned as she lifted a hand to her temple, where the pain seemed centered.

Instantly both men went silent and turned to her.

"Chloe," Wesley said, at the same time Diego asked, "Are you all right?"

She dimly noted that the angry tones both had been using were gone, replaced by gentle ones. "Head hurts. A lot," she mumbled as she tried to sit up. A hand came to rest on her back and helped her upright. Only then did she realize she was on one of the tables used for autopsies. Her stomached churned and she closed her eyes until it settled. When she glanced up, she saw Wesley's concerned face, complete with yellow eyes. Her brow furrowed, but her mind was too muddled to think clearly. "Your eyes are yellow."

He smiled, but it was clearly forced. "It happens when I get upset. It'll go away in a minute."

Diego stepped up beside Wesley. "I can try to ease your headache, but given the cause, it might not do much."

"Please," Chloe murmured, leaning into Wesley's hand. She felt almost boneless. Sitting up, much less standing up, was going to be a problem for later.

He placed his fingertips on either side of her forehead, and she felt a gentle warmth radiate outward from them at the same time she felt the tingle of his magic. The headache eased but didn't disappear completely. It was bearable, though, and enough to let her think a little more clearly. It did nothing for the rest of her body, though.

"What happened?" she asked after Diego withdrew his hands.

"You passed out," Wesley answered, still supporting her.

"But why?"

"What's the last thing you remember?" Diego asked.

She frowned and tried to think back. "I felt sort of high on the power. You two were saying...something...then the magic

170

broke or something and I absorbed even more power. Then nothing."

He pressed his lips tightly together and nodded. "There was more power in the shield than expected, and you absorbed too much, too quick. You took enough that I thought I could dispel the rest, and it worked, but something, some combination of your power, my power, and the power in the shield, turned explosive. I felt the rest of the power hit you. It must have overloaded your system and knocked you out." He inclined his head to the sheriff. "Wesley was able to catch you before you fell."

Chloe gave Wesley a shaky smile. "Thanks. How long was I unconscious?"

Neither man answered right away, and neither looked happy.

"How long?" she pressed.

"Almost an hour," Diego said quietly.

Her eyes widened. "Seriously?" She paused. "Wait, you guys have been arguing for an hour?"

Near identical looks of embarrassment flashed over their faces before Wesley answered, "We were worried about you."

She almost rolled her eyes. "Did you at least check the body?"

The embarrassment deepened and Wesley actually shuffled his feet while Diego's cheeks colored.

"Are you serious? I went through all that and you didn't even see what was behind the shield?" she asked, voice rising in both pitch and volume.

"Now you can look with us," Diego interjected. "Here, let me help you over there," he said, lifting her off the table and setting her down. Her legs were shaky and didn't quite want to support her, so she clung to his arm as they moved to Jeremy's body, with Wesley sticking close to her other side.

Once the sheet was drawn back, they all went silent.

Chloe spoke first. "Is that…are those…?"

"Fang marks," Diego said, voice clipped, ruthlessly controlled.

The mark where they had believed a knife had been stabbed into Jeremy's heart was gone. Bruises had appeared that weren't

171

present before, ringing both his biceps and throat. But the worst part of it, the thing that had Chloe swallowing in an attempt keep her breakfast down, were the two ragged marks on his throat. There was nothing neat about them, no tiny set of punctures like movies portrayed. The flesh had been torn open with no care for the victim.

"Do they always look like that?" Chloe asked, unable to look away.

"No," Wesley said in a low growl. "Most vampires are able to feed from willing partners, given that it's normally enjoyable—very enjoyable—to both parties. Those fang marks cause the least amount of damage possible. You'd see two small holes, maybe a bit of bruising around them, but that's it. But this?" He shook his head. "I don't know if they did this because they're a messy eater or because they wanted him to bleed out."

Chloe closed her eyes so she didn't have to look any longer. "There was a lot of blood on the leaves where his body was found, but could it be both? Could they have wanted him to bleed out, but only after they'd…eaten their fill?"

"It's entirely possible," Diego said with a nod. "I'd even say likely. But that's not the biggest question right now."

Curious, she opened her eyes to look at Diego. "No? What's the biggest question, then?"

"Who shielded the body," Wesley answered.

That answer was obvious to Chloe, but something about their demeanor made her rethink it. "Whoever killed him would have, right? To try to keep it from being obvious it was a vampire attack?"

"No, it couldn't have been the same person who killed him. Not unless they're just mimicking a vampire attack."

"Which is entirely possible," Diego said. Seeing Chloe's confusion, he explained. "Vampires don't have magic like this. Their powers are largely focused on their bodies—making themselves stronger or faster, usually—or magical persuasion. This? This is some sort of extremely strong illusion. It affected more than just the ears and eyes. It *felt* real. Which is just not something any vampire I've ever heard of can do."

"Oh. So, unless this is someone with illusion magic trying to frame a vampire, we've got two killers?" Chloe asked.

"It sounds like it, yes."

She turned to face Wesley and arched a brow. "Like maybe two people who could have been arguing in the woods behind my house that Jeremy saw before he died?"

"I said I was going to look into it. Now, I have a little more to go on," Wesley said, his eyes fading back to their normal color. It could be because the concern and anger in his voice had been replaced by mild annoyance, though.

"What argument? How do you know what Jeremy saw before he died?" Diego demanded.

"She dragged Lexi out there and she talked to Jeremy's ghost," Wesley answered.

"He said he remembered two people arguing about my grandmother, but couldn't remember who they were, just that there were two of them," Chloe added.

"I think this proves that he was correct about two people being there, then," Diego said, nodding.

"It does," Wesley agreed. "But we can't exactly just question every vampire on Salus. Besides that, I don't want to start a panic, so this has to stay just between us and the council."

"Agreed," Diego said.

"I'm sure as hell not going to tell anyone. And even if I did, who would believe me? They'd think I was trying to deflect guilt off me onto someone else," Chloe said darkly.

"Unfortunately, you're probably right," Diego said gently. "And...I hate to say it, but given how we were fooled by this body for almost a week, perhaps we should check Emma's body while we're here. Just to be safe."

Wesley scowled, but rather than arguing, he asked Chloe, "Are you up for it?"

Chloe grimaced but nodded. "As long as I don't have to break anymore shields, I'll try. Though if I can do it while sitting, that'd be better."

She let out a soft yelp of surprise when Diego easily picked her up and carried her over to the rolling chair the coroner must use when doing paperwork, carefully depositing her in it.

"If you need to take a few before we start, that's fine," he told her as he moved to a mini fridge and peeked inside. He grabbed a bottle of water out and offered it to her.

"I'm going to insist you take a few," Wesley said. "And before you bitch at me about bossing you around, remember that you were out cold for an hour. Taking five minutes isn't a bad thing."

"I can still bitch," Chloe muttered before she opened the water and took a drink. "You know, in any other town, this wouldn't be happening. A murder suspect helping to investigate the very murders she's accused of."

Wesley shrugged. "You've got skills no one else on Salus does, along with education that makes you useful. And there's no direct evidence linking you to either murder, so you're less a suspect and more a person of interest. Especially since aethers don't have fangs or illusion magic."

"And you have very good reason to help us find the murderers, since that will clear your name and make life a little easier for you," Diego added.

"All true. Okay, let's check out Emma." She got to her feet, a little steadier than before. "I don't know whether to hope she's got a shield on her, too, or not."

"A spent round was found during the autopsy, but if the illusion was as powerful as you two say, then it's entirely possible I didn't actually test it like I thought I did," Wesley said.

"Okay, now I am hoping she's got a shield, just so it's one set of killers, not two," Chloe said. "Where's she at?"

Wesley led her and Diego over to one of the drawers and pulled it out but didn't touch the sheet. "It's probably best if I leave her covered. Unless it's going to affect the magic?"

Diego shook his head. "It's just cloth. Ordinary cloth or clothing generally won't affect magic use."

Chloe let out a sigh of relief. She wasn't ready to see her grandmother's friend as a lifeless corpse.

"Good. Anytime you two are ready, then," Wesley said with no trace of impatience.

She nodded and closed her eyes. She tried to ignore the magic from the men and other body and focus on what was right in front of her. It took her only a moment to shake her head. "There's something there, but it feels more like an echo. Like when a woman's wearing perfume and leaves the room. You can still smell it lingering, but it's not there."

"I have to agree," Diego said with a nod. "She may have used magic to try to defend herself, or had magic done to her, but there's nothing on her right now."

Wesley pushed the body back into the drawer and closed it. "Which doesn't mean it wasn't the same people, just that they didn't feel the need to hide a bullet wound." He focused on Chloe. "Unfortunately, you are still a person of interest, since vampire involvement doesn't completely rule you out."

"But I can't perform illusions! I wouldn't know how even if I could," Chloe protested.

"I still can't rule you out completely. But for what it's worth, I don't think you did it. Either of them, for that matter."

Since it wasn't said angrily or mockingly, she subsided. "Okay. Thanks. And I know, still can't leave town, blah, blah, blah."

Wesley cracked a smile while Diego chuckled, which had been her intention.

"Come on. I have to write this up, so I'll take you back to your car," Wesley said. "Unless you're not feeling up to driving yet?"

Chloe mentally prodded at herself. "No, I think I'll be good. I'm actually starting to *feel* good."

"I'd be surprised if you weren't," Diego said. "You took in a hell of a lot of power. You should be flying high for the rest of the day."

"I don't know if I'd go that far, I just feel good."

His brow furrowed, but he smiled only a second later. "I'm glad. I'll see you later. Try to play nice with magic for a few days, hmm?" he teased.

"I make no promises," she said, laughing as she followed Wesley out.

Chapter 24

Chloe's first stop after she retrieved her car was the gym. Unfortunately, Garrett wasn't there, so she wasn't able to apologize to him. Deflated, she tried to do some more investigating, including discreetly getting the names of vampires who lived on Salus, she didn't come up with much. There were as many vampires on Salus as there were anything else, which didn't narrow things down any. The only one she'd personally met was Francois, but she hated to even consider the fact that it might have been him.

After a few hours, she went home, surprisingly exhausted after her power boost, and slept through the night and nearly until noon. She was woken, yet again, by a knocking on her door. Since the last few times she'd been woken this way had meant someone was dead, a sense of dread settled as a hard knot in her belly. More coherent than she expected after just waking up, she hurried downstairs to open the door. Instead of Wesley, she was face to face with Ted, the man who'd given her the ferry ticket.

Too confused to respond at first, she only stared at him.

His mouth split in a grin and he shook his head. "Not the reaction I normally get, but it's better than some." His gaze settled a few inches above her eyes, and she saw his lips twitching. "Were you still sleeping?"

"Huh? Oh. Yeah, I was." It clicked what he must be staring at and lifted a hand to her hair. Yep, she had a major case of bed head. She scowled and tried to flatten it, but it didn't do a whole lot. "Not to be rude, but…what are you doing here?"

"Oh, you've got a letter. Normally I just pass it onto the ferry and someone picks it up on this end, but when I saw it was for you, and since it was my lunch break, I thought I'd deliver it." Ted's amusement dimmed. "Wanted to see how you were doing. I half expected to see you back on the ferry the day after you showed up."

Chloe grimaced. "It was tempting, believe me, but I owed it to Granny to stick around for a bit." That's how it had begun, anyway. The rest didn't matter, and Ted was nearly a stranger. He didn't want to hear her life's story. "I'm doing…okay, though. Adjusting to Granny's loss and the supernatural." No way was she mentioning the murders. If he didn't know she was a suspect, she wasn't going to tell him. "You said I got a letter?"

"Yeah," he said, offering over an official looking envelope. "Look, I know you don't know me, and there are plenty of people on the island, but if you need someone to talk to, I'm not hard to find."

Touched, Chloe smiled. "Thanks. I'm doing all right for the moment, but if that changes, I'll definitely keep you in mind."

Ted grinned. "Good. Now I'm going to go find some actual food and get back to work. Take it easy," he said, walking back to his car.

Chloe went into the kitchen and started a pot of coffee before she looked at the letter. It took a second to recognize the name of the sender as Granny's lawyer, and a moment more to recall that he was sending her a check. A very big check. She grabbed a butter knife and slit the envelope open to find a brief letter full of legal jargon, and a check with more numbers on the left side of the decimal than she'd ever seen. Luckily, she'd seen a bank in town. It wasn't her bank, but given how oddly everything else operated in this place, she had no doubt she could get the money where it belonged. On the other hand, people in Salus were, apparently, gossips, and it might be better for her to leave the island to deposit it. Which meant sneaking off or sweet-talking Wesley. Both options were appealing, she admitted to herself, but she was in enough trouble without being caught out of town by Wesley.

After pouring her first cup she retrieved her phone from her bedroom. She'd just started to call the sheriff when Lexi's picture popped up and the phone started to ring.

"You've got good timing. I just picked up my phone," Chloe said before taking a drink.

"Calling someone hot, I hope."

"Actually, yes, though not for the reasons you're hoping for."

"Aww," Lexi said, and Chloe could envision the pout on her face. "That's no fun."

"Probably not, but that's okay. What's up?"

The playfulness vanished. "Did anyone tell you there's going to be a town meeting tonight?"

Chloe frowned. "No, this is the first I've heard of it."

"Then I'm glad I called. It's at seven at the school. The gym's the only place in town big enough to hold enough of us."

"There are that many people in Salus?"

"Mmm. In the town? No. On the whole island? A couple thousand. Most of them probably won't come, though. We've got a lot of hermits on the far side of the island. They don't deal too much with town business."

Chloe leaned against the doorframe. A couple thousand? And almost all of them supernatural in some way? She hadn't realized there were so many people on Salus. "That's...a lot."

Lexi laughed. "Not really, but I guess it could seem like it. The meeting's about the murders though, so I'm not sure if you want to go or not."

"Yeah, I guess if I go a lot of people will be giving me the stink eye. Probably a lot of them will be thinking I'm the murderer."

"Probably," Lexi said sympathetically. "But it's completely up to you. I'll be there, so if you go, you won't be alone."

"Thanks, Lex. I really do appreciate all the support. I've sure as hell needed it."

"That's what I'm here for. To be awesome and get people having fun."

Chloe smiled. "You do it very well. And I'll see you there. Can't hide forever."

"Thanks! And I'll get there a little early, just to be on the safe side."

"Okay. Thanks Lexi. See you later."

"Later."

She disconnected and blew out a breath. Maybe the meeting was exactly what she needed. Wesley would surely give them the facts, right? That might make some of them realize she wasn't automatically a murderer. Of course, it could have them turning on the vampires, which wouldn't be good either, but that was going to happen whether or not she was there.

Chloe straightened. No, she wasn't going to hide. Her true self had been hidden long enough.

It was hard waiting so long for the meeting. It was harder since she didn't have anything specific she needed to get done beforehand. She tidied up the house, showered, paid some bills online, but that only took a couple of hours. She didn't want to venture into town just yet, not if people were upset enough to need a town meeting, so she took a drive in the opposite direction. Until now she'd only seen the town and area around Granny's house, so she figured she was past due to see what else was on the island.

Forty-five minutes later, she concluded it was mostly trees. Not that she minded trees, but to her urban mind it was a little creepy. Things hid in the woods. There were dozens, if not hundreds, of horror movies that showed that clearly. She had to admit it was pretty, though, at least in the daytime. There weren't any huge buildings that blocked out nature or the sky, no traffic jams, and no rush. The cliffs she found at one point were pretty, too, in a stark, dangerous sort of way. She kept away from the edge of those. Heights had never bothered her before, but up until now she'd only dealt with them by being in tall buildings or a ladder. Being on the edge of a hundred foot tall cliff was a whole other story entirely.

Somewhere in the middle of the island she came across a well-worn dirt road. Since she was in exploration mode, she turned down it, despite it apparently heading deeper into the woods. She felt drawn to go that way, though she tried not to think too hard on that. When the road ended, she got out and wandered to a clear path easily visible from the road. She didn't want to go too far from the car, not when there was a killer on the loose, but she looked down the path, to try to figure out what was down there.

All she saw was a tree, separated from the others, but ringed by them. Curiosity got the better of her and she found herself taking the path. When the trees around her opened up, she got her first good look at the one in the middle. It stood alone in a clearing, though the branches that reached the farthest brushed those that circled it. It was an oak, she was sure of it, though she knew next to nothing about trees. It was also absolutely massive. Next to it, all the other trees seemed somehow tiny in comparison, even the ones that were taller. But what drew her closer to the ancient tree was the power she could feel radiating off of it. She'd never felt anything like it. It wasn't like any magic she'd felt before, not in strength or type, but it felt warm and somehow familiar.

Chloe stopped a few feet from the tree, just out of touching distance, and stared at it. Other than its size, physically it didn't look like anything special. There weren't any markers or plaques nearby to explain the point of the tree, either. It was visited frequently, she knew that from the clearness and size of the path, but why? It had to have some purpose or meaning.

Slowly she lifted a hand and reached for the tree, hesitating just before contact. Nearby, a crow cawed loudly, startling her enough that when she jumped her palm made contact with the trunk of the tree. She gasped loudly at the rush of power that spilled into her. Unlike the previous day, this magic didn't overload her. It was gentle, warm, and flowed over and through her as easily as breathing. She felt as though she'd just woken up from the most restful sleep ever, full of energy and optimism.

A soft noise came from above her and she glanced up to see the leaves rustling, though there was no wind. And perched among those leaves was a crow, staring back at her. The same one, she assumed, that had surprised her just a moment ago. It cocked its head and let out another caw, but it sounded strange to her. She couldn't put her finger on it, but the cry was distorted somehow.

The weirdness of the moment struck her then and she jerked her hand back. The flow of power ended. The lack made her feel empty, alone, but the energy remained. The crow called to her again and she backed away. She was so careful to keep her eyes on the bird that she didn't see the root of the tree and stumbled over it, falling backward and landing hard on her butt.

This time it almost sounded like the crow was laughing.

Chloe scrambled to her feet and shot a glare at the bird. "Sure, laugh it up, birdbrain. Ha ha, it's so funny when the new girl gets freaked out, huh? Bite me," she called up to the bird, knowing she was being ridiculous, but she couldn't help it. She turned on her heel and stomped back to the car, relieved no one had seen her interaction with the bird. Some of them already thought she was a killer. No reason to let them think she was crazy on top of it.

Chapter 25

A few hours later, Chloe left for the school. It was easy to find, though she had to wonder at how different it was from human schools. Somehow, she doubted it was quite like Harry Potter, but surely there was some sort of magical education. Elemental Magic 101 or Vampire Eating For Beginners: How Not to Kill Your Meal, maybe.

The parking lot was already packed. It took her a good five minutes to find a spot so she could head inside. The gym was just as easy to find, since she could simply follow everyone else, but even on that short trip she'd started receiving some nasty looks. Spotting Lexi waiting just outside the doors relieved her, and she quickened her pace to join her friend.

"I wasn't sure you were going to make it," Lexi admitted as she gave Chloe a quick hug. "I don't know if I'd have come in your place."

"I thought about it, but I'm not going to hide. Besides, you want me to stay on Salus, right? Which means joining the community and doing community things. So...meeting."

"I hate it when you turn my own points against me," Lexi mumbled, though her annoyance was playfully feigned. "Let's get inside. They're going to start anytime now."

Chloe followed her inside and to a spot that Zane had been saving. "Hey Zane," she told him as she sat, sandwiched between him and Lexi.

"Hello, Chloe. How are you doing?" he asked, concerned.

"I'm hanging in there. Remind me later though, there's something I want to ask you," she said, thinking about the oak.

Curious, he nodded. "I will."

The din of voices started to die off and Chloe looked toward the center of the gym to see Wesley standing with the four councilors she'd met, and a blonde woman and redheaded man she hadn't.

"Who's that?" she whispered to Lexi before she nodded in the blonde's direction. She was tiny, around five feet tall, if that, Chloe figured, but there was no way she'd be missed in a crowd. She was petite, yes, but with very obvious attributes that marked her as woman rather than child. There wasn't a lot of color to her, given that her skin was nearly bone white and her long hair was an extremely pale blonde. She even wore nothing but black, though the pantsuit did look good on her. In fact, the only color to her were her lips and eyes. Not all women could pull off a stark blood red lipstick, but the woman managed it. Still, it was her eyes that really made her stand out. Chloe had never seen someone with purple eyes before, but even from several yards away she could tell this stranger's eyes were a vivid violet color.

"Hmm? Oh, Kyra Christensen," Lexi answered. "The vampire councilor."

Chloe nodded but before she could ask about the man, Diego turned on a microphone. Part of her wondered why he didn't magically amplify his voice, but she didn't get a chance to wonder long before his deep, smooth voice filled the gym.

"Thank you all for coming. I know for some of you it's early, but we'll be as brief as possible." He looked around at the faces surrounding him before continuing. "As all of you know, we've lost two of our own in the last week. Both Jeremy and Emma will be missed by us all. I know you're all concerned, even scared, but I promise you that Sheriff Adams is doing his best to find the people responsible. And with that in mind, I'll give him the floor now."

He handed the microphone over to Wesley who looked mildly uncomfortable to be the center of attention, but his voice was strong regardless. "Thank you, Councilor. As he said, I'm doing everything I can to find the ones responsible and utilizing every resource available in order to do so. In the meantime, simple precautions should be taken. Both Jeremy and Emma were apparently alone when they were killed, so if you leave your house, especially at night, go with someone else."

Chloe frowned. Emma had been killed in her home, so that advice wouldn't necessarily keep someone safe. But she understood why he said it. People needed to feel safe, and to feel like they were taking steps to be safe.

A man stood. Chloe didn't recognize him, which didn't surprise her. He looked like he was in his thirties, despite his short, stark white hair. He wore simple clothes that did nothing to hide the beginnings of a beer belly and his eyes were filled with contempt when he glanced at her. His voice carried even without external amplification. "Why should we do any of that? We all know who did it. We all know who killed Jeremy," he called. "But for some reason she's sitting right there," he pointed accusingly at Chloe, "rather than in a jail cell! Why is that, Sheriff?" he asked, the title said mockingly.

Chloe froze at the hatred in the man's eyes. When she felt other pairs of eyes, some neutral, some unfriendly, she lifted her chin and looked back to the councilors.

Wesley sighed but kept the microphone from his mouth so it didn't carry. "Keith, there's no evidence that she committed either murder." He motioned to the redheaded man beside him. "Both my deputy, Jack, and myself have searched thoroughly, and the council has been given access to the evidence we've collected. Nothing points to Miss Chadwick."

The man who had been sitting beside Keith stood. He was a little taller than his companion, and in much better shape. "Well, who else could it be? We hadn't had a murder here in decades and you know it. Then she shows up and we have two?" He shook his head. "We all know enough to know there's no such thing as coincidences. I say you arrest her!"

A few voices cried out their agreement, calling for her arrest, and Chloe ground her teeth together as a cold knot formed in her belly. She could protest her innocence until she was breathless, but she knew it wouldn't change anyone's mind. She glanced back, in time to see a familiar woman with red hair joining in. Peyton had helped her in the woods, but clearly she wasn't Chloe's biggest fan.

The chill eased marginally when Zane scooted a little closer to her, clearly showing whose side he was on. It was replaced altogether when Lexi leapt to her feet and started yelling back. "You idiots don't know what you're talking about! Chloe wouldn't kill anyone! Just shut up and let the sheriff do his job!"

Chloe almost smiled. Almost.

There were only twenty or so voices calling for action, but she heard a few who added their cries to Lexi.

Colin took the microphone from Wesley and snarled into it. "Silence!" The yelling began to lessen until all conversation had stopped. "We know you're all scared. We get it. We know you want the murderer in jail. We get that, too. But putting an innocent woman in jail won't solve the problem. It'll just take focus off finding the real murderer."

The outcries started to pick back up, but he just shot a glare at the loudest offender and they subsided. "I'm not saying she's innocent or guilty, because right now we don't have enough evidence to arrest anyone. But she's not going anywhere, now is she? If, *if* she's guilty, then she'll be arrested, I promise you that. But we're not going to start a witch hunt just so we can make you all feel better. We'll arrest the guilty person *when* we find them."

Kyra took the microphone next. "You all elected us to the council for a reason. You trusted us to represent you, to lead you. So let us do what you elected us to do. If you have concerns, we encourage you to bring them to us after the meeting, or at any other time at the council building," she said in a smooth, sultry voice.

Chloe frowned as she felt a faint cold chill tease at the back of her neck. There was no draft in the gym, so the vampire councilor had to be doing magic. But to do what? She was so focused on the magic that she didn't notice at first that Kyra was staring at her, her eyes cool and far from friendly.

Erick took the microphone next and Chloe had to suppress a shudder. There really was no reason for him to creep her out, but she couldn't deny that he did. "We will be here for the next hour, or until we've spoken to anyone who has concerns. And if any of you know anything about either murder, or see anything suspicious, please let us or Sheriff Adams know immediately."

Some began to trickle out when he was done, though it seemed half of those gave her suspicious looks. Others sat talking to each other, including the men who had spoken up about her and Peyton. She saw the trio huddled together, glancing at Chloe now and again.

Zane bumped her shoulder lightly with his. "Hey, it'll be okay. They're just scared and don't know you. If they did, they'd know you couldn't have done this."

"But they don't. I'm worried someone's going to try to take care of this themselves. It doesn't seem as though Granny's house is exactly hidden. They all know where I'm staying," Chloe pointed out.

He frowned and glanced at Lexi, but neither could refute that statement. "Maybe you should think about staying somewhere else," he suggested. "Just for the time being."

Lexi nodded. "That's a good idea. You can come stay with me. I've only got one bedroom, but the couch is surprisingly comfortable."

Chloe considered for a moment before she sighed. "I can't."

"What? Why not? It'd be fun."

"It would, I'm not arguing that. But I can't put you at risk like that. If someone found out I was staying with you, they could still come after me." Chloe shook her head. "No, I'll stay at my house."

Zane frowned but didn't argue. "You can still come visit us, so you're not alone in that house all the time."

"I don't think that'll be a problem," Lexi murmured, but

neither Chloe nor Zane caught it.

Chloe did notice someone was coming their way and looked over to see Diego approaching with a sympathetic smile.

"Chloe, I'm so sorry you had to go through that," he said as he stopped in front of them.

"It's not your fault. People are scared. They aren't always themselves when they're scared."

He arched a brow but nodded. "True. Most people wouldn't care about that, though."

Chloe shrugged. "Not my fault most people don't follow logic."

Diego chuckled. "True." He nodded to the others. "Lexi, Zane. How are you both doing?"

Lexi grinned. "I'm doing great. I just need to go talk to Joel about my schedule tomorrow," she said, motioning toward a shorter man with a stocky build. "Be right back." She got to her feet and took a few steps before she glanced back to Zane and glared at him.

It took a moment for him to notice the pointed look being directed at him, then his eyes widened. "Oh, um, I needed to talk to Lexi. About something. Too," he said awkwardly before he got up and quickly followed after. They didn't go far, but had a short, rapid-fire conversation that didn't go above a whisper.

Lexi wasn't at all subtle, and Chloe just shook her head.

Diego looked bemused as he watched them. "Couldn't be anything I said. I hardly said anything."

"No, it's not you," Chloe assured him. "And thank you, for coming over to see if I was okay. I'm going to hold tight to any friendly faces I have here. They're way too few." Though she saw another one close by. Sort of. Wesley was talking to Erick, and both were currently looking in her direction, neither looking particularly friendly.

"I think there are more than you realize."

She shifted her focus back to Diego and cocked her head. "Oh?"

"Not everyone speaks up the same way Lexi does, but that doesn't mean that they disagree with her. And I've had a few people mention that they didn't think you did it. Though I'll admit part of that is due to knowing your grandmother and just thinking that Lydia's granddaughter couldn't be a murderer." He grinned. "Beyond that, I like to think I'm more than a friendly face."

Chloe couldn't help but smile. "Oh yeah? How much more?"

"That all depends."

"On what?"

"On if you agree to have dinner with me tomorrow night," he said with a wide smile.

She laughed. "And if I say yes? What does that make you?" she asked, enjoying the flirting. It occurred to her that even this bit of flirting was more enjoyable than the entire date with Erick had been.

"Hopefully it makes me the man you're dating."

"I don't know about that, but we can talk about it after the first date."

He grinned impishly. "Does that mean you're going to have dinner with me tomorrow?"

Chloe laughed softly. "Sure. It could be fun. Though, as much as I enjoyed Banquet, maybe not there?"

The grin dimmed to an understanding smile. "Of course. How about you come over for dinner around seven? I'm a decent cook. I may not be on Francois's level, but I have a few dishes that are edible."

"Sounds good to me. I never argue about a home cooked meal."

"Fantastic." Diego pulled his phone out. "I'll text you directions." Someone called his name and he glanced over and nodded to them. "After the meeting," he clarified as he slipped his phone away. "I should get back to it, actually. This many people hanging around means there are still scared people who want answers."

"Of course. I'll see you tomorrow," Chloe said with a bright smile.

"Until tomorrow," he said before returning to the other councilors.

She watched him walk away, which is how she noticed the looks on both Wesley and Erick's faces. Erick was frowning deeply, and she was struck by how badly it marred his normally attractive appearance. Wesley wasn't frowning, but he looked extremely grumpy and she thought it looked like his eyes had a yellow tinge to them.

Chloe scowled but was distracted by the return of Lexi and Zane.

The bubbly woman beamed at her. "Did I hear what I think I just heard?"

Bad moment broken, Chloe laughed softly. "Yes, you heard Diego asking me out and me saying yes."

Lexi let out a happy squeal and threw her arms around Chloe. "That's awesome! He is absolutely one of the hottest guys on the island. I tried for a year to get him to notice me, but no spark. Dammit." She sighed. "But he is a good friend," she added as she drew back.

"He is a nice guy," Zane confirmed.

Chloe grinned at him. "I know you think so. Otherwise, why would you have called him to help me last week?"

He flushed a little but grinned. "There is that."

She stood and leaned against him briefly, head resting on his shoulder. "Thank you for that, by the way. I'm starting to get the hang of this power thing."

The blush deepened and he shoved his glasses up his nose. "You're welcome."

"Now. What do you say we get out of here? Grab some pizza or something?" Chloe suggested when she straightened.

"Sounds good. I'm in," Lexi said, popping to her feet.

"Me too," Zane added before he impulsively offered an arm to each of the women who took them with happy smiles, allowing him to escort them out.

189

Chapter 26

The next day proved busy for Chloe. After going through her morning routine of coffee at her house, then breakfast at the diner, she went to the bank. She wasn't exactly hopeful they could help her, so was pleasantly surprised when she was told they dealt with transferring deposits to other banks regularly. Most of the residents of Salus used the bank on the island, but they often had visitors from off the island who used more mainstream banks. Family who had moved away usually, but sometimes friends visiting from outside the supernatural communities. Fortunately, she would also be able to withdraw money from the bank if she needed, which relieved her. Everyone took credit cards so far, but it never hurt to have options open.

Unconsciously, she was leaning more toward staying than leaving, even after she was cleared of the murders and got her powers under control, so she went on another shopping trip. Boxes were first on her list, because she knew she couldn't keep all of Granny's things out forever. As it was, it was hard to look at some of them. Beyond that, Granny hadn't updated the house in quite a while, which included the electronics. The TV was ancient and had only a VCR hooked up to it. Since all the movies

Chloe watched were on DVD or streaming services, and she had been spoiled by a high-def screen, the old TV had to go. She could have watched whatever she liked on her laptop, but she wanted a real screen.

After lunch she started worrying about her date with Diego. True, she'd just be going to his house and not some fancy restaurant, but she wanted to look nice. The dress she'd bought was a little too much, while the jeans she had with her weren't enough. Fortunately, Christie wasn't working when she went to Emma's boutique since it was a school day, but the woman who was working—a slender blonde with resting bitch face—wasn't any better. The clerk, whose name tag read 'Brittany', kept giving her the stink eye and making snide comments. Chloe did her best to ignore the woman, picking out a nice pair of skinny jeans, a pair of black boots, and a nice teal sweater that clung nicely to her figure. If she could get her hair to cooperate for once, she'd look good. No, she'd look better than good, she decided as she looked at the outfit in the full-length mirror, her lips curving. Diego wasn't going to know what hit him.

Diego texted the directions to his house as she was applying her lipstick—another of her purchases that day, since she almost never wore makeup beyond a little eyeliner—and she grinned at herself in the mirror. Even if his food was barely edible, she had a feeling this was going to be a good date. She'd even managed to control her hair with liberal use of the blow dryer and hair spray.

His house wasn't too hard to find. It was actually near the cliffs she'd found the day before. Most of the houses she'd seen on Salus had looked old-fashioned, while his just looked rustic. It was a cabin, nestled into the trees, but it was a very nice, two-story cabin, complete with a wrap-around porch and flower boxes on the windows.

Chloe got out of the car and walked up to the door, knocking. A moment later the door opened. Diego had gone with jeans as well, along with a long-sleeved shirt, though he'd rolled the sleeves up to his elbows. Chloe had to admit he looked good, but then, she had to agree with Lexi that he was just hot, period.

His gaze raked over her before he gave her a heart-stopping smile. "You look gorgeous, Chloe. Come on in."

"You look good, too," she said as she stepped into the house. "Really good," she added, leaning in to smile at him.

He grinned and shut the door behind her. "Always happy to please a beautiful woman," he said, resting his hand lightly on the small of her back to guide her through the house to the kitchen.

The colors inside were warm and masculine, heavy on earth tones. The walls hadn't been covered with drywall, but were smooth, golden wood. He had a few things here or there, just enough to make the place feel homey without making it cluttered. She saw he'd lit a fire, and it crackled away happily, providing the only music in the house.

When they reached the kitchen, it was much the same, and he'd even taken the time to put the chrome and steel of the appliances behind wood. This room was obviously not just for show and making coffee, but was well-used. She could tell that easily enough by the fantastic smells coming from the stove, but it just had a lived-in look to it she appreciated. Not that she could cook, so a kitchen like this would have been wasted on her, but she still liked it.

"Something smells amazing," she said as he stopped by a trio of stools that sat in front of a raised counter.

"I'm glad to hear you say that, since it's dinner," he teased as he reached behind the counter and pulled out a bouquet of flowers wrapped in tissue. "Hopefully these smell just as good," he said and offered the flowers to her.

No roses, she noted. He'd gone with sunflowers, daisies, and some small purple flower she couldn't identify. But the result was something bright and cheery, and she couldn't keep herself from smiling. "They're beautiful, Diego. I love them."

"Oh good," he said, feigning extreme relief, but she could see the glint of humor in his eyes. "I knew I couldn't get you something as ordinary as roses, but these made me think of you." He reached out and gave one of her curls a gentle tug.

"Maybe it was just the closest I could get to the gold of your hair."

Chloe laughed. "Whatever the reason, I really do love them. But do you have something I can put them in until I leave?"

He held up a finger in a wait gesture, then reached beneath the counter once more, pulling out a vase, already filled with water. A blue vase, that was actually pretty close to the color of her eyes, she noted with amusement. "Got you covered," he said and set it in front of her.

"Should I be flattered that you got flowers to match my hair and a vase to match my eyes? Or should I be reporting a stalker to Wesley?" she teased as she unwrapped the flowers and carefully placed them in the vase.

He chuckled and went to the stove, stirring whatever was in the pot. "I'm hoping you'll settle for flattered, personally. Though I'd have to be blind to miss your hair or your eyes. They're both striking."

"Then thank you. So, what are we having for dinner?"

"Shrimp alfredo. I thought I'd go relatively simple." He glanced over his shoulder at her and smiled. "Didn't want to go too complicated and risk having to just order in pizza."

"I'd be okay either way. I like pizza. Anyone who doesn't is just crazy."

"It just so happens that I agree, but I wanted something nicer for tonight," he said as he pulled garlic bread out of the oven and started plating. "Do you like wine?"

"Love it."

"Great." He carried the plates over to a table she'd barely noticed when she came in, and now she saw there was a bottle of wine there, along with everything they'd need for dinner. Aside from the plates he was carrying, anyway.

She smiled and slipped off the stool to follow him, and he pulled her chair out for her. "Such a gentleman. This is just like going to a nice restaurant, but without the wait time or strict dress code."

"Hopefully it won't be exactly like a restaurant," he said as he took his own seat.

"Oh? Why not?"

He grinned as he opened the wine and poured. "If this was a restaurant, you'd be leaving soon after you ate, and I was hoping you'd stay, maybe watch a movie with me."

She took a sip of the wine, found it delicious, and tried not to smile too brightly at him. "Assuming the food is good, I suppose I could stay for a movie."

"Wonderful."

They started eating, and Chloe couldn't help but make a sound of pleasure at the first bite. He was a really good cook. Or he'd had help, but she didn't care which it was. For several minutes they ate and asked easy questions, mostly about how their days had gone. Then Diego asked, "So how are you settling in here? Certain incidents aside?"

"Not too bad, actually," she answered. "I have started making some friends, and I'm getting to know the town. The island, too, but not as much."

"Why not?"

"Well, pretty much everything I've needed has been in town, or close to it, like my house. I have done some exploring, though." She smiled. "There are some really pretty spots on the island. And some unusual ones."

"What's your favorite so far?" he asked as he motioned to her drink and topped it off when she nodded.

"That's a hard one. I like the cliffs, think they're beautiful, but they make me a little nervous. Not used to heights like that. But it didn't...grab me...like this tree I found."

Curious, he arched his brows. "A tree?"

She nodded. "Found this dirt road and followed it to a path. They both looked like they were used a lot. Led to this really big oak tree."

The beginnings of a smile started to form on his lips. "What grabbed you about the tree?"

"For one, it was huge. I'd never seen an oak that big. There were taller ones around it, but it still seemed massive. And it was radiating power."

He nodded and motioned for her to go on.

"I felt sort of drawn to it, so I got close. I wasn't going to touch it, but this damn crow cawed and made me jump. It was..." Her eyes closed and she felt an echo of the power she'd gotten from it. "I'd never felt anything like it. The power I got at the morgue was one thing, and it was strong, don't get me wrong, but the tree? It felt...you're going to think this is stupid."

He leaned forward and shook his head. "I won't. We deal with weird stuff all the time on Salus, remember? What did it feel like?"

"Like coming home," she admitted reluctantly. "I'd never felt so good. It was like a cup of coffee after the best sleep ever while waking up in a nice, warm bed next to your favorite person."

Diego chuckled. "All that?"

She nodded. "I'd still been feeling a little sick after being attacked, but after I touched that tree, I felt amazing. But it scared me a little, too. And that damn crow didn't help either." Her voice dropped to a mutter. "Laughing at me."

He blinked and his lips twitched as he fought not to smile. "What was that? Did you say the crow laughed at you?"

"Okay, no. I know crows don't laugh, but it sounded like it was laughing at me."

"It may have been," he corrected. "But why did the tree scare you?"

"It was too much. Too big, too powerful, too weird." She wasn't going to mention the distorted cawing from the crow. That was a little much. "What is that tree? None of the other trees radiate power like that."

"Actually, some of them do, at least on Salus, but that oak is special," he agreed. "Most of the supernatural communities like Salus have a sort of sponsor when they're founded. A god who approves of us banding together or likes the reason we join as a town. When they do, they often give a gift of some sort. In our case we received an oak tree from Zeus."

Stunned, Chloe could only repeat, "Zeus." She was pretty ignorant about mythology, but even she knew who Zeus was.

He smiled and nodded. "The king of the gods, yes. One of his symbols is the oak tree. He gave it to us to help protect everyone on the island. It acts as a sort of anchor for the wards which keep us hidden from the human world. So, it's not surprising that you'd feel it radiating power that strongly. And as for the feeling of coming home...well, maybe you are home, and the tree was trying to tell you that."

"You and Lexi. Neither of you are going to be happy until my permanent address has Salus in it somewhere, are you?"

"Probably not," he answered cheerfully. "And we could use an investigator here. Maybe even a deputy. Wesley's only deputy is a vampire, which does limit the hours he can work."

"At least you're honest," she said with a low laugh. "And I'll keep that in mind."

"Honest and a politician. Boggles the mind, doesn't it?" he asked as he stood and cleared their plates from the table.

"How did you get to be a politician, anyway? I mean, sure you're charming and intelligent, but why the council?"

"You know elections are held every five years, right? And each race votes for their councilor and the omni councilor?" She nodded. "A few elections ago, the old witch councilor was ready to retire. She was getting older and wanted to travel. Otherwise, I can tell you she would have won again. But when she decided to go, she basically picked her successor. I'd been learning from her in any case, though magic, not politics, and she decided I would be the best to replace her. She told the others, and, apparently, they trusted her enough to vote for me. I've tried not to let her—or them—down."

"Ahh, so no thirst for power, then?" she teased.

He chuckled and walked back to her side. "Not even close. I just try to do my best, that's all." He reached for her hand and gently tugged her out of her chair. There wasn't much room between them, so if she took a deep breath their bodies would be touching. He brushed his thumb over her fingers before lifting his other hand to cup her cheek. His expression was serious now, his hand warm on her skin. "I've been wanting to do this since I saw you," he murmured before he bent his head.

Diego gave her plenty of time to recognize his intention, but unlike when Erick kissed her, she wanted this. She wanted it a lot, actually, so she met him halfway, surprised by the jolt of pleasure and desire that zipped through her body. It was vastly different from Erick's kiss. She moaned softly and he took it as the acceptance it was, deepening the kiss. His hand slid into her hair, his other arm wrapping around her, pulling her in against his body. She trembled at the contact and slid her arms around his neck, holding him close as he kissed her until every thought flew out of her head.

When he pulled his lips from hers, they were both breathless and clinging to each other. "I don't want to stop," he admitted in a low voice, "but if I don't stop now, I'm not going to."

"You don't have to stop," she whispered. It had been too long since she'd really been attracted to a man. Too long since she'd slept with a man. So no, she didn't want to stop.

He groaned and rested his forehead against hers. "But I do. You've been through a lot in the past week. I don't want to be the man who just helps you forget for a few hours. I don't want you to regret this later," he told her quietly.

Rather than dousing her desire, his reasons for stopping only made her want him more, but she understood those reasons. Worse, he wasn't wrong. She liked him, yes, and was definitely attracted to him, but would she be using sex to forget? As nothing more than stress relief? It only took a moment for her to realize she would. Chloe drew in a shaky breath and nodded. "Okay. You said something about a movie?" she asked as they slowly, reluctantly, released one another.

"I did," he agreed, smiling, though it was tight with restraint. "And I must say, your eyes look absolutely beautiful like this."

She cocked her head and gave him a confused look.

"They're violet," he explained, the smile relaxing some. "Strong emotion, remember?"

"Oh. Violet? That does sound pretty." She didn't really care much at the moment, since she still just wanted to jump him.

They moved to the living room and sat on the couch, close enough that their bodies brushed. It was a form of torture, but it felt too good to sit beside someone like this.

"What sort of movies do you like?" Diego asked as he turned

on the TV.

"Action, sci-fi, fantasy, comedy...I'm pretty easy to please, just no gore."

"I can get on board with that." He found an action movie with plenty of funny moments in it and they settled in to watch. Halfway through the movie they'd moved closer, with his arm around her and her head on his shoulder. When the movie was over, they decided to watch the sequel, and before it was done, they'd fallen asleep right there on the couch.

Chapter 27

Chloe woke when sunlight shined on her face. Her eyes slowly opened, and she was confused as to where she was, and why there was a crick in her neck. It was only when she started to sit up and had an arm tighten around her waist that she remembered.

Diego was still asleep, though he'd fallen to one side at some point during the night, so his head was pillowed on the arm of the couch. She'd been laying half atop him. It wasn't uncomfortable, either, aside from the odd angle of her neck. He looked peaceful in his sleep, and she had to be amused that even unconscious he'd tried to keep her from moving away from him. True, it could just be that she was warm and her absence would leave him chilled, but she preferred the first explanation.

"Diego?" No answer. She repeated his name a little louder, but he only made a small sound and turned his head toward her voice. Lips twitched and she debated the best way to wake him up. She could think of a surefire way to accomplish it, but it probably wouldn't be smart to start something she couldn't finish. Instead, she twisted and squirmed her way out from under his arm so she could get to her feet. The moment she did, his eyes opened.

"You moved," he mumbled, making a half-hearted grab for her, but she laughed and danced out of reach.

"I had to. It's morning. I need a toothbrush and cup of coffee. I don't even care what order it's in."

He groaned and lifted his head so he could see the clock on the mantle. "It's just before seven. How are you so…awake?"

"Refreshing company?" she asked playfully.

"If you're going to be this cheerful this early, I need coffee," he muttered as he got to his feet. He swayed and she reached out to steady him. The moment she was within reach, he snaked an arm around her, pulled her in close, and gave her a quick, firm kiss. "And that. That's better than coffee," he murmured against her lips before he released her.

Chloe shoved playfully at his chest but grinned. The kiss had been pretty good, but better than coffee? That was blasphemy. "I'll go make coffee. Do you happen to have a spare toothbrush?" she asked as she headed for the kitchen.

"Actually, I do. Under the sink in the bathroom. If you want to do that, I'll take care of the coffee."

"Sounds good."

By the time she got done in the bathroom she smelled not just coffee, but bacon. "You're really bucking for a second date, aren't you?" she asked as she walked into the kitchen.

He grinned. "The first one went so well, how could I resist trying for another?"

She moved over to him and leaned up, giving his cheek a quick kiss. "At this rate, you'll get it."

They ate breakfast before Diego walked her out to the car, handing her the vase of flowers and stealing one more light kiss before she left.

Lexi's car was sitting in front of her house, and the woman herself was leaning against the hood of her car, her phone in her hands, thumbs busy tapping away.

Chloe's phone dinged at her and she smiled, knowing just who the text would be from. She pulled up beside Lexi's car and got out holding the flowers.

Lexi grinned broadly and straightened. "Spent the night, huh?

200

And got flowers? You go girl! Tell me he's as good as every woman on the island has hoped he would be."

Chloe laughed and shrugged. "Sorry, but all our clothes remained on, so I have no idea." Lexi looked so disappointed at that answer that Chloe added, "I can say he's an amazing kisser, though."

"That's something, anyway," Lexi said with a long-suffering sigh. "But if you guys didn't get naked, why are you just now coming home?"

"We fell asleep on the couch. Watching movies, sorry, no naughty reason for that either," Chloe said with a grin.

"That's all right. At least you gave me a minor thrill. Good date then? Can't imagine you staying for a movie if it was a bad date."

"No, it was a great date. He cooked, and—" She broke off when a crow landed on the hood of her car and her eyes narrowed at the bird. "Seriously?"

"What?" Lexi asked as she turned to look at the bird, too. "Yeah? It's a crow. They're around."

"I know they're around. They've been following me."

Amused, Lexi turned back to her. "Following you?" she echoed.

"Yeah. I keep seeing them. Saw one yesterday at the oak tree—and yes, I know what it is, Diego told me. Damn, meant to ask Zane about that," she muttered, but shook it off. "But I saw one when I first got here, at the murder site in the woods...they're just all over the place and watching me."

"Seriously?" Lexi gave the crow a longer, considering look. "Could be a crow or raven shifter is curious about you and using them to learn more about you. Otherwise, I don't know. If you were a shifter, or even a witch, I'd just say that you had an affinity for them or something, but as an aether?" She shrugged. "No idea."

"I don't know if I like that idea. I've got enough attention on me without someone using birds for spies." Chloe ran a few steps toward the crow, waving her arm at it. "Go on! Get out of here and leave me alone!"

The crow just cocked its head and watched her, not bothered by her display.

"Come on, give me one freaking day without a feathered spy laughing at me," she yelled angrily.

"Laughing at you?" Lexi asked, amused again.

"Long story," Chloe said, dropping her arms when the crow gave no reaction.

"I wouldn't worry about it too much, to be honest," Lexi said, walking over to Chloe and slinging her arm around Chloe's shoulder. "They'll get bored, or whoever they're spying for will. And either way, stressing about it won't do you any good."

Chloe sighed. "Yeah, I guess you're right. You want to come in?"

"I can't. Gotta get to work, I just stopped by to see how the date went." Lexi grinned. "I'm glad it went well. Hopefully the next date goes even better."

Chloe laughed and shook her head. "You and Diego are two peas in a pod," she said as Lexi walked over to her door.

"And you adore us both," Lexi sang happily. "You should stick around and see where it goes," she added, ducking into the car and shutting the door before Chloe could reply.

"I'm not going to get any peace until I move here," Chloe muttered as Lexi drove away. She went into the house, put the flowers on the coffee table, and ran upstairs to wash her face and change. She wanted to see if Wesley had learned anything more, and she wasn't about to do it in yesterday's clothes, with her makeup faded and her hair a mess.

Half an hour later she grabbed her bag and headed out.

Chloe walked into the sheriff's office with a little smile on her face. She felt good. Part of it, she figured, was what remained from the power received from the oak, but the rest was just a good mood caused by a good date. She had a cup of coffee in one hand and a paper bag in the other. As it turned out, Salus had a bakery, and a damn good one at that. Which meant she could bribe a cop for info the way he was meant to be bribed—with doughnuts.

"Hey Wesley," she called as she stepped inside and crossed the office. He looked up and gave a faint smile, but was clearly distracted, so she added, "I come bearing gifts." She sat the bag down in front of him and offered the coffee to him.

Wesley took the coffee and started to take a sip when he stopped and sniffed. His eyes narrowed and flashed yellow for just a moment. "Thanks," he said, voice clipped, and sat the coffee down without even tasting it.

She arched a brow at the sudden surliness. "Uh…you're welcome. There are some doughnuts in the bag, too. Figured it was the least I could do considering how early I was showing up."

"What are you doing here, Chloe? In case you've missed it, I've got two murders to solve. And you're my only suspect."

The venom in his voice had her taking half a step back. "Excuse me?" she asked incredulously, her own temper rising. "You did *not* just say that to me. Your only suspect? You know damn good and well I'm no killer!"

"I don't know jack," he retorted, his voice louder now, too. He pushed out of his chair and stomped over to the coffee pot, adding insult to injury when he poured a cup of what she knew was subpar coffee instead of drinking the cup she'd given him. "I only have your word that you were ignorant before coming here. For all I know, you were friendly with a vampire before you ever stepped foot on the island," he said with a sneer as he turned back to face her.

Chloe stalked over to him and jabbed a finger in his chest. "You better get whatever crawled in your ass out, because I am not going to just stand here and let you bitch at me because you're in a bad mood, Yogi."

He sputtered in shock. "Yogi? Did you just fucking call me Yogi?"

"I did, yeah, because you're acting like just as much of an idiot as that bear!"

"I'm not an idiot," Wesley snarled, his eyes pure yellow now, no trace left of their usual gray. "But you can't come waltzing in here with doughnuts and coffee, expecting to sweet talk me into giving you information on an ongoing police investigation when you smell like him!" he roared, slamming the coffee down.

"What the hell are you talking about?" she asked, too angry to be confused.

"Diego," he snapped before he grabbed her arms and yanked her close, crushing his mouth to hers. Her eyes widened in shock before her senses registered the feel of his lips against hers, the brush of his beard against her skin. The taste of him. Just as suddenly as he'd kissed her, she was grabbing hold of his hair and kissing him back. He growled and turned them around, pressing her against the wall and pinning her to it with his body. Only then did his grip gentle, though the kiss remained stormy, wild, with that undercurrent of anger beneath it all.

His fingers dipped beneath her shirt and brushed against her stomach, which jolted her back to reality. She tore her mouth from his and, breathing heavily, she planted both hands on his chest and shoved. He stumbled back a few paces and stared at her. His lips were swollen, his eyes still yellow, and he looked like he was only a breath from kissing her again.

She remembered then what Lexi had said about bears and their senses of smell. Even though she'd changed, she must still smell like Diego after sleeping against him all night. What confused her was that Wesley had never shown the slightest bit of interest in her as a woman, so why had he cared who she smelled like? Bigger question, why had he kissed her?

He took a step back toward her and she held out a hand to ward him off. "Stop. I can't," she said, though her lips tingled with the memory of his kiss. "I'm not the sort of woman who bounces between guys."

That made him stop, then retreat a step. "Shit." He ran his hand through his hair. Gray bled back into his eyes gradually, until they were back to normal.

She pressed her lips together, trying to erase the feel of his kiss. It didn't work. "I didn't know…" She trailed off, not sure how to continue.

Wesley shook his head and dropped his hands to his hips. "No reason you should have." He started to say more but paused and walked back to his desk. Very deliberately he picked up the coffee she'd brought him and took a drink. "Did you have to call me Yogi?" he asked, sounding so aggrieved she had to smile.

"I really kind of did. Teddy bear didn't really suit you, but I think Yogi does," she teased, hoping to lighten the mood a little more. She couldn't deny she was attracted to Wesley—a lot, actually—but the timing was horrible. Even if she hadn't just started seeing Diego there was the whole murder thing to contend with. People were pissed enough that she wasn't behind bars. How pissed would they be if she started dating the sheriff?

He sighed and dropped down into his chair. "There's nothing I can do to convince you not to call me Yogi, is there?"

Chloe shook her head and cheerfully said, "Nope!"

"Then I demand you keep bringing coffee and doughnuts whenever you come by to nag me for information," he said, opening the bag and selecting a jelly filled.

She grinned. "I think I can do that. Except I don't nag," she insisted as she sat in the visitor's chair.

"That's a matter of opinion," he muttered. "So, what did you come here for? I know it wasn't just to bring me coffee and doughnuts," he said, carefully avoiding the kissing issue.

"I was hoping you'd learned something new," Chloe admitted. "And I was wondering if I should be worried. A lot of the people at the meeting weren't happy."

"No, they weren't, and I can't really blame them. No one likes the situation. Some people are starting to avoid vampires, even, which is ridiculous. One vampire shouldn't change the town's opinion on the whole race."

"It shouldn't, no, but scared people don't always think logically."

"No, they don't," he agreed dryly. "I'm not even sure how they found out a vampire was involved. But on a good note, I did find a bullet casing at Emma's house." She sat forward eagerly, but he shook his head before she could speak. "There was a partial print on it, but not enough to match it to anyone. I brought in a psychometrist who—"

"What's a psychometrist?" she interrupted. The word sounded familiar, but she couldn't place it.

"Someone who can touch an object and read impressions off it. Who handled it or made it, strong emotions that occurred near it or while it was being touched, what it was used for…things like that. Sometimes they can get readings off places, too, but that's rarer."

Right, Lexi had mentioned them. "I don't get it. Why not just send this psycho—"

"Psychometrist. And her name's Uma."

"Why not just send Uma to the murder scenes and let her tell you who done it?"

He shook his head. "It's not that easy. She might be able to do exactly what you're asking, but the problem is there's a very real chance she'd relive the murder. And I don't mean she'd see it happen, I mean she'd live it, as the murder victim. Would you want to willingly experience death like that?" Slowly she shook her head. "Would you be able to ask someone to experience it? Especially knowing that some psychometrists go insane because of the things they see?"

"No," she admitted with a sigh. "Okay, scratch that idea. You brought this Uma in. Did she learn anything?"

"Not as much as I'd like. All she could get was anger and obsession from whoever handled the bullet. She couldn't get a look at their face, or even tell what gender they were."

Chloe grimaced and nodded. "But it gave you something, at least. Anger could mean anything, but obsession?"

"Agreed. The only question is what was the killer obsessed with? Emma? Or was she simply the means to an end for them?"

Discovering that, she knew, would likely lead to the murderer. "I hope we find out. Before another person dies," she said grimly.

Chapter 28

The encounter with Wesley left Chloe feeling a little out of control and lost, so she went to the bookstore. Zane was starting to feel like the brother she'd never had—and never thought about wanting as a child. Even better, he had an odd way of centering her. Maybe it was all the magic practice they did, or how he was so awkwardly adorable that she just forgot to be freaked out. Or maybe the fact that he was just her friend with no undercurrents between them, but he helped. To her relief he was there and happy to keep her company. A lot of their conversation was had while he worked, but she didn't mind. After a little while she even chipped in to help him unpack books and put them on shelves, while sliding a few to the side to buy when she left.

Before she knew it, she'd spent four hours with Zane. She paid for the books she'd set aside earlier—a history of Salus, a book on Greek mythology, one on elementals, and a fantasy novel that looked like a mix of truth and misconception—and headed home.

When she got out of her car she was singing softly to herself, her mood vastly improved. She was a few steps from the front door when she realized it wasn't closed. Keeping her eyes on it she set the books on the ground and dug out her pistol, happy she'd gotten it back from Wesley and had cleaned it. She flipped the safety off and started to creep forward before she paused, remembering that she had another tool to use. Searching for magic was still easier for her with her eyes closed, but she didn't dare put herself at a disadvantage now. Instead, she reached out with that new sense of hers, but after a minute she came to the conclusion that there was no more magic here than normal. She moved forward slowly, the pistol held in a practiced grip, aimed downward, and eased the door open a little wider with her elbow. The sight that greeted her made her gasp.

Her house had been thoroughly trashed. She could only see the living room and part of the kitchen without actually going inside, but someone had completely wrecked it.

All of the little knick-knacks her grandmother had collected and lovingly placed around the house were on the floor, and from what she could see, every one of them was smashed. The pictures and paintings that had hung on the walls were on the floor, the glass broken, and in some cases, the pictures had been ripped into pieces. The TV she'd just purchased had an end table sticking out of the screen and it looked like someone had stomped on the DVD player. The chairs were overturned, the fabric slashed, and the couch was absolutely destroyed. They'd even ripped apart all the books, so torn pages lay all over the place, along with stuffing from the throw pillows that had rested on the couch.

The chest she'd brought from the house in Boston was little more than kindling.

The flowers that Diego had given her just the day before were shredded, the beautiful vase in pieces.

The kitchen was just as bad, from what she could tell. Dishes lay shattered on the floor and drawers had been yanked out and tossed around. She could only see one chair, but it was in pieces, so she didn't have much hope for the others.

Chloe wanted to rush in, to see how bad the damage was. She wanted to find the person who'd done this and beat the shit out of them. Instead, she fought the urge, backed up, and pulled her phone out, calling Wesley.

Wesley's voice was mildly annoyed and impatient. "I don't have anything new, Chloe."

"I do," she said, trying to keep her voice even, but anger and the sense of being violated put a tremor in her voice.

"What is it?" he asked, instantly going serious.

"Someone broke into my house. They trashed it. They trashed the whole damn place, from what I can see." Tears formed in her eyes, as much from fury as grief, and her hands trembled with the urge to punch someone.

"I'm on my way. Don't—"

"I haven't gone in. I'll wait for you," she said, barely holding onto her temper. She disconnected and put her phone away. Her gun was shoved into her bag, and she stalked away from the house, needing the distance.

They'd broken all of her grandmother's things. They weren't the only things she had from Granny, but they were still irreplaceable. And if they'd destroyed the photos she'd found upstairs, she really was going to hunt them down and break every bone in their body.

Her head fell back and she let all the rage she was feeling out with a scream. The sound echoed through the trees and faded to silence. A silence only broken when she heard a low caw from nearby.

Chloe turned and spotted the crow, sitting on the books she'd set down a few minutes ago. "Did the person you're spying for do this?" she demanded as though the crow would answer her. "Did you see who did? Did you see who destroyed all of a dead woman's possessions? And for what? For what?" she screamed at the crow who ruffled its feathers and bobbed its head. "If you know what's good for you, you'll stop spying on me," she said darkly, taking a step toward it.

The crow hopped off the books and closer to the car, before it flew up to the hood, so it was close to eye level with Chloe. It cawed again, and in some fanciful part of her brain, she thought it sounded like an apology.

She heard a car coming down the drive and turned. That

seemed to be a signal to the crow, who took off into the trees. "Coward," she muttered, just before Wesley's cruiser came into view.

The sheriff got out of the car and approached her, but after a few steps he slowed, until it looked like he was approaching a wounded, cornered animal. "Chloe?"

"What? Why are you looking at me like that?" she snapped.

"Because you're upset, and you need to calm down," he answered, his voice strained.

"Of course I'm upset. Take one look inside the house and you'll understand why!" she snarled, jabbing a finger in the direction of the house.

"I know. I get it, I really do. But you need to calm down." When she only glared at him, he tried another tactic. "I'm not going in that house until your eyes go back to blue and you stop tugging at my bear."

That caught Chloe off guard and she frowned. "What are you talking about?" she asked, though her tone wasn't quite so harsh.

"You affect magic. The part of me that can shift into a bear is magic. I can feel you pulling at me," he explained in a soothing voice. "I don't know if it would make me shift or make me unable to shift, but I'd rather not have either one happen right now."

That she could do either one, especially without meaning to, shocked her out of her rage. She knew when her eyes turned blue again because Wesley breathed a sigh of relief and relaxed. "Sorry. I didn't mean to," she said, ashamed of her lack of control. She knew her powers were unstable, that was why she originally agreed to stay on Salus. If she didn't have better control than this, she'd never be able to leave.

"I know, and it's understandable," he said as he finally walked up to her. "This is the biggest jolt you've gotten—emotionally, I mean—since your powers surfaced, isn't it?"

"Yeah."

"Then give yourself a break. Next time you'll be more aware and control them better."

She took a deep breath and nodded. "Yes, yes I will." She

turned back to the house. "The door was open when I got here, just a crack. I didn't sense any magic, so I bumped the door open with my elbow and looked inside. And before you yell at me, I did have my gun out and was ready in case someone had been in there."

"I still might yell," he said casually, "but I'll give you points for realizing that was a possibility."

"Gee, thanks," Chloe said sarcastically. "I saw that everything was wrecked, backed away, and called you."

"There might still be someone in there, but it's doubtful," he mused as he studied the house. "I'm not going to be an idiot and think you'll actually listen when I tell you to stay out here, but at least keep your gun holstered and stay behind me."

That irked, but she agreed. "But if you get hurt because you're acting like a macho man, I'm going to laugh. And I won't send you flowers."

He gave her a quick grin. "Noted."

They moved through the house, with Chloe keeping her word, but they didn't find any sign that anyone else was there. She managed to keep her temper when she saw her bedroom, though the bed had been slashed and some kind of dark liquid poured onto it. Her grandmother's bedroom had almost broken what little control she had, since it was just as bad as the rest of the house. But to her relief, the room with all the pictures hadn't been touched. She had no idea why, but she was grateful for it.

Wesley grimaced when they reached the living room again. "You weren't kidding. They really did a number on this place, but no one's here. I'll see if I can find some fingerprints or DNA, but I'll be honest, it's going to be hard to find anything."

"I know," Chloe said tiredly, leaning against the wall. "Do you think the psychometrist would help out with this?"

"She might, since it's not a murder. If I don't find anything, I'll give her a call," he promised. "How long were you out of the house?"

"A while. I was here for a few minutes this morning, before I saw you, but that's it. So, they've had all damn day to wreck the place."

He nodded with a scowl. "At the very least we can rule out vampires, though."

Which still left a lot of people as suspects, she knew. She straightened and watched as he searched for evidence, but whoever had done this was good. Wesley found a few fingerprints, but judging by the location, he said he was betting they were hers, though he'd check them back at the sheriff's office. Nor did he find any of the little things criminals often left without thinking like cigarette butts or gum.

"I'm sorry, Chloe. I'll call Uma, see if she can come out and take a look, but there's nothing here I can really go on."

Chloe smiled faintly and shook her head. "A lack of evidence isn't your fault. Don't suppose you could just smell who was here, then?"

His mouth tightened and he shook his head. "No. Whoever did this was surprisingly smart. I can smell you, of course, but the rest he covered up with Lydia's perfume. It's overshadowing just about everything. I'm scent blind, basically," he said, scrunching up his nose.

It was almost enough to make her laugh. "Okay. Thanks, Wesley. Can I start cleaning up?"

"Go ahead. I'd also seriously considered staying somewhere else, at least for tonight," he told her before leaving.

Chapter 29

After Wesley left the house Chloe turned back toward the mess. She didn't close the door behind him. There wasn't any point. Everything worth stealing had been destroyed, and a door wouldn't stop a supernatural from attacking her. She was happy her laptop had been in her car when the break in had occurred, but she'd seen only one pair of jeans and a tee-shirt that had survived. At least she had one change of clothes, but the more she saw the more depressed she got.

She leaned back against the wall, only to grimace and move two feet to the left when she saw a hole in the wall beside her. No blood, so probably not from a punch, but it meant she couldn't just toss all the destroyed things and be done with it. No, there were repairs to make now, too. Hopefully there was a handyman somewhere in Salus. They had everything else, so she was betting there was. But man, Salus really needed some sort of directory if it was going to stay off the internet. Or maybe they had one already. She'd have to remember to ask Lexi or Zane later.

Chloe sighed and went into the kitchen, grabbing a box of garbage bags, then went back into the living room. She started to

MEG M. ROBINSON

toss things haphazardly into a bag, her mood dropping with every fragment that disappeared into the black plastic. Most of what she was throwing away wasn't expensive, but Granny had kept each of these things for a reason, so it still stung. Especially when she had to throw away the pieces of photographs that had been lovingly framed and displayed. She was throwing away memories.

The first bag was only half full when she heard a car pull up. She scowled and set the bag down, fully prepared to tell whoever it was to go the hell away. She wasn't in the mood for company. She definitely wasn't in the mood for anyone else wanting to accuse her of murder.

When she reached the door, she was stunned. Wesley's cruiser was still there, with the sheriff leaning against it. Just pulling up was the SUV she'd seen in Diego's driveway, with him at the wheel and a familiar brunette in the passenger seat.

Lexi leapt out of the car and ran over to Chloe, catching her in a bear hug. "I am so sorry, Chloe! This sucks big time!" she said, her voice muffled by Chloe's shoulder.

Chloe was too startled to do more than absently pat Lexi's back and shift her gaze from Diego to Wesley and back again. "What are you guys doing here?"

"Wesley called us and told us what happened. We came to help you clean up," Lexi said when she drew back. "We grabbed pizza and some beers, but we're going to help first."

Diego shut the door to his SUV and nodded. "We are," he agreed, carrying over a couple of pizza boxes, along with a twelve pack of beer. He gave her a sympathetic smile. "I'm sorry, cariño," he murmured when he was closer.

Chloe closed her eyes, fighting back the tears that had begun to form. Never had anyone done anything so thoughtful for her. Granny had loved her, yes, and she'd dealt with all of the hurts and fears that come with growing up, but Granny had never had to comfort Chloe after anything quite as emotional as this. When she opened her eyes, she hugged Lexi tight. "Thank you, Lex." She moved on to Diego next, though he couldn't return the hug with his hands full. "Thank you." She drew back but didn't let go

214

of him completely. "They destroyed the flowers you gave me," she said sadly.

"I'll get you more. I'll get you a dozen bouquets if it makes you smile again," Diego promised.

She gave him a shaky smile then went to Wesley, who had been silent since Diego and Lexi arrived. She stood in front of him for a moment, remembering the awkwardness from when he'd kissed her, but she wrapped her arms around him, too, giving him a warm hug. "Thank you, for calling them. For knowing I'd need them." Yes, he could be a surly asshole a lot of the time, and there were issues between them, but he wasn't a bad guy. Far from it. If she enjoyed the hug a little more than she ought to, well, she was only human—sort of—and he was an attractive man who'd helped her. It was only natural.

Wesley rubbed her back once before he let his hands drop, well aware that they weren't alone. "You're welcome. But you're not getting rid of me so easily. I'm going to help clean."

Chloe drew in a slow breath and stepped back. "You two might change your minds once you see the house," she said grimly to Lexi and Diego as she led the trio inside, grabbing the books she'd left outside earlier as she went. She heard a soft gasp from Lexi, along with a low Spanish curse from Diego.

"You are not sleeping here tonight," Diego said darkly as he took in the carnage and Lexi echoed the sentiment.

She smiled wryly. "I couldn't even if I wanted to, not unless I slept on the floor, without a pillow, and with a tee-shirt for a blanket."

"I told you before, I've got a spare couch," Lexi offered, as she gaped at the destruction.

"I have a guest room," Wesley said. "You're welcome to it as long as you need it."

Diego shot Wesley an unhappy look before he stroked a hand down Chloe's arm. "I, too, have a guest room. And you're well aware how comfortable the couch is."

Wesley scowled but said nothing.

Trying to diffuse the tension, Chloe smiled faintly. "True, but I did wake up with a crick in my neck. But we'll figure that out after this place is a little less like the local dump." She eyed the hole in the wall. "Do any of you know a good handyman?"

"I do," Wesley said with a nod. "So do you, for that matter. At least a little."

"I do?"

"Colin. He's primarily a woodworker, but there's not much he can't do with his hands. He prefers making or fixing things to being a councilor, in fact. I'll give you his number before I leave."

"Thanks." She grabbed the bag she'd been working on earlier and resumed cleaning. Before long all four of them were loading up bag after bag of debris. They picked a wall and started piling the bags up, but they added up entirely too quickly for her liking. Still, the living room was clean an hour later of everything but the big pieces like the couch. Clean and bare. Diego promised to bring a trailer over the next day to help her haul everything off.

They paused to scarf down the pizza and beer before they moved into the kitchen, and from there the bedrooms and bathroom.

It was nearly midnight when they finished, and the living room was almost completely full of bulging black bags. Chloe was exhausted, mentally and physically, but somehow seeing the bags was better than seeing all her grandmother's possessions in pieces.

Altogether, aside from the storage room, all they'd managed to salvage were a few articles of clothing, a single can of Coke, and a tube of toothpaste. Whoever had done this had been extremely thorough or they'd had help. Which again made her wonder why the room with all the pictures had been spared. Had she come home before the culprit had started in that room? It didn't seem likely, but she supposed he could have slipped out the back door. But it was a mystery for another time.

Chloe stared numbly at the pile of bags and swayed on her feet.

"I think it's time you got some sleep," Lexi said as she leaned against Chloe, so they propped each other up.

"Past time," Chloe agreed. She sighed and forced herself to

stand up straight. "Wesley?" She waited until he turned and gave her a curious look. "I appreciate the offer—and yours, too, Lexi—but I think some people might be...even more vocal about wanting me in jail if they found out I was staying with the sheriff. And Lexi? I love you, but I'm not sleeping on a couch two nights in a row."

Wesley looked unhappy but nodded. "A valid point. But I meant what I said earlier. You need anything, you see anything off, give me a call, okay?"

She smiled. "I will, I promise. Though hopefully this is the end of it."

"I hope so, too. And before I forget..." His phone was pulled out, tapped on for a moment. Her phone dinged and she saw he'd sent her Colin's number.

"Thanks."

"No problem." He stretched, working a kink out of his back. "I'm going to head home. I'll let you know what Uma says," he told Chloe as he headed for the door. "Night, Diego. Lexi."

"Night, Wes," Lexi called.

"Good night, Wesley," Diego said. He turned back to the women. "Are you two ready to go?"

"Oh yeah," Lexi said with an eager nod.

"I am. I'll just follow you over. My laptop's still in my car, so I just need to grab my bag," Chloe told him as she went into the kitchen where she had stashed it earlier after they'd cleaned up a bit.

Twenty minutes later they'd dropped Lexi off and were pulling up to Diego's cabin. He hurried out of his SUV and over to her car, opening her door for her. He grabbed her bags, carrying them inside so she only had to worry about getting herself in the cabin. "Bed," she pleaded. "I know I could use a shower, but unless I can sleep and shower at the same time, it won't work."

He chuckled and led her to the guest room, setting the bags down in a chair in the corner. "I'll leave a pair of sweats and a tee-shirt in the bathroom for when you wake up. I know they'll be big, but they'll be clean."

MEG M. ROBINSON

"You are a god among men," Chloe said as she sat on the edge of the bed and pulled her shoes off. She collapsed back onto the bed and was asleep almost instantly.

Diego grinned and bent down, kissing her forehead before he turned the lights off and left, closing the door behind him.

Chapter 30

For the second time in as many days Chloe woke confused about where she was. Unlike the night before she didn't have Diego sleeping next to her—or under her, more accurately—to help remind her. She sat up and looked around, but couldn't place the room, not after the two minutes she'd spent in it before passing out.

She got up and stretched, but it wasn't until she opened the door and peeked into the hall that she remembered following Diego back to his house. A quick glance at her watch showed it was still early. Since he'd been so slow to wake yesterday, he was probably still sleeping. Hopefully he'd left the clothes as promised, because she was desperate for a shower.

Quietly she made her way into the bathroom and smiled when she saw the sweats and shirt sitting on the counter. "He is most definitely getting a second date," she murmured before taking a hot and lengthy shower. When she got out, she smelled like him, but since he always smelled so good, she couldn't mind too much. It didn't help her libido much, though. She changed and savored the feeling of being clean. It was a feeling so all too often took for granted. So, the clothes bagged on her. She didn't care. They, too, were clean.

Chloe emerged from the bathroom feeling marginally better mentally, but even that got a boost when she smelled coffee. She followed the scent to the kitchen and found Diego making pancakes while the coffee brewed. He wore a pair of loose cotton pants and a tee-shirt, and looked even more tasty than the coffee smelled.

"You know, you don't have to keep sucking up. I've already decided to give you a second date," she said as she padded over to him.

He grinned and reached over to get a mug out of the cabinet, setting it in front of the coffee pot. "Maybe I'm thinking ahead to the third date," he teased.

She laughed and poured herself a cup. "Good thinking. I wasn't sure you'd be awake. You didn't seem like a morning person yesterday."

"Normally I'm not," he admitted, "but I woke up almost an hour ago. When I heard the shower, I knew you'd be in begging for coffee soon."

"I could kiss you."

He flipped a pancake and arched a brow at her. "No one's stopping you," he pointed out, turning to face her.

She considered for a moment before she gave him a bright smile then took a sip, watching him over the rim.

He laughed good-naturedly and went back to the pancakes. "How are you feeling this morning?"

"Better, a little. I kept having dreams about Granny's house and the break in, which kept waking me up," she admitted. "But I'm glad we got everything cleaned up."

"Once we're done eating, we can go take care of the rest. And I know Lexi wanted to take you shopping."

She wrinkled her nose. "I don't want to buy too much, not until Wesley finds whoever's responsible. I'd hate to spend the time and money replacing everything only to have it wrecked again."

"An understandable worry," he said, transferring pancakes to plates. "I meant what I said last night, about staying here. You're more than welcome, for as long as you need."

Chloe studied him as he worked. "Okay, what's the catch?"

Confused, he glanced at her. "Catch?"

"You're hot, you can cook, you're charming, you're considerate, and you're a hell of a good kisser. There's got to be a catch. Are you secretly married? Part of a cult? I think this is something I should know before our second date," she said, only half joking.

He flashed her a brilliant smile. "And if I said there was no catch?"

"Ahh, there it is," she said with a knowing nod. "You're delusional. Everyone has a catch."

Diego laughed and carried the pancakes and syrup over to the table. "And what's your catch?"

"High maintenance," she answered without hesitation as she took a seat. "I mean, just think of all the work you've already had to put into dating me. I've been accused of murder, twice, been attacked, had my house broken into, and half the town is calling for my arrest. Isn't that enough of a catch for you?"

"When you put it that way…"

She grinned and snagged a few pancakes for herself and smothered them in syrup. "That's what I thought. Now eat up. I don't think I'm going to feel any better until I get it all out of the house."

"Never let it be said I kept a lady waiting."

Hours later they'd dropped off the last of the bags and hauled the couch and other ruined pieces of furniture out as well. Lexi called on their way back to Diego's house.

"Are you and Diego done?"

"Just finished," Chloe confirmed.

"Good. I'm stealing you for the rest of the day. Tonight, too."

"You are?"

"Mmhmm. Shopping first, then we're going out. You're going

to relax tonight no matter what. We're probably going to get more than a little drunk, so you're gonna crash at my place since it's closer."

Chloe was caught between irritation and amusement but focused on the amusement. "Okay, but just clothes and some necessities. Maybe a bed. I'm not restocking the whole house until the asshole's been caught."

"Makes sense. Okay, meet me at my place in thirty? I'll text you directions."

"Sounds good."

After she'd hung up, she grinned at Diego. "Looks like you're going to have to make do without my charming company tonight."

He just smiled. "Lexi's kidnapping you, I take it?"

"Yep. Overnight, even."

"Somehow I think I'll manage to contain my disappointment. I may hold your laptop hostage, though, just to make sure you come back," he teased.

"I'm high maintenance, not dumb," she said, laughing, as she got out of the car and walked with him toward the cabin. "Lexi is awesome, but even she would give me hell if I opted to stay with her over you."

He playfully preened and made her laugh as they went inside.

She changed into her one remaining outfit and borrowed a sweatshirt from Diego, since it was entirely too chilly to wander around in just a tee-shirt. She headed for the door, pausing awkwardly when she saw Diego on the couch with a book. They weren't truly in a relationship, even if they were temporarily living together. Even if they were living together, she had no past experience to fall back on with how to handle this. Yet, the thought of living together, even on a temporary basis, freaked her out. She wasn't ready. Hell, she didn't know him well enough even if she was. Fortunately, he made it a little easier.

Diego looked up and smiled. "Have fun," he said, before returning to his book.

The man was entirely too perfect. "I will," she told him before going outside to head to Lexi's. The woman was waiting outside when Chloe got there and happily hopped into Chloe's, since it was a little bigger.

"Tell me you're not one of those girls who hates shopping," was Lexi's hello.

"I'm not," Chloe assured her. "I like shopping." Sort of. "But like I said, just necessities."

"Would those necessities include something sexy to wear for a certain witch?"

"You seriously have a one-track mind," Chloe said, laughing.

"Hey, I've been having a dry spell lately. That's the problem with living in a small town when the people don't really change. Eventually you've dated everyone you're interested in. So...I have to live vicariously until someone else catches my interest,"

"Didn't you say you had a date the other night?"

Lexi shrugged. "Didn't pan out. Didn't figure it would, but had to give him a try. Now come on. This is going to be fun."

It was, Chloe had to admit it. She really did enjoy shopping, but clothes shopping with a girlfriend? It was a whole other level. She couldn't just try clothes on to see what fit, oh no. She had to model them and see what was cute, what was hot, and what just simply wouldn't do.

In the end she left with six outfits, a few new bras and panties, new toiletries, and—at Lexi's insistence—a little black dress and something sexy to put on under it. She did go ahead and order a bed, which would be delivered the next day. She couldn't just keep stealing people's guest rooms indefinitely.

They had lunch at Banquet—Chloe's treat—before they went back to Lexi's for a few hours, killing time until it was late enough to hit the bar. Salus didn't have a club, so the nightlife tended to consist of the bar or the small movie theater.

"So, things are going good with you and Diego, hmm?" Lexi asked as she meticulously painted her toenails a vivid shade of blue.

"You know things haven't changed that much since yesterday," Chloe pointed out as she attempted to paint her own nails, going with a bold red.

"So, nothing happened last night?"

"Just me passing out the moment my head hit the pillow. But…"

Lexi stopped and looked up, her expression hopeful. "But…" she prompted.

"This is just between us, right? I mean you won't tell *anyone*?"

"Do I have to cross my heart or swear in blood?" Lexi asked with a straight face before she grinned. "Yes, it's just between us."

Still Chloe hesitated. "I kissed Wesley yesterday."

Lexi made a sound Chloe wasn't sure even dogs could hear. "You did what?"

"Well, technically I guess he kissed me," she confessed.

The bottle of polish was set aside and Lexi turned to her. "Spill," she demanded.

Chloe told her everything, from the moment she'd walked into the sheriff's office to when they'd gone back to talking about the case.

Lexi let out a low, impressed whisper. "Damn girl. You don't waste any time, do you?"

"It's not like it was my idea," Chloe protested. "And I did stop him."

"You didn't want to, though, did you?"

Chloe let out a defeated sound and slumped back. "Not really, but I'm not the type to juggle two guys."

Lexi moved over beside Chloe and hugged her. "I wouldn't worry about it too much. You didn't sleep with him, and you've only had one date with Diego. Maybe it'll end up happening with Wesley, or maybe you'll have a bunch of little babies with Diego."

Chloe sputtered and felt the blood drain from her face. "B-babies?"

"I'm not saying have them right now, but it could happen," Lexi told her, grinning. "My point is that you should just relax, enjoy yourself, and let things go how they go. Otherwise, none of it will be any fun."

"You're oddly wise."

Lexi gave a slow, sage nod. "Of course I am. Madam Lexi

knows all, sees all," she said in her best mysterious voice.

Chloe laughed and shook her head.

"That's better. Now finish painting your nails so we can go have some fun! And we're dragging Zane with us, too. That boy is way too stuck in his books."

"Now that sounds like a *lot* of fun."

Chapter 31

Z ane took a little convincing, but between Lexi's persistence and Chloe giving him sad looks—only mostly feigned—he relented.

They piled into Chloe's car and headed over to On the House. There were already quite a few people there, which made Chloe nervous. Any one of those cars could have held someone who considered her a murderer. She began rethinking this whole night out thing, but Lexi looked so happy she kept her concerns to herself.

Inside, the place was surprisingly nice. No dive bar for Salus. It was a large area, with a bar made of gleaming wood dominating the left wall. There was a stage at the far end just big enough to hold a band, as it did tonight, one playing rock covers. A small dance area was in front of the stage—empty— surrounded by two and four-person tables. Only a few booths had been put in, all of them meant to hold larger groups. Only one was full at the moment, though more than half the tables had people at them, and almost all the barstools were taken.

They paused just inside and looked at the seating options. Chloe spotted a familiar face sitting at the bar. A face who just happened to have a few empty stools beside him. She smiled.

Maybe tonight wouldn't be so bad, she thought as she glanced slyly at Zane.

"Why don't we sit over there?" she suggested to her companions, pointing to the open stools next to Cole.

They looked over and Lexi started to shrug, but even in the dim light Chloe could see the flush staining Zane's cheeks. "I...I don't know. Maybe we should just find a table," he protested.

Lexi gave him a curious look, then glanced to the bar. Confused, she turned to Chloe, who mouthed 'Cole' and smiled. Lexi's eyes widened and shook her head. "No, I like the bar," she said, linking her arm with Zane. Chloe mirrored her and they led him over to the bar, working it so he ended up sitting on the stool closest to Cole.

The surly mechanic glanced over with a scowl, but Chloe was paying attention and noticed that it softened slightly when his gaze landed on Zane.

"Hi, Cole," Chloe said with a grin. "I guess you know Lexi? And Zane?"

Something in her tone made Zane look back at her suspiciously, but she just gave him a smile and faint nod. His eyes went wide with understanding before he gave her a shy smile.

"Of course. They've been here for ages," Cole answered in his gruff voice before he took a swig of his beer.

"How have you been, Cole?" Lexi asked with a bright smile before she ordered a round of tequila shots for all of them, Cole included.

He frowned at her but didn't turn down the shot. "I've been okay. Busy." His gaze slid back to Chloe. "People keep interrupting me when I'm working."

"Hey, don't blame me, blame my belt," Chloe said, holding her hands up in an 'I'm innocent' gesture. "Or you can blame Lexi for giving me your number."

"You owe me two shots then," he told Lexi.

"You're lucky she sent you to Cole. There's another mechanic on the island, but he's not as good," Zane said.

Cole arched a brow, but they were all distracted by the shots, lime wedges, and salt the bartender placed in front of Lexi. He reached for his shot, but Lexi put her hand over it.

"Nope, you have to do the shots right, and with us," she insisted.

He scowled. "Fine," he said grumpily, but he licked and salted his hand. Once the others had done the same, they tossed back the shots.

Zane didn't hesitate, which surprised Chloe. He also made a face, which didn't, but did make her smile. "Not a fan of tequila?" she asked after she disposed of her lime wedge.

"I can honestly say this is the first time I've had it," he admitted.

"That calls for another round, then," she declared and motioned to the bartender. "Another round. And two for Cole, this time."

The second round went down easier for all of them.

A song came on that Chloe liked and she got an idea. She nudged Lexi. "You afraid to be the first person on the dance floor?"

Lexi slowly smiled. "Can't say I am. Sorry boys, you'll have to deal without us for a little while."

"Whatever," Cole muttered as he knocked back his third shot.

Zane looked mildly panicked, but Chloe just smiled at him as she grabbed Lexi's hand and went out to the small dance floor.

"You don't really want to dance, do you?" Lexi asked, though she didn't hesitate to start moving with the music.

"Not really," Chloe admitted. "I like dancing all right, but I prefer singing."

"So, what's the deal, then? For a minute I thought you had a thing for Cole, but that's not it, is it?"

"Not even a little." She laughed. "I like him well enough, I guess, but I'm pretty sure Zane has a major thing for him."

Lexi stopped dancing. "What? Zane? Are you sure? How do you know?"

The sheer indignation in Lexi's voice at not having noticed drew another laugh from Chloe. "The way he reacted when I

228

mentioned my car breaking down the other day. And the way he reacted when we dragged him over to Cole. Didn't you see how freaked out he looked? Hopeful but scared?" She shrugged. "I just wanted to give them a few minutes alone. More than a few, if we can manage it."

"That's easy. When they're not looking, we'll just grab a table on the other side of the room."

Chloe glanced to the bar and saw the two men weren't paying them any attention, but were engrossed with their own conversation. "How about now?"

"Sure. There's one." They wove through people until they reached the table and sat down. "I'm glad you let me drag you out here tonight."

"So am I," Chloe admitted. "I needed this. The date with Diego was fun, but first dates are stressful, too. This is just fun." She spotted a face coming toward them and sighed. "Though I think the fun just ended," she murmured.

"Huh?" Lexi asked, looking around, just before Erick joined them.

"Hello, Lexi, Chloe," he said, nodding to Chloe but giving Lexi a little smile.

Chloe resisted the urge to roll her eyes. Some men couldn't handle being the most irresistible man around. But all she did was smile at him. "Hi, Erick."

Lexi looked surprised but smiled as well. "Hello, Councilor."

Erick's smile brightened as he turned on the charm. "Now, no need for formality. You've known me for years. And I'm not exactly acting as councilor now."

Though Chloe could see right through the thin layer of shine on Erick, Lexi looked like she was buying it. She laughed and nodded. "True. Erick," she said pointedly. "I didn't know you came to On the House."

"I don't, not often," he said, ignoring Chloe, nearly turning his back on her. "But now and again I like to get out of my rut and have some fun."

"That's why we're here, too," Lexi told him.

"Oh? I didn't think you had any trouble having fun," he said with a flash of a grin.

She laughed. "I don't, but Chloe needed to get out. This week has been way too rough."

He glanced at Chloe and the grin dimmed. "Yes, I suppose it has," he said, his voice cooling.

Hoping to avoid any future awkwardness—or worse—Chloe inwardly sighed. "Erick, I'm sorry. I know I should have called you after our date, but honestly things have just been so crazy it's a wonder I'm not forgetting basic things like eating and breathing. I enjoyed our date, but the…spark…just wasn't there. I hope we can still be friends, though." It wasn't entirely a lie. She did forget about calling him, and she enjoyed the food and meeting Francois. And she most definitely wasn't attracted to him.

Erick looked surprised at her words, but the expression disappeared after a second. He warmed a touch and nodded. "No, I understand. And I should have taken the current situation into account." He gave her a sheepish smile. "Unfortunately, men don't always act rational when they see a beautiful woman ending up on the arm of another man."

She forced herself to smile. "I know. But you're a handsome man, Erick. You'll find someone you have that spark with." And she'd pity the woman when he did.

"Thank you for that," he said, inclining his head to her. "I should leave you two ladies to enjoy your evening. Have a good night." He gave them one more smile then slipped off to greet someone else.

Lexi glanced between his retreating back and Chloe for a moment. "That was…"

"About as much fun as a fork in the eye?" Chloe asked dryly.

"I was going to say uncomfortable as hell to watch, but yeah, that too," Lexi agreed.

"I know, and I'm sorry. I really should have called him, but it honestly didn't occur to me. I was more concerned with whether or not I'd end up in jail than dealing with the feelings of a guy I went on one date with. Especially when he gave me the creeps."

Lexi frowned. "I know what you said about the date, and I

believe you, I do, but it's just hard for me to imagine him being creepy like that."

"I really don't know what to tell you there. It's not like I know him well. And maybe it's just me he's weird with."

"Maybe," Lexi murmured, uncertain.

"We should order some more drinks. You did say we'd be getting drunk, right? I'm not going to get drunk on two shots of tequila," Chloe said with a small smile, trying to regain their good mood.

"We should! And we are!" Lexi agreed, shaking off the funk without hesitation. "Do you want to…"

She trailed off and after a long moment Chloe frowned. "Do I want to…?" she prompted.

"Look," Lexi hissed with a big grin on her face, nodding toward the front door.

Chloe twisted around and about fell off her chair. Cole was leaving, which wasn't a big surprise. But he was leaving *with* Zane. Cole looked a bit less grumpy than usual, and Zane looked both shell-shocked and pleased. "Oh my god, it worked," she breathed.

Lexi bust out laughing. "It did something, anyway. But for Zane's sake, I hope it's exactly what we're thinking it is. He's been alone way too long. He deserves someone. For that matter, they both do." She frowned, her voice going serious. "I just hope Cole doesn't hurt him."

Chloe whipped back around, and by the startled look on Lexi's face, she assumed her eyes were violet. "Is Cole the sort to hurt him?"

"Oh no, I don't mean like that," Lexi quickly assured her. "I just don't know if he's the type to commit, but I know Zane is."

"Oh." Chloe mulled that over for a moment. "Nothing we can do about that. We helped give them a chance to find out, that's all. And if they don't work out, it's not like Zane will be alone. He'll have us."

"Damn right he will. And we're going to celebrate that chance with another round of tequila!"

"When I wake up with a hangover tomorrow, you're getting

me coffee, bacon, and aspirin," Chloe warned.

"Fuck that. I've got a hangover remedy," Lexi said absently as she flagged down a server.

"Old family recipe?"

Lexi snorted. "Hardly. I like drinking but hate hangovers, so I grabbed a couple hangover cures from the apothecary as soon as I decided I was taking you out."

Before Chloe could ask about the apothecary, since she'd been curious about that particular store, the lights flickered and someone yelled from across the room, "Who let that murdering bitch in here?"

Chloe's eyes closed and she sighed. She'd been afraid something like this would happen. At least she recognized the voice, so it wasn't a new enemy. And now she could identify exactly what he was, given the way little shocks were racing across her skin while the lights dimmed and flickered, seemingly at random. Electricity elemental. Joy.

Her eyes opened and she smiled tightly at Lexi. "How about we just grab a bottle of tequila and finish the shots at your place?"

"Chloe, you don't have to listen to people like him," Lexi protested.

"He lives here. I'm just visiting, for now. I don't want to get run out of town before I even decide if I want to live here," Chloe said, getting to her feet as Keith kept loudly insulting her and everyone who'd refused to put her in jail.

Lexi wasn't happy but she didn't argue. "I'll go cancel the shots and see if I can sweet-talk a bottle out of Anastasia. Meet you out at the car?"

"Sure." Chloe did her best to ignore Keith, who was only getting louder, until she got outside. She half expected to get jumped but reached her car without seeing another soul. That didn't mean there wasn't still trouble. That came when she saw her car. Someone had keyed it. Worse, in addition to random scratches, someone had written 'murderer' along the side and on the hood.

"Dammit!" she screamed, kicking the tire. It didn't help so

she did it again, and again, until Lexi came out.

Seeing Chloe's violent reaction to the destruction, Lexi ran over. "Chloe? What's wr—" She cut herself off and gasped. "Oh, my gods. I'm going to kill Keith!"

Chloe stopped kicking her tire and shook her head. "It probably was him, but he was hardly the only person pissed that I wasn't in jail," she said as she pulled out her phone.

"Who are you calling?"

"Wesley. Could be the bar has cameras and he can find out for sure," she answered as she called.

"Do you realize what time it is, Chloe?" came Wesley's groggy voice.

"You're asleep at ten?"

"I was, since I was up at five. What do you want?"

He sounded so irritated she almost told him it was nothing, but she wanted these attacks to stop. "Someone keyed my car."

Lexi leaned in and half-shouted, "They didn't just key it, they wrote murderer on it!"

That woke Wesley up, his voice more coherent when he asked, "Where was it parked?"

"Outside On the House. And that guy Keith is inside. He started calling me a murdering bitch, so we decided to leave," Chloe said. "I figure it was probably him, but…"

"Yeah, I know. You've made some enemies," Wesley finished. "I think they've got cameras outside the building, since we do occasionally have drunken issues, so I'll pull the footage and see if it caught the one who did it."

"Thanks. Do I need to stay here? Because I want to put some distance between me and Keith."

"No, you can go. Are you still at Diego's?"

"I'm staying with Lexi tonight."

"Okay. I'll let you know. Try to stay out of trouble."

"Trust me, it's my number one priority," she said dryly and disconnected. "We can go," she told Lexi as she unlocked the car and got inside.

"I guess it's a good thing Ana was being nice," Lexi said, cradling the tequila in her lap after getting in.

"Oh yeah," Chloe said as she started the car and headed for Lexi's. If she had her way, she was going to be in desperate need of that hangover remedy in the morning.

Chapter 32

The remedy from the alchemist that Lexi gave Chloe worked wonders. A moment after she drank the small vial, all traces of the hangover were gone. No wonder Lexi hadn't been worried when they'd drank a whole bottle of tequila between the two of them.

She got a call saying her mattress was on the way, so she told Lexi good bye and drove out to her house to meet the delivery men, except it turned out to be one man. He carried the mattress in like it weighed nothing, and refused a tip when Chloe tried to give him one. It had only taken him two minutes, he'd said, so why should he accept extra money for that?

It had just occurred to her that she had no sheets to go on the bed when Wesley called.

"Hey, Wesley. What's up?"

"Hi, Chloe. I was wondering if you could come over to my place. It's my day off, technically, and I figured I could make good on my favor."

For a minute she was clueless. "What favor?"

"Shifting for you?"

Her mood improved. "Seriously?"

The excitement in her voice made him chuckle. "Yes,

seriously."

"Absolutely! Text me how to get to your house and I'm so there." Sheets could wait. She was actually going to see a shifter change into an animal! It might not make up for everything that had happened to her, but it couldn't hurt.

"I will. See you in a few."

Chloe grinned as she locked up and got in her car. When the text arrived, she looked the directions over and saw he wasn't too far from the oak. She felt a little spurt of apprehension, but it didn't curb her enthusiasm.

Like Diego's house, Wesley lived in a cabin style house, though the sheriff's didn't look quite so new. It was almost as large, though. Wesley hadn't bothered with the flowers, and Chloe could see the glimmer of sun reflecting on something through the trees in the back. Water, maybe.

She got out of the car, grimacing at the sight of 'murderer' on the side of it. Deliberately, she turned her back on it, walked up the stairs, and knocked.

Wesley answered, and though there was a faint smile on his lips, he didn't seem nearly as excited as she did. Instead of his uniform he was wearing a pair of black sweatpants and a tee-shirt, and it struck her that it was the first time she'd seen him out of his uniform. He looked good in sheriff garb, but he made the simple clothing look good, too. Really good.

"Hey. Come on in," he told her, opening the door wide.

"You're going to shift inside?" she asked with surprise as she stepped inside.

"No, but I wanted to talk to you about something before we got to that," he told her, shutting the door. "Do you want some coffee?"

She was concerned about this talk, but she was still able to crack a smile. "Depends. Did you make it?" she teased.

"Sorry, but yes."

"Then I'll pass, though I'll take a Coke if you've got it." He did, grabbing one from the fridge. He was being entirely too accommodating, though, which worried her. "What do you want to talk to me about?"

He stuck his hands in his pockets. "I reviewed the security footage last night."

Chloe went on alert. "Did you see who it was?"

"I did. It was Keith, just like you thought. He confessed, since I had him on video." He hesitated then added, "I asked him about your house, and he denied that, but he was entirely too smug for me to believe that. I don't have any proof, though."

She cursed and clenched her fists, trying to prevent herself from kicking Wesley's furniture. It wasn't hers, and it was heavy, with lots of wood, so breaking a toe wasn't entirely out of the question if she hadn't restrained herself. "I knew it was him, I did, but..." She shook her head. "This is going a little far. The car? Okay, maybe. If he thinks I'm actually guilty but running around free, I can get the car. But my house? Granny's things? I just don't get it."

"I know," he said quietly. "Do you want to press charges? If you do, I'll have him in a cell by the end of the day," he promised.

Her first instinct was to say yes, hell yes, but she made herself stop and consider. "Has Uma been to my house yet?"

He shook his head. "Not yet. She'd actually left the island right after checking the evidence from Emma's house." His lips twisted into a grimace. "It's hard for her to deal with things connected to violent crimes, and she needed a break."

"Oh." She could understand needing a break after absorbing murder energies, though she was disappointed, too. There was no proof that Keith had been the one in her house. She blew out a breath and shook her head. "No," she finally decided. "Not for the car. I don't need more enemies in Salus, or to make the enemies I've already made hate me even worse. If you can get proof on my house? Then I'll press charges."

"That's a pretty logical decision. Very rational. Not many people would have thought it through like that."

Chloe smiled tightly. "I try to be rational. I can't say I always manage it, but I try." Her eyes narrowed. "This is why you're shifting for me, isn't it? Because I don't want your pity."

Wesley scowled. "I don't pity you, Chloe. Why the hell would I? I'm doing this because I promised I would." There was a long hesitation before he admitted, in a lower voice she couldn't really hear, "And because I hoped it would cheer you up."

"What?" she asked, not sure she heard right.

"Look, do you want to do this or not?" he asked in a gruff voice.

Deciding to choose her battles, she nodded. "I do. But before we get to that..." She trailed off, rethinking her decision to tell him about her latest theory.

He gave a long-suffering sigh. "Yes?"

Chloe stared up into his impatient gray eyes for several long moments. "Did you know that Jeremy apparently dated my mom?"

That clearly hadn't been what he'd expecting because all traces of impatience disappeared as he blinked at her. "What?"

"That's what I said, too," she said with a weak smile. "I was asking Lexi about him, since you said he and my grandmother didn't get along. I was wondering why they didn't get along, you know? Granny...she got along with everyone. All Lexi could think of was that he, and I quote, dated Lydia's daughter. Since, as far as I know, Granny only had one daughter, that means he dated my mom. And I...found a picture in Granny's house. It was Jeremy with his arm around my mom. They both looked happy."

Wesley frowned and shook his head. "I didn't know. They must have been discreet about it." He mulled over this new fact for a minute. "Why tell me, though?"

Again, she hesitated. "Why would my grandmother and Jeremy not get along just because he dated my mom? I mean, it doesn't sound like he was a bad guy, so why would Granny care? Especially with it being so long ago?"

Slowly he shook his head. "I don't know, but it sounds like you have a theory?"

"I do...Wes, is it possible that Jeremy was my dad? That he ditched my mom when she got pregnant, and that's why Granny hated him?" she whispered.

His eyes widened. "Shit. That's what you've been thinking?"

She nodded once, feeling way more vulnerable than she liked, but she had to tell someone about her theory, and Wesley was in a unique position to be able to help her find out if it was true.

He ran his hand through his hair. "I don't know. Obviously, I don't know, since I didn't know he'd dated your mother. But I can see your way of thinking," he admitted. Then he stopped and his eyes flickered yellow. "Chloe, you can't tell anyone else about this theory," he said seriously.

"What? Why not? I mean, I wasn't going to shout it from the rooftops, especially since I'm not sure it's true, but…" She trailed off and shrugged.

"But if people knew, it would make you an even more likely suspect for his murder," Wesley said bluntly.

"What?" she cried before she stopped to think about what he'd said.

"Think about it. If, *if* he was your dad and abandoned you and your mom when you were a baby, that just gives you even more of a motive to kill him. People will say you came back to confront him, he denied you were his, so you killed him. Or that he insulted your mom and you killed him. Or—"

"I get the picture," Chloe interrupted wearily. She'd gotten it just as he started talking. And he wasn't wrong. It would give people like Keith another reason to call for her arrest. "They'd even say that's why I killed Emma. Since Emma was Granny's best friend, surely she would have known, and she was going to rat me out to you," she said bitterly.

"Yes," Wesley agreed in a stiff tone. "So, you can't tell anyone about this, Chloe. I mean it. I'll look into it, and if need be, we'll do a DNA test, see if you two are related, but for now, this stays between us."

She nodded. "Okay."

"Good. Now, you want to do this? See me shift?"

She drew in a deep breath but nodded. She did, and it might take her mind off everything else, at least for a little while. "I do."

"Then come on," he said, not sounding happy, but he led the

way through his house—which was pretty spartan—and out into the back yard.

Chapter 33

C hloe stepped out onto Wesley's back deck and gasped. She'd wondered at his choice of living so far from town when he was the sheriff, but this view answered that question.

The deck was nice enough on its own. Large, with a swing, chairs set around a table with a fire pit built into it, and a recessed hot tub. But it was what was beyond the deck that had her staring.

Grass stretched from the deck to the small lake, the trees parting just enough to allow for this small clearing. A hammock hung between two trees off to the side, and across from it, near the lake, was a bench. But it was the lake and the trees beyond that gave the yard its real beauty. Waves gently lapped against the bank while sunlight played on the surface of the water. A small, simple dock extended out into the lake, an Adirondack chair set at the end of it. None of it was urban, so it was wholly alien to her, but it was serene and calmed some of the turmoil that had taken up residence in her belly.

Wesley didn't notice her preoccupation right away, so was off the deck and grabbing the bottom of his shirt to pull it off when he turned. Seeing her standing there staring had him dropping his hands. "Chloe? You okay?"

"This is gorgeous, Wesley," she murmured. "I envy you this."

His head cocked and he turned back, surveying the yard. After a moment he nodded. "It is nice. Honestly, I've lived here for so long I don't notice it that often," he admitted.

"You'd have to live here for a long, long time to take this for granted."

He grinned. "Like, say, a century?"

She hadn't realized he was so old, and her eyes widened, but she nodded. "Yeah, that would do it, I guess." She followed him off the deck. "So how do you want to do this?"

"Carefully," he said dryly. "I can shift with clothes on, but I get so big it'll literally rip them to pieces. Which means I could only shift once and you'd have to leave before I shifted back, assuming you're the shy sort. But you'd only get one shot at trying to keep me from shifting that way."

"I'm not all that shy," Chloe said with a faint smile. "I think I can handle seeing you in your birthday suit without going mad with lust or blushing so hard I faint."

Wesley slowly smiled, the expression so confident and sexy that she began to doubt the first part of her statement. "You sure about that? But, shy or not, you are dating someone. I didn't want to step on toes," he told her as he pulled off his shirt, which made her doubt deepen. The man was seriously built. Fit, muscular, and seriously strong.

"I...It's not like we're doing anything wrong. This is me practicing magic, which Diego supports me doing." Though they hadn't exactly talked about her practicing with a naked man. But this was Zane's suggestion, and it was a good one. If she got attacked by a shifter—and she wouldn't be surprised if that happened—then being able to keep them from turning into an animal with fangs and claws might just save her life. "So don't worry about it."

"Okay." Still, he kept that wicked smile on his lips as he pushed the sweatpants down and kicked them off, standing nude and unashamed. Not that he had any reason to be ashamed. Not by any stretch of the imagination. Clichéd it may be, but she could only think he was built like a freaking god. It was difficult but she kept her gaze above the waist, at least after her first look, and she bit her lip. "So…how do you want to do this?"

"Don't do anything the first time I shift. I imagine it'll be easier for you to do anything with the magic once you know what it feels like."

"Makes sense. I'm curious about what it looks like to see someone shift anyway. And to see you as a bear. I haven't seen a shifter in animal form yet."

"You haven't? I figured you would have by now." He frowned thoughtfully. "Actually, you probably have, if you've seen animals around, you just didn't realize it was a person."

She thought for a moment before she shrugged. "I don't know. Maybe? The only animals I remember seeing are crows though. They've been following me." And she looked around now, searching for some sign of her little black spy. She didn't find one, but that didn't mean it wasn't there.

"Might be, though I can't think of any crow shifters on Salus offhand. Anyway. You ready?"

Chloe nodded. "I am. Go for it."

He nodded and she felt the magic build rapidly, that feel of fur, and then he began to change. Dark brown fur spread across a body that grew taller and larger. When he was more bear than man he fell forward onto all fours, the last of the magic running through him. It had taken about fifteen seconds, and now Chloe stood only feet from a full-grown grizzly bear.

"Holy shit," she said, sitting down abruptly in the grass. "Holy shit," she repeated. "I've seen magic, but that was…holy shit!"

Wesley reared up on his back two legs and she saw he was several feet taller in this form than his human one, and even more intimidating. But then he plopped down on his backside, his huge front paws resting on his legs, and she let out a delighted laugh. The big bad grizzly looked freaking adorable.

Chloe scrambled to her feet and rushed over to him. "Oh my god! This is so awesome! I mean, I knew you were a bear, but seeing is definitely believing. Can I touch you?" Touching him when he was a man was definitely off limits, but like this? How could she resist?

She was close enough he was able to lean over, bumping her hand with his massive head. She took that as the consent it was meant to be and ran her fingers through the fur. It wasn't as soft as she'd expected but felt kind of rough. It wasn't unpleasant, just different. It actually felt just like his magic did. "This is so cool," she murmured as she walked around him. Once she'd come full circle, she threw her arms around his neck in a tight hug and laughed. "Thank you, Yogi. This is exactly what I needed."

He made a grumbling noise at her use of the nickname, but she just grinned, completely unrepentant. "Sorry, but you're a bear right now. Yogi it is. I'll call you Wesley again once you shift back. Probably" She leaned her full weight against him and he didn't even wobble. She sighed. "I guess I should stop playing around though, huh?" He rumbled again and she drew away from him, moving back a few feet. "Okay, let's just stick with me trying to stop you from shifting *into* the bear. Just to be safe."

He nodded and transformed back, getting to his feet. "Probably a smart idea. Just tell me when you're ready."

Chloe took several deep breaths then nodded, too focused on the magic to be embarrassed at the sight of him nude. "I'm ready."

He nodded and gave her a moment to prepare. When he started to shift, she didn't just watch, just feel the way his magic worked, but reached out toward the glow in her mind. She didn't want to hurt him, so rather than trying to absorb the magic she worked on dispelling it as gently as she could. When he didn't shift as quickly as before she felt relieved that she was getting the hang of this. She put more of her own power into stopping his and a moment later the magic cut off, leaving him standing there, still a man.

She beamed until he stretched a little and made a face. "Are you okay? I didn't hurt you, did I? I know Diego said it could be uncomfortable, but I tried to be as gentle as I could."

"Uncomfortable is a good word for it," Wesley agreed, "but I think that's more because I've never had anyone stop me from shifting. It was weird."

Still, she was concerned. "We don't have to keep going if it felt too weird."

He shook his head. "No, it's okay. Learning to control your power is important. We can go again."

She studied his face but read his sincerity. "Okay." He tried to shift twice more for her before she switched from dispelling to absorbing. She didn't know if it was strictly necessary, but the practice was good, and she was curious how his magic would make her feel. On that attempt she saw fur actually starting to sprout across his body before she got hold of the flow of magic. As she began to draw his magic into her, she saw the fur recede and the bulk he'd begun to gain disappear until he was fully a man again.

His magic felt good. So much better than the spell she'd absorbed from Jeremy's body, and even better than the small bit of Zane's magic she'd taken. It was hard to stop once she'd gotten her first taste of him, and it took a supreme act of willpower for her to cut it off. Stopping like that left her feeling drained rather than invigorated, and she sank down to the grass, breathing a little heavier than normal.

Worried, Wesley closed the distance between them and crouched down beside her. "Hey, what's wrong? You okay?"

Chloe waved a hand dismissively, too busy recovering to drool over his close-enough-to-touch body. "I'm okay. Just give me a minute."

He didn't look convinced but nodded and retrieved his pants, pulling them on. "Then what was that?"

"I tried to absorb your magic to stop you from shifting."

"Like what you did in the morgue?"

"Yeah, basically. The how is the same for both, but the results...varied."

"What do you mean?"

"In the morgue, I got overloaded, and the power...It was like sticking my finger in a socket. You get a jolt but it's not really fun. Your power? It was more mellow, but it was...tasty, for lack of a better word. Harder to stop taking it. A lot harder."

Though worry still showed in his eyes, Wesley grinned at her. "I'm tasty, huh?"

Yes, and not just his power either, but Chloe wasn't going to dive down that rabbit hole. She gave him the stink eye. "Your power is, anyway."

"Would it help if you ate something?"

"Maybe. I don't know. This is a first for me," she admitted.

"Then why don't I order some pizza and you can stay until you feel better?"

It was tempting, but she didn't want to complicate things between them anymore than they already were. "Thanks, but I should go." She slowly started to get up and Wesley offered her a hand, helping her to her feet.

"Okay. Then I'll go ahead and have a talk with Keith, warn him off messing with you."

"Isn't it your day off?"

He shrugged. "Yeah, but think of it this way. The less he messes with you, the less work I have to do."

Chloe smiled and nodded. "Makes sense. And thank you. For checking into it, for shifting, all of it."

"Not a problem."

Her steps were sluggish as she walked to her car, but mentally she was happy. She'd managed to dispel elemental, witch, and shifter magic. She was actually starting to figure this aether thing out.

Chapter 34

Chloe had just left Wesley's house and started back to Salus when Diego called.

"Hello?"

"Chloe. I just heard about your car. Are you all right?"

She smiled at the concern. "I'm fine. He didn't touch me, just my car. It looks...well, horrible, to be honest, but it's still drivable."

"He? You know who did it?"

"Yeah. Wesley checked the camera footage from the bar and verified it was Keith."

He cursed softly in Spanish. "Has he been arrested?"

"No. Wesley asked if I wanted to press charges, but I don't see a point. But if it comes out he trashed my house? Then you better believe I'll file charges so fast his head will spin."

"He should be in jail. Next time he might not settle for destruction of property."

"I don't think it'll come to that, and Wesley said he was going to warn him off, too, which should help."

Diego sighed. "At least you'll be staying with me and not alone."

She cringed. "About that..."

His voice went wary. "Yes? What about it?"

She pulled into her driveway and stopped, not wanting to have this conversation while driving. "I'm not sure it's such a good idea, me staying with you. Don't get me wrong, I like you, a lot, and I do want that second date, but this is too close to living with you and we haven't even known each other for two weeks yet."

He didn't answer for a long moment. "That's a very good point, and I confess, I hadn't even considered how much it resembled living together, even though we're not sleeping together."

"I know, and it might be different if we were sleeping together, but this is just still too new. And even if it wasn't...Dating is one thing, but I don't know that I should be trying for anything serious while dealing with everything else. It's just too much."

He sighed. "I understand. And I'm happy you do still want to continue dating. But where are you going to stay?"

"I ordered a bed when I was out shopping with Lexi yesterday. It was delivered a few hours ago." She smiled as he started protesting and broke in. "I told you I don't think he'll escalate, and I'll be sure to sleep with my pistol beside the bed. And if I hear anything or feel uncomfortable, I'll call you and the sheriff right away," she promised.

His voice held amusement now. "It sounds like you thought of everything. I'll hold you to that. Though you can call even if you just want company."

"Actually, company sounds good. Why don't you come over, hang out for a while? I'll order a pizza and we can...well, we can always watch a movie on my laptop."

He laughed. "That sounds great."

"What sort of pizza do you like?"

"I'm a fan of anything but pineapple and anchovies, so order what you like. I'll be over in a few."

"Great. See you then."

One of the numbers she'd been sure to get, given the lack of ability to search the internet for numbers, was the pizza place, so after she hung up with Diego, she gave them a call and ordered the food. She almost started driving up to the house when she remembered that she had friends who would worry, so she texted Lexi and Zane to let them know she was back at Granny's. That done, she continued down the drive. Before she got out of the car she looked around but didn't see anything out of place. No graffiti or obvious damage, no one lurking around waiting to attack. Just her grandmother's house.

Chloe got out and started for the door before she spotted the crow sitting on the windowsill. Her eyes narrowed. "What's the deal, huh? You guys don't seem to be bothering anyone else, just me. Or is it just one of you? Are you a shifter?"

The crow flapped its wings and cawed at her before it flew away.

"Stupid crows," she muttered as she went inside. The house seemed bare without all the things inside, but she tried to ignore that, and the hole that still remained in the wall. It was only then she remembered that she hadn't gotten any sheets for the bed. She'd have to make sure she went into town after Diego left to get some, because the idea of sleeping on a naked mattress didn't appeal to her. Luckily, she'd found a chest of blankets in the storage room, so she wouldn't freeze either way. For now, she grabbed a few out and took them downstairs. She spread one out in the middle of the living room floor and set the others nearby to use as makeshift pillows. The laptop was pulled out of the bag and set at the end of the blanket. She couldn't resist a smile. It wasn't fancy, but it would hopefully be cozy.

There was a knock on the door and she opened it to Diego. "Hey," she said with a smile. "You beat the pizza, but I've got a little picnic all set up," she said with a motion toward the blanket.

He stepped inside and laughed at her setup. "It's perfect," he said, kissing her cheek. "A picnic without ants or November chill."

"Mmhmm. If we end up feeling really adventurous later, we can start a fire and pretend to roast marshmallows in the fireplace."

"I think this may be the best date I've ever had already."

Chloe grinned. "This is a date, hmm?"

"Well, we are alone, having dinner, and spending time together," he pointed out with a smile. "I think that counts as a date."

"True." She heard a car pull up. "That should be the pizza. Why don't you take your shoes off and get comfortable?" she asked as she moved to the door.

He smiled and sat down on the blanket to do just that when she opened the door. The pizza was there, but the unfamiliar face she'd expected wasn't. Instead, it was Zane holding several pizza boxes and a couple bags, standing next to a happy looking Lexi.

"Surprise!"

"Lexi? Zane? What are you two doing here?"

"Um…" was Zane's answer, and he looked at Lexi with a shrug.

The brunette grinned. "I knew you were bummed about your car, and thought you'd be here alone, so I decided we'd get some pizza and come keep you company. Except I saw Diego's SUV so you're not alone, are you?"

"No, she's not," Diego called, which made Lexi laugh. "But I don't mind the company if Chloe doesn't."

Chloe looked back at him. "You sure?" He'd just been labeling this a date, after all.

He smiled. "I'm sure. I like Lexi and Zane."

"All right, you heard him. Come on in, make yourselves comfortable. Hope you don't mind sitting on the floor."

"Not at all," Lexi said as she swept inside with all the grace of a queen.

Zane smiled apologetically and followed after her.

Diego was already unfolding another blanket and spreading it out beside the first so there was plenty of room for all of them. Chloe gave him a bright smile and sank down onto the blanket. "Did you guys get an extra pizza? I only ordered enough for two people."

"Of course. One pizza wasn't going to cut it. I even brought over something extra special for you," Lexi said with a smile as she stretched out on the blanket.

Curious, Chloe asked, "Oh?"

"There's a coffeepot and some coffee in the car," Lexi said with a pleased grin.

"Oh god, I love you," Chloe said, half-lunging across the blanket to tackle Lexi in a hug.

"I see I went wrong with pasta. I should have just made you coffee," Diego joked as he sat down.

"I love them both, but I can't function without coffee," Chloe said as she sat back up and reached for one of the pizza boxes, pulling out a slice. She took a bite and focused on Zane. "You're being pretty quiet today. I think all you've said so far was um."

Zane flushed and awkwardly joined them on the blanket. "Sorry. Just…have my mind on things. That's all. I am happy to be here though, and sorry about your car."

"It's okay. Wesley's going to have a talk with Keith and hopefully that'll be the end of it. But what sort of things are on your mind, hmm?"

"Oh yeah, I'd forgotten that you left with Cole," Lexi chimed in with a mischievous grin. "How'd that go?"

From the darkening blush on his face, Chloe was betting it had gone very, very well, but just smiled.

"It was good. I'm, uh, going to see him again tomorrow night," Zane muttered. "But don't think I don't know what you two did."

Chloe schooled her expression into one of innocence. "What we did? We didn't do anything. Do you remember doing anything, Lex?"

Lexi made a show of thinking it over before she shook her head. "No, can't say I do. We just went to the bar, danced a little, had some drinks, and left."

"Uh huh," Zane said, not fooled. "Thank you."

Chloe smiled. "You're welcome. But he better be good to you, or I'm going to kick his ass." Not that she'd ever been in a fight in her life, but hurting Zane was like kicking a very tall puppy dog, so she'd damn well try.

Diego watched it all with a curious look, but said nothing, just grabbed a breadstick.

"So, anything exciting happen today?" Lexi asked curiously as she grabbed food for herself.

Zane shook his head and Diego said, "Nothing for me. It's been quiet, as Saturdays should be."

"I saw my first shifter shift today," Chloe said, giving a sidelong look to Diego. "Was able to stop him from shifting, too, so yay."

Unsurprisingly, Diego frowned, though she had to give him credit for attempting to hide it, and for keeping his voice casual. "Wesley?"

Lexi arched a brow and glanced between Chloe and Diego but stayed quiet.

"Yeah. Guess he thought it would distract me after he told me that it had been Keith who keyed my car."

"Ah." He was quiet for a moment before he smiled. "And did it distract you?"

Relieved that he wasn't going to act the jealous boyfriend, Chloe grinned. "Seeing a man turn into a big ass furry bear? Yeah, it was kind of distracting. And I like the fact that I'm getting my powers under control. Seems like one of the few things that *is* under my control lately."

He leaned over and kissed her cheek. "Things will settle down soon enough."

Zane nodded. "He's right. It'll come out that you didn't kill anyone—for sure, I mean—and people will go back to their lives. But I'm glad you took my advice and practiced with shifter magic."

"And if they don't play nice, I'll punch them all in the nose for you," Lexi promised solemnly. "Or send a couple ghosts to haunt them until they're crazy."

Chloe laughed. "I love you guys. You're the best friends I've ever had."

Lexi stuck her nose in the air. "Of course we are." She held the snooty pose for only a few seconds before she broke down laughing. "Seriously though, we've got you."

"I know. And thank you."

"Yeah, yeah. Enough sappy stuff. Let's pig out!"

Laughing, Chloe did just that.

Chapter 35

Everyone stayed for several hours before leaving, with Diego being the last to go. By that point Chloe was too tired to even consider going shopping for sheets, and just burrowed under blankets while promising herself she'd go into town tomorrow.

The next morning, after making good use of Lexi's gift of a coffeepot, she went outside, prepared to get all her errands done all at once, but stopped a few feet out the door. Cole was sitting on a toolbox beside her car, meticulously applying what looked like painter's tape to the door.

"Cole? What are you doing here?" she asked as she slowly approached. He didn't respond at first and she noticed the wire going from his ear to his pocket, so she continued toward him until she could tap his shoulder.

He jumped a little and yanked the earbud from his ear, scowling at her. "Don't sneak up on me," he said in his usual surly voice.

"Wasn't trying to," Chloe said, retreating a step and holding up her hands in surrender. "I talked to you, but with the earbuds in…" She shrugged. "What are you doing?"

"Fixing the damage to your car," he said, shoulders hunching defensively, which made it seem like he was displeased to have been caught doing something nice.

"Seriously? You can do that here? I thought I'd have to take it to a paint shop or something," she said, moving behind him so she could better see what he was doing. So far, she just saw the tape, which looked like he was using to outline the gouges in the paint.

"Yeah. I mean, it's not going to be perfect, but it won't be so fucking noticeable, you know?"

"Hey, no, I'm totally fine with just less noticeable," Chloe said quickly. "And thank you. I knew I'd need to get it fixed but haven't really had the time to do more than put it on my to do list."

Cole jerked a shoulder. "Yeah, well, I'm already here, so you can check it off your list," he muttered. "Were you about to go somewhere?" he asked with a nod toward her messenger bag.

"Into town. Got a new bed to replace the one that got destroyed, but don't have sheets. Have a few other errands to run, too. It's all right though, it can wait."

He leaned to the side and fished a set of keys out of his pocket, offering them to her. "Take my truck. I'll be here for a while. If you're not back when I'm ready to go, I can grab a ride back to the shop."

She took the keys. "You sure? I don't want to put you out," she said, though she was inwardly suspicious. Cole was doing something nice. It was just too weird.

"I said it, didn't I? Take the damn truck."

A grin split her mouth. "You had fun the other night, didn't you?"

His hand jerked and he pulled off way more tape than he'd intended. He glared at her. "I don't know what you're talking about. Now would you just go so I can get back to work?"

"Sure thing. And thanks, Cole. I really appreciate you making it so I don't have to drive around with 'murderer' on the side of my car."

"Yeah, yeah," he grumbled. "Now go."

She went, grinning.

Other than getting sheets, there wasn't much Chloe really had to do in town, but she refused to cower in her house and let Keith think he'd won, so she made herself as visible as possible. She got the sheets then went and grabbed a couple more outfits and some food to replace what had been ruined.

When lunchtime came, she went to the diner, and made a point to chat up Lexi, the other waitress who was working, and any of the customers who happened to sit next to her. A few were wary of talking to someone with her current reputation, but by the end of the conversations she thought she'd won over at least a few of them. Or at least had them rethinking her apparent guilt.

After lunch she went to Zane's and took her time browsing the shelves and selecting a few more books for her slowly growing collection. It took a while, considering she kept chatting with him and the other customers, but when a grumpy old man smiled at her, she felt victorious.

Dinner wasn't eaten at Joel's, but at Banquet. She'd enjoyed the food and knew the restaurant attracted a different sort of clientele than the diner. To her delight, Francois came to her table once more.

"I was hoping I'd see you back in my restaurant."

Chloe grinned at him. "How could I resist? I told you this was the best food I'd ever eaten. I like the diner, don't get me wrong, but eating here? Amazing."

Francois chuckled. "Now you're just trying to flatter me so I'll send more chocolate cake your way."

Her eyes widened hopefully. "That's a possibility? I ate that cake for breakfast and didn't feel the least bit guilty."

"I have to say, that's a first for me," he admitted, delight sparkling in his eyes. "But I'm glad you enjoyed it." He sobered. "I just wanted to say that I know you had nothing to do with the murders. I know what some people are saying, but it's obvious those people have never even met you."

"No, they haven't," she agreed quietly. "And I appreciate the support. I know it's just a couple people being extremely loud, but sometimes it feels like there's a lot more people who are against me than are with me."

He rested a hand lightly on her shoulder, squeezing reassuringly. "I think you've got more support than you realize, though part of that is because of the reputation your grandmother had. Lydia was a wonderful woman. For anyone to think her granddaughter could murder anyone, much less Lydia's best friend, is ridiculous."

She gave him a small smile. "I couldn't agree more. And thank you, again."

"You're very welcome, chérie," he said, giving her a half bow. "Now I'll leave you to enjoy your dinner."

She smiled at him as he left, but her appetite had diminished. When her waiter came around next, she signaled for the check, but when it was brought to her, it came with a fat slice of chocolate cake in a to-go box, along with a note that said 'Try to save some for breakfast'. She burst out laughing, which drew a few disapproving looks from a few people near her, but she didn't care. With a single, simple gesture Francois had repaired her mood.

Chloe sang along with the radio the entire way home and was grinning as she parked and got out, holding her cake protectively against her chest. She continued the last song that had been playing, singing at the top of her lungs and not caring who heard her. Probably no one, since her closest neighbor was almost a mile away.

She dug her phone out and used the flashlight function to look at the side of her car. It may not be perfect, but Cole had done a damn good job getting rid of the damage. She couldn't tell it had read 'murderer' only that morning. That further improved her mood.

She was nearly to her door when she heard the all too familiar cawing. Turning abruptly, she yelled, "What? What do—" She cut off as she got a cold chill she'd only felt once before—at the school gym, when she thought she was feeling vampire magic. The memory of Jeremy's vampire-torn throat flashed in her mind. Her cake was forgotten as she fumbled in her bag for her gun, but she had just managed to pull it out when she got hit by what felt like a truck.

The cake and gun both went flying somewhere into the trees as Chloe's back hit the ground hard, knocking the breath out of her. As she struggled to suck in air, she fought to see who or what had slammed into her. In the darkness all she could tell was that it was a small person, shorter than Chloe by several inches with a petite build.

Not one to give up, even though her back throbbed, Chloe lashed out with a fist, which wasn't just blocked, but caught by her assailant.

"You have been a pain in my ass since you got here," a woman hissed as she reared back and slapped Chloe. It hurt badly enough Chloe had to wonder if the woman had broken something. Whoever she was, she was strong as hell.

"Screw you," Chloe said through gritted teeth, jaw aching with every word, as she twisted and bucked, fighting to get the woman off her. It was sheer luck that had her elbow connecting with the woman's jaw, surprising her just enough for Chloe to shove the attacker off her and scramble to her feet. She wanted, desperately, to search for her gun, but knew that taking her eyes off the other woman would be a mistake.

The woman gracefully stood and stalked closer to Chloe, enough menace in her pose for Chloe to feel like prey, despite being the larger of the two. "You're not my type," the woman said, just as she passed a shaft of moonlight.

It was Kyra, the vampire councilor, but her eyes were solid black and her fangs were fully visible.

"What the hell are you doing this for? You're supposed to protect the town, not attack its residents!" Chloe snapped.

"Ah, but you're not a resident, are you, Chloe Chadwick?" Kyra hissed. "You've resisted becoming part of our little community, haven't you? But that's all right, because you're not going to be here for much longer." She lunged at Chloe, who

258

tried to fend her off, punching and kicking at the smaller woman, but the vampire had more experience in fighting. She didn't actually strike Chloe again—it seemed that she was toying with her—but neither was Chloe able to land more than a single blow, which turned out to be a bad thing.

Kyra snarled as Chloe managed to knee the smaller woman in the side, but it only pissed the councilor off. The next thing Chloe knew, was she was being held from behind with arms that felt like steel around her. "Now you've made me angry." She pressed her face against the side of Chloe's neck and whispered, "And hungry. I wasn't going to kill you, but now?" She struck, her fangs sinking painfully into Chloe's throat, making her scream, but no matter how hard Chloe fought, she couldn't escape Kyra's hold.

Mouthful after mouthful of Chloe's blood was drained from her and her struggles grew weaker. Her strength, her very life was being stolen while her head had begun to spin from the blood loss. Just when she felt on the verge of passing out, she heard a noise she couldn't quite place, not until the crow attacked Kyra.

Sharp claws dug into Kyra's scalp and pulled at her hair before the crow started to peck rapidly with its beak, aiming for the vampire's unprotected eyes. It may not have done much damage, but it did draw blood and had to have hurt. Kyra tore her mouth from Chloe's throat, ripping flesh open and sending more blood spilling down Chloe's body. She screamed in anger and swung her arm at the bird, hitting its delicate body and sending it spiraling away from her.

Even with Kyra distracted by the small attacker, Chloe didn't move. She could barely lift a hand, much less fight off an angry vampire. But as she stared at the crow while it tried to get to its feet, anger and desperation flipped a switch in her brain.

Kyra had to be the vampire who killed Jeremy, and most likely she'd been involved in Emma's death, too. And now she'd decided to kill Chloe? Rage took hold deep within her, and she noticed something was starting to light up her front yard. It wasn't until Kyra screamed in agony and stumbled back from

Chloe that she realized *she* was the thing lighting up her front yard. Somehow her skin was glowing, and Kyra didn't like it. It was hurting her a great deal more than Chloe's amateur punches had. And the vampire just kept screaming, her skin blistering as her legs gave out and she collapsed to the ground.

"Please!" Kyra shrieked as she curled around herself, protecting her face from the brightness that was Chloe. But only a few seconds after her frantic cry, she went limp.

Confused, Chloe stared at her, swaying on her feet for a moment before she went down to one knee. The glow began to fade and she dug out her phone, sparing the crow a glance. It was on its feet now, watching her. It hopped closer and she gave it a weak smile before trying to dial Wesley's number. As the phone rang, she fell forward, catching herself on her free hand, but her arm shook and wouldn't support her for long.

"Chloe? Don't tell me Keith did something else."

"Help," she gasped weakly. "Kyra…attacked. Drank…blood."

"What? Kyra? The councilor? Where are you?" he demanded, his voice switching abruptly from aggravated to worried.

"House. Yard. Help…The crow…"

"The crow? Never mind. I'll be there as soon as I can," he said, and she could hear the sound of him running, the jingle of his keys in his hand, the sound of a car unlocking.

"Can't…Sorry…" she murmured, before the phone slipped out of her fingers and she hit the dirt, unconscious, blood flowing from her neck.

Chapter 36

The sound of sirens helped Chloe stir, though everything felt fuzzy, and she couldn't remember at first why she was laying on the ground, or why she was hurting so bad. Nor should she figure out why her clothes and neck were wet.

Tires skid to a stop and Wesley leapt out of the car and ran toward her, his deputy close behind him.

"Check her," Wesley barked as he knelt beside Chloe. "Chloe? Hey, come on. Wake up for me, honey," he said, his voice gentler than it had been for Jack, but it was too worried to truly be soothing.

"Awake," she mumbled, though she couldn't manage to open her eyes. It was hard enough to get the single word out.

"Shit," he hissed and tugged his shirt out of his belt and yanked it open then off, ripping off buttons. He folded it quickly and pressed it firmly against her neck. She whimpered at the sharp sting it caused but he didn't relent. "I know. I know it hurts, but we've got to stop the bleeding." He looked over to Jack, who was cautiously checking Kyra over. "She alive?"

"Seems to be, but she's got burns over every exposed bit of skin," Jack called back. "If it wasn't so late, I'd say she'd gotten caught out in the sun. As it is...some sort of accelerant, maybe?"

261

"She going to live?"

"If she gets blood soon," Jack answered, though he didn't sound too certain.

An SUV pulled up and Diego had barely put it into park before he was jumping out and running over to Wesley and Chloe. "What happened?" he demanded as he brushed Chloe's hair back from her face.

"I'm not sure. She called, said Kyra attacked, but mentioned a crow, too. But that is definitely a vampire bite on her throat. She needs to go to the hospital," Wesley answered.

Diego glanced at the burned body nearby then back to Wesley. "I'll take her. You can handle Kyra."

"Call me as soon as you know something," Wesley said in a tone that suggested Diego not argue.

"I will." Diego looked down at Chloe. "I'm going to pick you up now, cariño. I'm sorry if it hurts," he murmured as he gathered her in his arms and carried her to the SUV, but she was so out of it she barely felt a thing. Wesley followed, opening the door so Diego could set her inside as gently as possible.

"I'd hurry," Wesley whispered. "She's lost a lot of blood."

"I will."

Diego made it to the hospital in record time and carried her inside. The nurse in reception looked surprised to see them but didn't sit there and stare either.

"What happened?"

"Vampire bite. Maybe more, but that's the worst of it, I think," he said, laying Chloe down on the gurney the nurse pulled over.

The nurse nodded and yelled down the hallway. "Deirdre! Vampire bite! Severe blood loss!"

A short woman with brown hair rushed out of a room and over to Chloe. "How long has it been since she was bitten?" Deirdre asked as she gently pulled the shirt away from the wound, grimacing at the sight.

"I'm not sure. She called the sheriff about ten minutes ago, so maybe a few more than that," Diego answered, reaching for Chloe's limp hand. She was in and out of consciousness so couldn't respond. The most she could manage was opening her eyes for a second or two at a time.

"Okay, let's get her back in a room. I'll heal the bite and see what we can do about the blood loss," Deirdre said briskly and started to wheel the gurney back and into a room. "What race is she?" she asked Diego.

"Elemental."

She got the table in place and focused on Chloe. "She's going to be fine, Councilor, so don't look so worried," she said absently as she held a hand over Chloe's throat. Beneath the blood, both fresh and congealing, the torn flesh started to knit back together. The process was slow at first, but the more that was repaired, the quicker the healing went, until the only sign Chloe had been bitten was the blood and stark white of her skin.

Diego stroked Chloe's hair while Deirdre worked, saying nothing so he didn't distract her. "Come on Chloe, wake up for me. Don't let her win," he whispered to her, and she gave him the tiniest of smiles.

"Councilor?" When he didn't respond immediately Deirdre said, "Diego!" He looked up and she continued. "I can either give her a transfusion or, if you're willing to lend me some power, I can replace some of the blood she lost. She'll still be anemic and a little weak for a few days, but it'll be bearable."

He took Deirdre's hand, ignoring the blood on his own, and nodded, pushing what power he could into the other witch while he watched Chloe's face.

After a minute Chloe's skin started to regain its normal color, and a minute after that her eyes fluttered open.

"That should be good enough. Though I sense some bruises I'm going to take care of real quick," Deirdre murmured as she released Diego's hand.

He nodded absently and moved around so Chloe could see him better. "Cariño, how do you feel?"

"I ache," she croaked. "Where am I?"

Deirdre smiled and stepped back. "You're in the hospital, I'm afraid, but we've gotten you pretty much patched up. In a few minutes you'll be fine."

Chloe started to sit up but was still too weak to manage it until Diego helped her. She frowned as she tried to recall why she would be in the hospital, then her eyes widen. "Kyra!"

Diego nodded. "I know. It's being handled. Just relax, okay?"

Chloe gripped the front of Diego's shirt and shook her head. "No, you don't understand. I need to talk to Wesley. I need to talk to Kyra."

The urgency in her voice got to him and he looked at Deirdre. "She won't be driving. Can I take her? This really is important."

Though tiny, not even five feet tall, Deirdre was no less formidable as she gave Diego an unhappy look. "Honestly, she should probably stay here for a while longer, but if you say it's that important, I'll agree. However," she said before he could move. "I want to see her back in here in two days to make sure she's recovering. And I want to hear sooner if she feels dizzy or passes out again."

"Yes, anything," Chloe mumbled. "Thank you, doctor."

Deirdre gave Chloe a gentle, maternal smile. "I'm not a doctor, but you're welcome. And Diego? You're using a wheelchair. No reason to carry her out," she told him sternly.

He did as she asked, pushing Chloe out to his SUV. It was still running, so it was an easy process to lift her from wheelchair to vehicle before he joined her.

"They probably took Kyra to the jail. Vampires can heal most things with blood, and Kyra's more powerful than most," Diego told her as he drove for the sheriff's office. "Did she really attack you?"

"Yes."

"What happened?"

Chloe shook her head. "I only want to go through this once."

Diego nodded and reached over to take her hand. "Of course. Save your strength."

She gave him a tired smile and closed her eyes for the remainder of the short drive.

When they arrived at the sheriff's office they saw Wesley's cruiser in the parking lot, which meant Diego had been right. He started to carry her inside, but she protested.

"I can walk," she muttered as she slowly got out of the car.

"Fine," he said, voice clipped with concern, "but I'm going to help you."

"Fine," she echoed quietly. He wrapped his arm around her and she leaned heavily on him as they made their way inside.

Wesley was standing in his undershirt by one of the cells. In it was Kyra, who lay on the cot, with Jack kneeling beside her, his wrist at her mouth. Most of the burns were gone, but she wasn't quite conscious yet.

The sheriff turned when the door opened, and relief bloomed on his face when he saw Chloe. "You're okay."

Chloe smiled faintly and nodded. "More or less. Though I'd love someone for forever if they got me a chair."

Diego led her closer to the cell while Wesley dragged the visitor's chair over, and they helped her into it. Even that short walk had sapped the last of her strength, so for a minute she just breathed and watched the vampires.

"How is she?" she asked with a frown.

"She'll survive. Hopefully she'll get enough blood in a minute or two to wake up," Wesley answered. "You said she attacked you?" She nodded. "Do you feel up to telling me what happened? If you don't, it's fine. I know you lost a lot of blood."

"No, it's fine," she answered, though her voice was still weak. "I'd just gotten home. A crow cawed at me on my way to the front door."

Wesley frowned. "The one you said has been spying on you?"

"Yeah, but I think it was trying to warn me." She shook her head slightly. "I *know* it was trying to warn me. I felt vampire magic, then she hit me. Hard. I lost my gun." Which she'd have to remember to retrieve when the sun was out. "She said I'd been a pain in her ass, and we fought. Sort of. She was a lot better at it."

"That's easily fixed," Wesley assured her.

"The sheriff's damn good at that sort of thing," Jack added, though his focus was still on Kyra.

"Thanks. I guess she got tired of playing with me, because she bit me." Her throat throbbed at the memory, but she ignored it.

"How'd she get burned?" Diego asked quietly.

Chloe frowned and took a minute, as much to try to sort it out in her head as to catch her breath. "I was getting weak, from the bite, when the crow went after her. She stopped drinking long enough to hit it." Her gaze slid from Kyra to Wesley. "Did you see it? Was it okay?"

"I didn't notice. I'm sorry," he answered apologetically.

She nodded. "When she went to bite me again..." She remembered the glow she'd been putting off, but she also remembered the mysterious stranger in her dream. Somehow, she thought it might be bad if it came out that she was a human glow stick. Especially since she had no idea how she'd done it, or what, exactly, *it* was. It probably wasn't a normal elemental power. She decided to give them the partial truth and hope they believed it. "This light came from...somewhere. It seemed to hurt her because she screamed and let me go. That's when I called you, Wesley."

Wesley nodded. "She'll be awake soon and we can ask her why she attacked you."

"I think she might have been the one to kill Jeremy."

"It does seem likely," Diego agreed.

"Jack, she's had enough. Get out of there before she wakes up," Wesley said, unlocking the cell.

Since the burns were almost entirely gone, Jack didn't hesitate to straighten and leave the cell, but he was looking a little paler than usual. "Boss, she needed a lot."

"Go eat. I think we can handle her," Wesley told him as he resecured the cell.

Jack nodded then rushed out of the office so fast he was a blur.

"Do you need anything, Chloe? I'm not sure coffee's a good choice, even if you liked mine, but I've got soda and water," Wesley offered.

"Water would be good. And do you have any...Damn that bitch!"

The outburst left Diego and Wesley both looking confused. "What's wrong?" Diego asked.

"Francois gave me chocolate cake. A big fat piece, too," she pouted.

Diego fought against a smile, but Wesley just grinned. "I don't have cake, but I've got some jerky and some chocolate candy?"

Though the chocolate beckoned, she said, "Jerky, please." Hopefully the protein would help with some of the weak feeling, otherwise she was going to be pissed at missing out on chocolate.

Wesley brought her the jerky and water, but she'd just opened the bottle when Kyra woke. It wasn't a slow return to consciousness, but abrupt. One second, she was out cold, the next she was awake and sitting up.

Chloe braced herself for the insults and anger she'd dealt with back at her house, but when Kyra saw her, her eyes went wide and she rushed to the bars, slim fingers wrapping around the metal. "I'm sorry, I'm so sorry," she said, her voice holding an accent it hadn't before. Even Diego and Wesley looked confused by her words.

"You nearly kill me and you're sorry?" Chloe asked slowly.

Kyra shook her head. "It wasn't me, I assure you. I have no desire to kill you. I didn't want to kill Jeremy either."

Wesley broke in. "You confess to killing Jeremy?"

"I do. He...overheard something he shouldn't have."

"And Emma?"

"Yes, that was me, too." Her gaze turned back to Chloe. "There's something you should know," she said hurriedly. "Your grandmother, she didn't die in a car accident. Neither did your mother."

Chloe felt like she'd been slapped again. "What?" she

267

whispered.

"I know, it's hard, but it's the truth. She was killed, to find out what she knew."

"Knew about what?" Diego demanded. "And who helped you, Kyra? You can't cast illusions, so we know there was someone working with you."

"Knew about the man...who..." Kyra trailed off and her eyes went wide with terror. "It was—" The next word was replaced with a scream that surpassed the one Chloe had heard earlier. The vampire clung to the bars as her body contorted in pain, gashes opening all over her body. Blood poured out of her as more and more of the cuts appeared, until the screaming stopped and what remained of Kyra's body collapsed to the floor. It had all happened in seconds.

Chloe whimpered and Diego tried to shield her from the sight, but she shook her head. "The power...from Jeremy's body...I just felt it," she whispered, rubbing her arms as she tried to ease the prickling feeling that danced along her skin. The lightheadedness wouldn't be going away, she knew, not with the blood loss helping it.

Diego grimaced at Wesley. "Her accomplice knew we were talking to her. That she nearly gave him away."

"I know," the sheriff answered grimly. "The only question is who is it?"

"Could it be your deputy? He was just here," Chloe pointed out.

Wesley shook his head. "He's a vampire. He couldn't do something like this."

"But she had his blood inside her," she insisted. She'd read enough books to know that had to be significant.

"Yes, but this is still beyond anything a vampire could do," Diego said, though he looked thoughtful.

"I think that, for now, we should keep most of what she said between the three of us," Wesley said. "Confessing to the killing, yes, we absolutely share that since it proves Chloe's innocent, but not the rest." His gaze softened and he asked Chloe, "Did you have any idea? About your mom or grandmother?"

"None," she whispered. "Though now I have to wonder if Granny knew about my mom. If that's why she never told me about Salus, about any of this."

"If she thought it was possible, it would make sense," Diego answered. "But you should get some rest. It's been a long night." He tried to smile, but it was thin. "I'm going to have to insist you come home with me. Just for tonight, given your condition."

"I'm too tired to argue," she agreed with a small smile. Nor did she protest when he scooped her up again.

"Wesley, will you inform the remaining councilors of Kyra's death?"

"Of course. You just take care of her."

"I will. As well as she'll let me," Diego said wryly.

Chloe rolled her eyes. "I'm not that difficult," she muttered.

"Yes, you are," both Diego and Wesley said together.

Diego was grinning as he deposited her back in his SUV and drove her to his house. When he got around to the passenger side to help her out, he hesitated.

"What's wrong?" Chloe asked.

Instead of speaking, he cupped her face, leaned in, and gave her a thorough, gentle kiss. It wasn't chaste, far from it, but he was so very careful with her, like he was worried she'd break if he kissed her too hard. When she was breathless from the kiss he drew back. "I've wanted to do that since the moment you opened your eyes and I knew you'd be okay," he admitted as he lifted her out of the vehicle and carried her inside. "Would you consider sleeping with me tonight? And I do just mean sleeping," he added before she could protest. "You came so close to...I just don't want to let you out of my sight just yet."

Chloe couldn't resist the fear in his voice and rested her head against his shoulder as he carried her inside. "Okay," she whispered.

Inside, he sat her on his bed, leaving long enough to get a bowl of water and washcloth. He carefully washed the blood off her neck and shoulder. When he'd cleaned off all he could, he got her another shirt and pair of sweatpants, leaving the room so she could change. The moment she called out that she was done, he was back and tucking them both into bed. When she fell asleep only a few minutes later, it was with his strong arms wrapped around her.

Chapter 37

D iego decided Chloe was to be spoiled the next morning. When she'd woken, she'd found that he'd already been into town and returned, with a thermos full of caramel coffee and a variety of goodies from the bakery. While he let her get up to go to the bathroom, he'd insisted on feeding her breakfast in bed. Since she'd never had breakfast in bed before, she just smiled and enjoyed it. It was probably good for her to relax in any case and regain her strength after the blood loss, though she had to admit she didn't feel as bad as she had expected.

Later, after she'd showered, they curled up on the couch to watch movies, though her mind wasn't really on the TV. "Who could have done that to her?" she asked half an hour in.

"I don't know," Diego admitted, pausing the movie. "A vampire seems most likely as far as controlling her goes—and it does appear that she wasn't in control of herself when she killed Jeremy or Emma, or when she attacked you. Some psychics have mental control gifts, though, as do some witches. And no vampire could have done to her what was done in the end. And it's not likely a psychic if they were the same to control her. But I can't think of any witches who have the power or ability to do what was done. I've never seen anything quite like that. A witch or some elementals who were in the room with her? Perhaps. But someone who wasn't even there in person?" He shook his head. "I honestly don't know."

Chloe sighed and leaned her head against his shoulder. "At least people will know now that I didn't kill anyone, though I feel sort of responsible for Kyra."

Diego frowned and straightened to look at her. "How in the hell do you feel responsible?" he asked, surprising her by cursing.

"It's stupid, I know," Chloe admitted. "But it just feels like if she'd done whatever she set out to do, if we hadn't questioned her, that she'd still be alive. And I know, I know. It's not on me, it's on whoever killed her. I guess I should say it feels like I was the reason she was killed."

"Perhaps you were, I can't really argue that, but you are not responsible," he said firmly.

They were both surprised by a knocking on the door.

"Wesley?" Chloe suggested.

"Maybe. It could be other council members, too. We are down one," Diego pointed out as he got up to answer the door, but it wasn't Wesley or the council. It was a tearful Lexi.

"Is she here? Tell me she's here," she pleaded.

"On the couch," Diego said understandingly, motioning her inside.

Lexi brushed past him and made a frantic sound when she saw the still pale Chloe. She ran over to the couch and jumped onto it beside Chloe, flinging her arms around the blonde. Chloe returned the hug, trying to sooth her friend. "I heard about Kyra," she said, voice muffled by Chloe's shoulder. "I went to your house, saw the blood on the ground, and freaked out. Tell me you're okay." She sat back and looked Chloe over from head to toe. "You're pale." Diego was on the receiving end of an accusing glare. "Why is she still pale?"

Diego held up his hands in an 'I'm innocent' gesture. "She looks a lot better than she did. It'll take her a day or two to recover from the blood loss, that's all."

"He's right. And I do feel better. Just a little tired, that's all,"

Chloe promised with a smile. "And hey, I've been cleared of murder, so that's a major plus."

Lexi sniffed. "Only idiots really thought you were guilty." She turned and flopped down onto the couch beside Chloe. There was enough room on the other side of Chloe for Diego, and he took it a moment later. "Do you really feel okay, though?"

"I do. Diego took me to the hospital and everything. I wouldn't be here if I was in any danger. I don't think anyone would've let me leave if I was."

"Deirdre may look tiny and small, but I don't think there's anyone on Salus who would argue with her," Diego confirmed with a smile.

Lexi nodded her agreement. "She's kind of terrifying, but in a good way." Her head tilted to rest on Chloe's shoulder. "But what now?"

"What do you mean?" Chloe asked.

"Well, you're no longer a murder suspect, which means you could leave if you wanted. Are you going to?"

A very good question. "I...don't know. I'm getting better with my powers, but I'm still not great with them. It's safer to work on that here," she said slowly, working through it all in her mind. "I also haven't really had time to think about it," she admitted.

"Oh yeah?" Lexi asked with a grin. "Someone been keeping you distracted?" she teased, shooting Diego a wink. To his credit, he only smiled fondly and gave Chloe his attention.

"Yeah, having a vampire try to rip my throat out was a little distracting," Chloe said dryly.

"No doubt." Lexi sighed and slumped back into the couch. "I just know you've been thinking of running this entire time, and that the whole murder thing was the big thing keeping you here. I guess...I'm just afraid you're going to bail the moment you're feeling better."

It was an understandable fear. Chloe had resisted the idea of moving here every single time it had been brought up. But she'd also made some connections here. After just a few weeks Lexi was closer to her than anyone else had been in years. Zane was both a good friend and a mentor, and she didn't want to lose him, either. Then there were Diego and Wesley.

She sighed and dropped her head back, but frowned almost instantly. "Do you hear that?"

"What?" Lexi asked, cocking her head to listen.

"I do. Sounds like something tapping," Diego said, nodding.

The sound got louder and more frequent before Lexi gasped. "It's your spy!" she said, pointing toward the window.

Frowning, Chloe looked over and blinked. "I don't think it's a spy, actually. It may have saved me last night. It sure as hell helped, anyway. But what's it doing?"

"I think it wants in," Diego mused as he got to his feet and walked to the window.

The crow stopped and watched him as he opened the window. The moment it was open enough, the crow darted in and flew directly for Chloe. She shrieked and ducked, throwing her arms over her head to protect her face, but the crow landed calmly on her knee and stood there, looking up at her.

Slowly Chloe lowered her arms and peered down at the crow. "Uh...hi?" She looked helplessly at Lexi, then Diego. "What's it doing?" The crow cawed and she turned her attention back to it. It nudged her arm gently with its beak. Hesitantly she stroked the tip of her finger down its back and its eyes closed in apparent pleasure.

"I think it likes you," Lexi said, amused.

"I think she's right. Is this the same crow that's been following you?" Diego asked thoughtfully.

"I don't know. I think so? I never really got close enough to get a good look." But Chloe paid better attention now and saw the crow was holding one wing a little awkwardly. "I think this is the same one from last night. Kyra hit it pretty hard, and this one looks like he's got a hurt wing." As soon as she said that she felt a surge of emotion that felt like agreement and her eyes widened. "Holy crap. I'm almost positive it's the same one. I just...felt...him agree that he was there last night." Because whatever that had been, the crow felt male.

Diego smiled. "Chloe? I think you've got yourself a familiar."

"What? A familiar? But I thought that was mutual on both sides? I wasn't looking for a familiar."

Lexi laughed. "I think he did the looking and you petting him was enough agreement for him."

"She's right," Diego said with a nod. "You should name him, see what he likes."

Chloe bit her lip and considered the crow. "Are they right?" she asked, staring into his eyes. "Are you my familiar now? Do you want to stay with me?" The crow responded with a caw and another mental wave of agreement before he did something that truly shocked her. He said her name. It was a little distorted, but it was clearly her name. She'd known crows and ravens could talk, but this was just astonishing.

"I think that's a yes," Lexi said, grinning.

"You were there, weren't you? At the Oak?" Chloe asked, recalling how the crow there had sounded odd.

"Yes," the crow said, bobbing his head.

"I thought your voice sounded familiar!"

"What are you talking about?" Lexi asked.

"I found that big oak, the one Zeus gave Salus, and he was there. I heard him cawing, but it sounded different. I just couldn't put my finger on what the difference was until now," she explained.

"Oh, that tree. That thing gives me the creeps," Lexi said, wrinkling her nose.

That amused Chloe. "The girl who sees ghosts is creeped out by a tree?"

Lexi shrugged. "It is what it is. But enough about that. What are you going to call him?"

Chloe considered for a moment. "Do either of you know Greek?"

Diego gave her a surprised look. "Greek? Why?"

She shrugged. "The first time he and I really connected it was at the tree given by a Greek god. Seems appropriate I give him a Greek name."

He smiled. "I know some. What were you wanting?"

"I don't know. What's Greek for...protector or avenger?"

"Ahh...protector is prostatis."

She wrinkled her nose. "Crow?

"Koraki."

"Nuh uh. Um...Black?"

Lexi laughed. "You're really getting creative here, aren't you?"

"Hey, give me a break. I've never named anyone or anything before," Chloe protested. Well, there was her business, but Chadwick and Hall Investigations wasn't creative, either.

Diego chuckled. "Black is mavros."

She brightened. "I kind of like the sound of that." She looked back to the crow. "What do you think? Do you want to be Mavros?"

His head tilted before he flapped his wings and cried, "Yes!"

"Mavros it is," Chloe said with a sharp nod. "Well, Mavros, Lexi was just asking me if I should stay in Salus. You want to weigh in?"

His head bobbed again. "Stay," he agreed.

"I love this bird," Lexi declared. "Mavros, I'm bringing you all sorts of special treats. As soon as I hit the net to find out what crows eat."

He made an odd sound that Chloe interpreted as a laugh and she grinned. "I guess I'm staying."

"About time," Diego said with a smile as he sat down again. "Salus will be lucky to have you."

"And you'll be lucky to have us," Lexi added, so happy she was bouncing.

"And you're very pleased to have gotten your way," Chloe said with a grin.

"True," Lexi said without shame. "So, when are you going to make it official?"

"Don't even think about going anywhere today," Diego said with a frown.

"No, I won't. I don't think I could make the drive even if I wanted to," Chloe said with a nod. "Tomorrow though, if I'm feeling well enough. Though I'll be gone a few days. I've got to clean out Granny's house in Boston and my apartment in Philadelphia. Not to mention deal with the business. I'll just sign that over to my partner."

"If you need help, or just want company, say the word," Lexi told her. "I'm sure I can talk Joel into giving me a few days off."

Diego scowled. "I'd offer the same, but with us being down one council member there's no way I can get away for a while, even for a day. But don't forget you need to go see Deirdre tomorrow, too."

Chloe smiled and gave his hand a squeeze as Mavros settled down in her lap and seemed to go to sleep. "I know, and it's okay. And yes, I'll stop in to see Deirdre before I go. And then? I'll be back for good."

And saying it, it felt right. She'd been fighting against the idea of staying, but now that she'd given in, something loosened in her chest and she could only smile.

Epilogue

Chloe had spoken to Wesley. He assured her that she was one hundred percent off the hook and that everyone had been informed that she was innocent. They knew Kyra was responsible, but the details—including the fact that while it had been her that had performed the killings, it hadn't been her will—had been kept from them. It was safer, he'd said, for Chloe. And another way to investigate who the man involved was without him being aware of it. Unless he'd been eavesdropping somehow, but neither brought up that point.

He'd been surprised to see Mavros, but pleased for her, too. He'd been more pleased when he'd been told Chloe was moving to Salus, and that both Mavros and Lexi were going to accompany her. It wouldn't be easy to hide a crow in either Boston or Philadelphia, but the women thought they could manage it all right.

Wesley had further surprised her by telling her that he'd talked to Colin, and that while she was gone, he was going to repair the hole in her wall. When she got back there would be no sign of the destruction other than the emptiness of the house.

When she asked him if he'd found anything to prove or disprove her theory about Jeremy, he'd grimaced. "I haven't, no. But if you leave a DNA sample, I'll see what I can do."

Chloe thought about that for a moment before agreeing and letting him swab her cheek. If the DNA test didn't turn anything up, she had one more avenue to pursue. Talking to Granny's ghost was a last resort.

Back at her house she'd searched the trees and found her

pistol. She'd also found the cake, or what remained of it. Scavengers had enjoyed it as much as she had hoped to.

The next morning Lexi showed up bright and early, bearing coffee and a bowl of blueberries for Mavros. To Chloe's surprise she'd only brought one bag, though she said she wasn't against doing some off-island shopping while they were gone. Luckily, they'd already planned to make several trips, so they weren't worried about finding space for everything.

At Zane's suggestion they'd hit the pet store, which had all manner of supplies for both pets and familiars, and they'd gotten Mavros a perch. He didn't need a proper cage since he was more intelligent than his mundane counterparts, so the perch was sufficient. They set it in the back seat so he had somewhere to rest on the drive, but Chloe had a hunch he wouldn't be using it much. Who knew lap birds existed?

Another surprise was when Mavros accompanied her into the hospital. He'd insisted, and though she protested, vehemently, he couldn't be swayed. Yet not a single person in the hospital looked shocked or annoyed at having a crow in the place. Even Deirdre had only smiled and greeted him before she examined Chloe and pronounced that she was essentially as good as new. Relieved, Chloe had thanked her, and promised to take it easy for a few more days more.

It wasn't much after nine when they pulled onto the ferry, Chloe smiling, Mavros dozing, and Lexi beaming with excitement.

"I haven't been off Salus in years. This is going to be fun," Lexi said as they waited for the ferry to cross over to the mainland.

Chloe laughed. "You do remember the main point of this is getting my junk from Philly to Salus, right?"

"Well yeah, but we're not going to be doing that twenty-four hours a day, now are we?"

"True," Chloe had to admit. "Though I'll be happy when it's over and I'm back."

Lexi grinned. "This place has really grown on you, hasn't it?"

Chloe twisted around to see the island receding behind it and

she smiled. "It really has."
It was home.

Coming Soon:
Waking Salus

After spending weeks packing up her human life, Chloe Chadwick returns to her new home on the supernatural-inhabited island of Salus. Except when she arrives, she discovers that everyone and everything on the island has fallen victim to powerful magic which has locked them all into an unnatural sleep.

Her unique powers allow her to stay awake, but she's too new to magic to solve the case on her own. She must figure out how to wake those she trusts, so they can help her investigate the cause of the magical slumber, as well as who's responsible for it.

It won't be easy, as things are even more complicated than they appeared at first glance. Even figuring out how to wake one person up will be hard enough, but when plots overlap with plots, will Chloe's skills and abilities as an elemental be enough to wake the island?

About The Author

Meg is a fantasy author who lives in north Georgia with her husband of eighteen years, teenage son, and a zoo full of critters. She's unapologetically goofy, which amuses her family to no end.

Her favorite hobbies do revolve around writing, as she reads more than she cares to admit. When she's not working on her next story, or enjoying someone else's, she enjoys playing video games, camping with her family, or being crafty, in a very literal sense. Fortunately, she currently has a job which allows her to plot and write at work, which gives her plenty of time to work on the next story.

.

She's loved Greek mythology and any story of the supernatural (with the exception of pure supernatural horror) since she was a child, and tries to incorporate the myths she's heard into her stories. It was actually the mystery surrounding Stonehenge that led her back to writing and helped her finish her first novel-length story. She's always on the lookout for a new myth or mysterious artifact to help spark her creativity. Her catch phrase when it comes to writing is "What if?", as it opens up so many possibilities.

You can find more about Meg M. Robinson and her upcoming novels here:

www.megmrobinson.com

www.facebook.com/megmrobinson

Made in United States
Orlando, FL
02 January 2022

12718842R00174